SOMEONE TO TEMPT

MICHELLE MAJOR

To the ones who've been told you're too much or not enough. In case you need to hear it today:
you are perfect just the way you are.

1

IRIS

TO THE OUTSIDE OBSERVER, this might look like any other Tuesday morning at the mayor's office in Skylark, Colorado. Spoiler alert: it's not. Because the mayor—that's me—is waiting, not so patiently, for the most important meeting of her life to begin.

I straighten an already perfectly tidy stack of papers on my desk and lift an arm to sniff. Damn. Nervous sweat is the worst. Digging into my emergency stash of toiletries in the desk drawer, I pull out a travel-sized deodorant. But when I flip off the lid, powdery clumps scatter over my navy blue suit.

Ugh. Ocean breeze scented snowfall.

I stand up, hoping the crumbs will fall to the ground without incident, but no such luck. My skirt is dotted with the chalky white bits, and everything around me smells like soapy springtime rain invaded a florist shop.

Why is it that women are stuck with products like lavender blossom and spring meadow, while guys are living their best deodorant lives with glacier punch and sharknado?

I'd like to glacier punch something at the moment, but there's no time for sharknado ramblings.

I have exactly three minutes until the woman who holds the key to my political future arrives at the mayor's office—my office of the past five months. I need to make a good impression, something that's eluded me with former U.S. Senator Gloria Johnson. She makes me more nervous than a group of middle schoolers at their first coed dance, hence the anxiety sweat.

Today I need to wow, connect, and convince her I'll make an excellent state senator, and hope she agrees to back me in the next mayoral election. It's an important first step if I want a career in Colorado politics, and I'm not sure I can manage it without her. Not with my limited connections and a family background I wish would fade into the sunset forever.

I rush to the tiny closet in the corner of the room where I keep a spare outfit for times like this. For the record, there's never been a time like this because I'm always prepared. Of course, now that the moment is upon me, I'm too nervous to do anything right. The skirt's zipper catches, and my button-down shirt strains across my breasts as I yank the offending fastener more forcefully.

Two minutes.

Voices float in from the other side of the office walls. I've got to get this skirt off and the other one on before Jodi Moore, my assistant, walks through the door. She never knocks.

The zipper finally gives, and the silk fabric pools around my ankles. I flip off the dark pumps that match the skirt I was wearing, but not the beige one I'm about to tug on. Gloria won't notice my shoes if I stay behind my desk.

The door clicks open just as I've got the new skirt hitched up to my knees.

"What's going on out there?" I demand, hating the sharp edge that gives away my tension. Talk about sharknado—Jodi is like a great white smelling blood in the water when it comes to catching me off guard.

She stares, mouth agape, before pulling the door closed behind her. "You're half-dressed," she hisses, making it sound like she caught me doing naked cartwheels across the thick rug.

I yank the skirt the rest of the way. "Fully dressed now. What's the deal? Is Gloria here?"

I'm discombobulated. Otherwise, I'd notice the gleam in Jodi's teal green eyes.

"Oh, yes." She preens. *Preens.* "Senator Johnson is here. Along with a half-dozen disgruntled residents."

My head snaps up. "Disgruntled? What are you talking about?"

"I guess they heard about you cutting funding for the community spirit budget."

"I haven't cut anything."

"But you're *planning* on it, and it's not going over well."

"First." I hold up a finger, then curl it back into my fist when I realize I'm trembling. "How does anyone know about that plan? We're still in the draft phase."

Jodi shrugs. "It's a small town."

"Second, I'm not trying to mess with the town's spirit. I'm all about community spirit."

She gives a disbelieving snort, as if I don't care about this town when I've spent every waking second trying to make sure it thrives.

I just happen to believe in practical solutions over feel-good fluff. "I'm trying to find a way to fund the library's early learning literacy program since the state cut funding."

"By sacrificing Skylark's reputation as one of the happiest towns in America," she insists.

A couple of online articles give a town a made-up title and people go nuts. It just so happens those people aren't responsible for the town's budget.

"No one and *nothing* is being sacrificed," I counter through gritted teeth.

She pretends to study her nails, and I remember the moment last week when she asked to leave early to have them done to match the outfit she was wearing to the Apple Harvest Parade.

to be associated with my mom's legacy or her affair with former Mayor Moore."

Mom hasn't been back to Colorado for over a decade, but her reputation as a fun-loving free spirit lives on. Only her version of fun left me and my brother without care or food half the time and made enemies of married women in every town she blew through.

"Skylark can't be the place where fun goes to die, Iris." Gloria steeples her fingers on the polished cherry table. "I also cannot back a candidate who has a reputation for killing community spirit. Do you know why Skylark's leadership first started actively investing in the town's image?"

I do. As a way to distract the town from his brother's scandal with my mother fourteen years ago, newly appointed Mayor Homer Moore began instituting prescribed events to bolster community spirit and build a reputation for wholesome small-town fun.

In the last decade, we've gone from hosting the usual seasonal festivals and an occasional juried art show, to at least one event a month funded by the town for the purpose of bringing a smile to the faces of residents young and old. I'm not a fan of forced fun, but I've attended most of the events, at least in passing, because of my position. Thanks to social media and a bajillion online lists ranking small-town life, plus the fascination with romantic movies centered around the very same thing, Skylark has grown in popularity. Our reputation and designation as one of the happiest towns in the country is a source of pride for many residents. But others, like me, have festival fatigue.

"Not every event brings in enough revenue to offset the costs associated with them. Plus, sometimes they prevent us from supporting the people who live here in a meaningful way. That's all I'm trying to do. Isn't that what good politicians do? We take care of our constituents."

She inclines her head to study me. "You're a smart girl. I didn't expect you to show such Pollyanna tendencies."

"I'm not—"

"This isn't Camelot, Iris." She closes her eyes for a minute. "Politics is as much about impressions as intention. You have to get elected before you can do the work, and you aren't going to get elected in a town like Skylark if everyone thinks you're the grim reaper of fun."

"I'm fun," I insist, but the words come out like a snarl.

She cracks a real smile. "Oh yes, that tone will convince people. Figure it out, Iris, and then we'll talk. Is the life of a career politician in the public eye *truly* what you want?"

I frown and force myself not to argue. "Of course, it's what I want."

Okay, maybe that hasn't always been the case. But once the members of the town council appointed me interim mayor, I realized this was how I could both *do* good and show that I *am* good. Prove to everyone in town that I'm not my mother, who still subscribes to the belief that sex, drugs, and rock and roll are the only kind of fun worth having.

Mom was like a holdover groupie from the decade of free love. Only instead of collecting famous notches on her belt, my mother collected married notches.

"I *am* fun," I insist. "And if I need to stay sunup to sundown at every event this town sponsors to prove it, I will."

She lets out what I can only describe as a disappointed sigh, confusing me all the more.

"Isn't that what you want from me?"

"I want you to do something for *you*. Something that lights you up and takes you out of your comfort zone."

Her blue eyes bore into me like she's imparting some great wisdom, but for the life of me I have zero clue as to what lights me up.

I think about my book club's bucket list challenge. We're meeting tonight, and I need to be ready to tell them what I'm going to do. I haven't been able to come up with anything that

4

JAKE

"CATCHING UP WITH AN OLD FRIEND," I announce to the crowd, feeling like the outsider I am in this town. "Remember to always use a crosswalk."

A few onlookers wave and nod before moving down the sidewalk or returning to the stores lining the street. I'm not sure if anyone recognizes me as Gilbert Byrne's grandson or remembers the summer I spent raising hell in this town after my brother died. Either way, it doesn't matter.

Skylark has been my grandfather's home for the past twenty years, but it isn't mine. I've come to Colorado for him and our family's legacy, and then I'm out of here. The beauty of the remote age of office work is I can run the foundation from Austin just as easily as I can in Skylark.

My grandpa explained how Iris had been appointed mayor months ago, but somehow I figured I could avoid her during my visit. She shot that plan all to hell when she rushed across the street without looking. I'm sure she didn't expect someone to come barreling around the corner, especially someone who *had* been texting and driving. Not that I'm admitting it to her. I want to claim no hard feelings about how things ended between us, but the sharp ache in my heart after seeing her only reminds me that where Iris is concerned, the emotions are like a dry, crusty scab over a cut that just won't heal.

Glancing at my watch as I climb back into the truck, I toss my phone on the bench seat next to me—there's nothing I need it for anyway—and start the six-mile drive to my grandfather's ranch. Thankfully, the pastry box on the passenger side floor wasn't jostled in my near miss with Iris.

The Colorado scenery never ceases to amaze me. Jagged peaks of the nearby Flatirons dominate the horizon, and the mountainsides display patches of vivid yellow as aspens stand out against the dark pines. Clusters of cottonwoods border the creek that winds to the south of the highway, golden leaves shimmering in the bright afternoon sun. The light is less intense than in the summer months, everything bathed in a gentle glow. I can feel the change of seasons in the air and hope to tap into that energy. I'm going to need it.

As I pull to a stop in the wide gravel driveway, I tell myself I'm ready for this. Despite my run-in with Iris, I'm ready to prove I'm not the screwup everyone thinks I am.

Everything about my grandfather's sprawling ranch is picture-postcard perfect, except for the man stepping out of the front door. I grab the bakery box, roll my shoulders against the tension that has immediately gathered there, and adopt a sneer—the expression my father expects from me.

"Hey there, Daddio," I call good-naturedly. Neither of us are fooled.

"Well, look what the cat dragged in."

I hold up the box. "Can I offer you a donut?"

It's Dad's turn to sneer. I doubt he's allowed even a crumb of white flour, let alone processed sugar, to pass over his lips into the temple of his body. When we were kids, Mike would use his allowance to bribe the housekeeper into bringing us candy, cupcakes, and cookies. We'd sit on the floor of his closet and laugh because I hate my resemblance to him. He's the last person I want to see gazing back at me.

"Why are you really here, Jake? Did you run out of yachts to party on? And what makes you think you're remotely qualified to handle the foundation?"

"I'm qualified because I *care*."

His eyes narrow. "You don't care about anything or anyone but yourself."

My chest tightens, and for a moment, I can't speak. "I know you blame me for Mikey's death," I say, my voice low. "Maybe I should have been able to save him. But I didn't, and I live with that every day. Running the foundation is my chance to do something good. Mikey believed in helping people. I want to honor him. And I'm done letting people think I'm a screw-up."

"Your brother was ten times the man you'll ever be, even as a kid."

Heat rises in my cheeks, but I force my shoulders to stay relaxed. "Great catching up, *Dad*, but I've got some donuts to deliver." I glance at my watch. "Nearly ten-thirty. Might be time to rip the day's first bong hit. I know you appreciate a schedule."

His lip curls into a sneer before he turns and walks away, his boots crunching on the gravel. I stand there, watching him go. My chest feels tight, like the weight of his disapproval is crushing me. As I head toward the house, the stupid, secret part of me that has always hoped my father and I could find a way past our mutual animosity gives a limp protest. I shove that mangy beast into the dark cave where I've kept it all these years.

My grandfather is at the kitchen table, finishing his green tea and the *New York Times* crossword puzzle. I smile when he looks up and try not to let guilt prick tiny holes in my righteous anger. The truth is, I've mostly seen my grandfather when he's come to Texas for visits with the foundation staff who work in the satellite office in downtown Austin. Skylark holds too many memories—most of them not good—for me to feel comfortable here.

"Did you know they put a second stoplight on Main Street?" I ask. "This town is coming into its own."

"You doing okay?" He takes off his glasses and rubs two fingers over his eyes. "You probably realize I sent you on the pastry errand not because I had a hankering for donuts. I knew your dad was coming by this morning but hoped he'd be gone by the time you got back."

I place the box on the table and grab the other half of the maple donut. I'm already feeling sick. Might as well continue the fun.

"How do you know we had a run-in? Were you peeping out the front window?"

His grin widens, and he pulls a cell phone from under the newspaper. "No peeping necessary when I've got cameras on my doorbell. Makes it feel like I'm watching a movie playing in my driveway. Looked like a standoff at the O.K. Corral out there."

"No standoff," I answer, unsure whether to admire or fear that my eighty-five-year-old grandfather is embracing modern technology. "I gave up fighting with him or trying to prove something a long time ago."

Grandpa doesn't argue, but I'm not sure he believes me. I'm not sure I believe me. "I'm glad you're here, Jake."

"He won't do right by the foundation, Grandpa. We both know it."

"And you will?" He gives me the same arched brow treatment I gave Iris. It's a small comfort knowing I look like my grandfather as well as my dad. "You haven't shown much interest in our philanthropic efforts before now."

I incline my head. "Talk to the grants manager in Austin. I've been doing more—learning the ropes." Maybe it's not enough, but I'm trying.

"Dad wants the glory. He doesn't care about truly helping people."

"I appreciate that." Grandpa sighs, and that exhalation of

breath feels like it carries a deeper message.. "But it's going to take more than donuts. You want to learn...I'll teach you." He taps his pen on the newspaper. "But first, I need some help with this. It's a four letter word and the clue is 'a mountain for the mind.'"

Is he punking me?

"I'll take a jelly donut, too," Grandpa says as he waits. It doesn't look like he picked this crossword clue because he's trying to subtly give me a clue as to what's in store for this visit.

I take a plate from the cabinet, set the jelly donut on it and then slide it in front of him.

"Test, Grandpa." I make sure my tone stays light and ignore the gleam in his eyes. "The word you're looking for is test."

It won't be easy, but I hope I pass the one I'm facing here in Skylark.

5

IRIS

I WALK into the back entrance of Cover to Cover fifteen minutes before seven, our regular book club time. I had Sadie drop me home after the run-in with Jake because I needed to fix my face, as my mom would say, before returning to the office. To make sure no one could see the toll this morning took on my heart.

I'm normally one of the first to arrive at our meetings. Tonight, the five other members are already seated around the large oak table Sloane—the founder of our Cool Girl Book Club— uses for meetings, classes, and other events.

I stifle a groan as the conversation stalls and five pairs of eyes turn to me. "I'm fine. No need for an intervention or whatever this is. Everything's fine."

Maybe if I say the words over and over, I'll believe them.

"How about a glass of sangria?" Single mom Molly McAllister points to the pitcher sitting next to a bowl of chips in the center of the table.

"Sure," I say with a laugh. "One glass might help me improve on fine. But only one. The way this day is going, chances are I'll end up with a DUI if I even sniff a second glass."

"I'll drive you home," Sloane offers, and I swallow back the emotion that threatens to choke me. Any of these women would give me a ride, just like Sadie did earlier.

But Sloane is my best friend in the group. In the world, actually. She's the first real friend I made in my life back when I spent that one fateful summer in Skylark.

Now she's thin and pale, her head wrapped in a thick scarf to cover the fact that we shaved her head months ago after the chemo left her mahogany waves falling out in chunks. But her sky-blue eyes are bright and filled with affection as she winks at me.

I hate that my friend battling cancer still feels like I'm the one who needs to be taken care of. I love that she's so willing to step up to support me, but I should be helping her feel better, not the other way around. It's what this whole bucket list challenge is about.

"One is plenty," I assure her, taking the plastic wine glass Molly hands me. "Really, I'm fine. Today was no big deal. A small setback, but I'll figure out how to fund the important programs while keeping the town's reputation intact."

"We'll get to town business in a minute," Avah Harris says. "First, let's talk about you and the hot stranger having it out on Main Street." With a slender build and an effortlessly chic sense of style, Avah seems like she'd be more at home in a sleek urban setting than in a quaint town nestled in the foothills of the Rocky Mountains.

I shoot a glance at Sadie, who shakes her head. "They didn't hear anything from me." I believe her. Sadie is one of the kindest and most loyal people I know.

"I heard it from Susanna Monroe at the bakery." Avah rolls her blue eyes, clearly annoyed at having to elaborate on her request. Patience isn't one of her strong suits. "You know how Suze loves gossip, and she said customers were glued to the front window like they were watching a reality show brawl."

"It wasn't that bad," I insist, but swallow back another groan. I'm not only not fun, now I'm going to have a reputation for making a fool of myself in public. Just what voters want from their mayor.

"Who was it?" Sloane asks, genuinely curious.

"Somebody I used to know."

She holds up the front edge of the scarf. "You have to give the bald cancer patient all the details when she asks."

I choke out a laugh then take a long sip of the sangria, hoping it will calm me. I don't want to rehash my run-in with Jake, especially with Sloane. "Are you seriously going to use cancer as an arm-twisting tactic?"

"I'm absolutely using cancer." She points to the empty seat across from her. "Its advantages are few and far between, but manipulation, coercion, and outright getting my way are perks that cannot be ignored."

Molly, ever the peacemaker, leans over and hugs her. "So that you know, we'll let you have your way even after you kick cancer's ass."

"I'm going to hold you to that. But right now, Madame Interim Mayor, spill those type-A guts."

I lower myself into the chair next to Taylor Maxwell, local librarian and most reserved of our friend group. "It was Jake Byrne. He's in town visiting his grandfather."

Sloane's full mouth thins. "Jake's back?" She's the only one who understands what this means to me—to my heart.

"A guy who loves his grandpa." Avah taps her chest. "That gets me right in the feels. Bonus that he's hot."

"Why were you arguing and how do you know him?" Taylor asks quietly. "His name doesn't ring a bell."

Taylor, Sadie, and Avah are the three Skylark natives of our group. They might have heard of Jake—or the hot gossip that punctuated his short summer in Skylark—but his family used their influence and buckets of cash to quiet the potential scandal.

Except Jake wasn't the only one involved that night, and the aftermath wrecked my brother's life as surely as if a tornado had touched down in our midst.

"He and Nick were friends in high school," I say, careful to keep any emotion out of my voice. "Today he was driving like an idiot and almost ran me over."

"That's not the whole story," Sloane says, her voice almost a whisper.

This is why I don't make friends. When people know you, particularly your weaknesses, they have the power to hurt you. Sloane would never—at least not on purpose—but Jake Byrne is another story.

I vowed to stop giving away my power a long time ago. And when I've mis-stepped on that promise to myself, it comes back to bite me. Every single time.

Still, I trust these women. So I take a deep breath, and with an encouraging nod from Sloane, try to explain the story of Jake and me without revealing the damage knowing him did to my heart.

"Jake came to stay with his grandpa for a few months right after Mom moved us to Skylark."

"The summer before senior year of high school," Sloane adds.

I nod. "He and my twin had a bromance from the jump. Two charming party boys looking for trouble." I roll my shoulders when I feel them hiking up to my ears, then continue, "They found more than their share."

Sadie reaches out and places her hand on my arm. "What kind of trouble?"

"It was stupid stuff. Breaking into the country club after hours to use the hot tub. Borrowing Jake's grandfather's Porsche to go joyriding on the two-lane highways outside of town."

Avah scoffs. "I'm guessing they didn't ask permission to *borrow* the Porsche."

I nod. "Correct."

"Kids still race on those roads," Molly says, "even though the sheriff's office sets up regular speed traps out there. We can hear the engines on summer nights. Someone's going to get killed."

Since moving to Skylark with her twins after her husband's death, Molly has lived with her mother-in-law on a small farm outside town. Her eyes widen as she makes the connection. "Oh, crap. Was it *that* kind of accident?"

"No one was killed." I grip the edge of the table like it can ground me. "They picked up a trio of college coeds in town for the rodeo. Lots of partying and even more alcohol. Someone had the brilliant idea to go drag racing after the barn dance ended."

"Alcohol and good decisions are somewhat mutually exclusive," Taylor murmurs.

"More than somewhat in this case. A deer ran across the road, and the driver swerved to avoid it. Ended up losing control and rolling the car several times before smacking into the cattle fence bordering the highway."

"I vaguely remember hearing about that." Avah frowns. "But no one had details."

"Because Jake's family *handled* the situation." I use aggressive air quotes around the word handled.

"You said the driver lost control." Molly leans forward. "Who was driving—Jake or your brother?"

A familiar wave of anger washes over me, hot and ugly like it was right after the incident. You'd think time would diminish my emotions. It heals all wounds, right? But not all wrongs.

"The official line was that Nick was behind the wheel." I blow out a long breath. "We found out later Jake had been driving, but his dad convinced my brother to take the fall."

A chorus of disbelieving gasps greets my revelation.

"He can't do that," Avah insists.

"Oh, he did it." I shake my head. "I confronted Nick, but he claimed he couldn't remember who was driving, so it might have been him."

"Did you talk to Jake?" Sadie asks. "Were the two of you close like him and Nick?"

"Not like that," I say carefully, keeping my gaze away from Sloane's.

She knows the truth about my feelings for Jake Byrne, and I can't bear to see that truth reflected in her blue eyes. "But I did demand the truth. He refused to confirm or deny anything. Totally shut me out, and by then it didn't matter."

"Why?" Taylor whispers.

I release my grasp on the table when my fingers start to ache. "Both of them were facing serious consequences, Nick especially. That's when the Byrnes worked their *magic*." More air quotes. "Jake's grandfather handled the cops and the girls' families. His dad stepped in and arranged for them to spend the rest of the summer—a month—at one of those wilderness camps for troubled teens. I hated the idea of Nick being sent away, but Jake's dad made it seem like there was no other choice."

Molly shakes her head. "What did your mom think?"

I force a smile like this part doesn't bother me anymore, even though the ramifications are still turning up like a bad penny. "She was so distraught by the whole thing she felt the need to take comfort in the arms of Skylark's very married mayor."

"Pew, pew," Avah whispers.

"It was devastating in more than one way," Sloane tells the group.

"All the ways," I agree. "I don't care what Jake and Nick said or refused to say. My brother got a bum deal because we didn't have the money to pay for our scandals to go away."

"So not exactly a happy reunion for you and Jake," Avah says.

That's putting it mildly. "He still can't drive for shit, but the rest of it is water under the bridge."

Sadie refills her cup and offers the pitcher to me, but I shake my head. "How does your brother feel about Jake and the Byrne family?"

"He won't talk about it." I wrap my arms around my stomach like that can protect me from the memories that have haunted me since that night. "He had a rough time at camp. I don't think he and Jake stayed in touch, not with how Nick spiraled after that summer. And I haven't given Jake Byrne another thought until I just about lost my kneecaps to his truck's bumper."

Avah hums a sound of disbelief but doesn't call me out on the lie. They all must know I'm telling one.

I drain the last few drops of my sangria, hoping the alcohol will warm the chill in my veins.

Taylor drapes an arm around my shoulder. "Okay, now that we've established that Jake Byrne is a total piece of shit, do you want to talk about this morning at the mayor's office?"

Another laugh bubbles up inside me, this one more resigned than forced. "Long story short, my lovely assistant threw me under the bus with the Community Spirit Committee. But I have a plan for managing that, and it involves the bucket list."

Sloane grins. "The bucket list can solve everything."

Avah rolls her eyes. "You're giving Kristen Quinn way too much credit."

Avah is the most skeptical that *The Year of Losing It*—the book club selection that inspired Sloane to start this bucket list challenge —is anything more than a montage of superficial clichés and Pinterest-level wisdom. But she's going along with the program for Sloane's benefit. Just like the rest of us.

"Are you going to make training with you for an ultramarathon part of Jodi's job description?" Molly winks at me.

I'd tentatively mentioned participating in one of Colorado's popular endurance races as my bucket list challenge. "She deserves that kind of torture, but no."

I pull the book that has inspired all of this bucket list talk out of my bag. "On page one-thirty-four, Quinn says, 'When we allow ourselves to embrace joy, laughter, and play, we recharge our minds and hearts. It makes us more resilient, creative, and open to life's challenges. Fun isn't a distraction. It's a strategy for living boldly.'"

"She's right," Sloane murmurs.

"I hope so." I close the book again. "Because for my bucket list challenge," I announce with a flourish like I'm revealing the showcase showdown prize on *The Price is Right*, "I'm going to have fun. And as my challenge, I am signing up for an ultramarathon."

A mix of anticipation and nerves makes my heartbeat riot against my ribcage, and I scan my friends' faces, waiting for the cheers or support I'd anticipated—well, hoped—they'd give me. Instead, an awkward silence greets my words, punctuated by only a few exchanged glances that sting worse than outright disapproval.

They don't get it, and why should they? No one—not even Sloane—knows the depth of my hatred for that word. *Fun*.

Molly finally speaks, her cautious tone making me feel even smaller. "Are you sure a marathon counts as a fun challenge?"

"You guys don't have to understand." Heat rises up the back of my neck. "Or approve. I'm doing this for me."

But that doesn't stop the hollow ache from settling in my chest, a reminder that I'm always the one who doesn't quite belong. Doing life wrong.

Why can't I be like everyone else instead of the odd puzzle piece in a box full of perfect fits?

6

IRIS

"Do we need to look up the definition of fun in the dictionary?" Avah grabs a handful of pretzels and pops one in her mouth as she narrows her eyes at me. "Because there's no way in hell—"

Molly elbows her. "Iris is right. Her challenge, her choice." She offers me a gentle smile. "Tell us more about why a long-ass run feels fun to you."

"Because it sounds awful AF." Avah takes Molly's arm when the redhead starts to elbow her again. "But also something you could handle with no issues. The challenges need to push us out of our comfort zone." She wiggles her eyebrows. "Like Sadie's V-Card."

"Training for a fifty-mile run will push me," I insist. "And accomplishing that kind of task will be fun."

"Debatable," Taylor says with a shudder.

Molly makes a similar face. "As much as I hate to admit it, Avah's right."

"Is someone recording this moment?" Avah demands.

"An endurance event would show people that I'm resilient and dedicated. I don't flake out once I commit. Doing hard things is fun."

"Reread the quote," Sloane tells me. "The part about joy, laughter, and play."

I oblige, then close the book and thunk it against my forehead. "Why is fun so hard for me?"

If I'm being honest, I already know the answer. How many times as a kid did I beg my mom to give up the nomadic life she loved so much? To prioritize paying bills and keeping us in one place for an entire school year. Her derisive response was that I needed to loosen up and have fun. But her kind of fun meant disappointing the people counting on you. Joy and play meant damaging your kids because you only cared about yourself.

"Do people in town really think I want to kill fun?" I ask my friends.

"Kill is a strong word," Molly answers.

Not precisely the fervent denial I'd hoped to hear. My gut tightens as I ask, "What do they think?"

"The bucket list challenge isn't about other people," Sloane offers.

"I want to know. Maybe I chose fun as my challenge because of what happened earlier, but I can't be associated with the slogan 'this is where fun comes to die.'" My gaze settles on Avah, the truth-teller of our group. "I can't fix my reputation if I don't know what it is."

"People might have the impression you're a little intense," Avah says. The fact that she worded the criticism so mildly strongly suggests that hella-intense is more like it.

"Rigid," Molly adds.

"Standoffish," Taylor whispers.

Each of their words hits like a punch, but it's sweet Sadie who delivers the knockout blow.

"A lot of residents chose this town because it feels like home and they love it here. It sometimes seems like you came back because you have something to prove." She shrugs apologetically.

"Once you check us off the list, you'll leave Skylark in your rearview mirror without a backward glance."

"Oh." I reach for my sangria glass—which Taylor has just refilled—because I need something to do with my hands, but my fingers are trembling too hard to pick it up without the liquid sloshing over the sides. I could argue that I do love it here, but I haven't let myself love anything or anyone for a long time.

I don't even want or need to examine the reasons why. Because if these women—my friends—think these things about me, I'm guessing most people in town would straight up call me a bitch.

"We know your intentions are good," Molly assures me, "but some of your words and actions might come off harsher than you intend."

"Harsh. So I need to prove to people that I'm fun and playful. Not harsh and rigid and..." I glance at Taylor.

"Standoffish," she repeats, then bites down on her bottom lip like it's painful to tell me the truth.

Not half as painful as it is to hear.

"You can do this," Sloane promises, but she doesn't look convinced. She knows me best, is why I'm in the book club and bellying up to the bucket list challenge. It's not a great sign.

"Think about what brings you joy," she encourages. "Or a time when you did something for the simple reason that it made you happy without worrying about proving yourself in the process."

"Okay," I agree. "I can do that." I hope to God I sound more convincing than I feel. Growing up in a state of constant chaos, fun doesn't come without worry in my life.

It didn't help that my larger-than-life mother tied a sparkly bow on the madness to convince Nick and me we were having fun. But a shit sandwich loaded down with colorful condiments still stinks like crap.

"It might feel impossible now." Sadie reaches across the table and grabs my hand, as if she can sense my anxiety and unease. Like I'm one of her dog clients and she needs to whisper me. She's not wrong. "But I'm proof that amazing things can come from putting yourself out there in a new and scary way."

I take a moment to admire the diamond sparkling on her finger. The one former NFL quarterback Ian Barlowe put there at the end of the summer. Not only did Sadie succeed in checking off her bucket list item, but she also managed to fall head over heels with a man who absolutely worships her.

It's a high bar. And while I have zero chance of matching her success, my competitive drive kicks in. Yes, I want to have fun. I also want to be elected mayor and convince Gloria Johnson to mentor me. I'm not sure I can or want to separate the two.

Still, the thought of Gloria triggers a memory. One that fits the criteria Sloane just gave me.

"I'm going to dance," I blurt.

"Yes, queen." Avah's velvety voice takes on an even huskier note as she bops her head from side to side to music only she can hear. "Let's go clubbing in Denver. That would be a metric shit ton of fun."

"But not exactly the spirit of the bucket list challenge," Sloane murmurs.

"Iris could set the goal to dance on every bar, Coyote Ugly style," Molly offers.

Avah nods and starts the head bopping again. "And dance with the hottest guy in every club." She jabs a finger in the air. "Or the hottest girl. That would be fun, at least to watch."

I wish it was as easy as going dancing for the evening, but even without Sloane's reminder, I know I need to do better.

"I'm going to take dance lessons," I tell them. "I've been thinking about it for a while." And by *a while*, I mean approximately ninety seconds, but I don't mention that.

"There's an adult class that meets twice a week at the community center, and I've invited them to perform at the Skylark Fun Fest the first weekend of November." At least I plan to do so when I enroll in the class tomorrow morning.

Taylor makes a soft sound of distress next to me. "I thought you were canceling this year's Fun Fest so you could put that money toward the library's literacy program."

"I'll find another way to fund the library," I promise, taking her hand. "Fun Fest is happening."

Sloane takes a drink from her mug of tea. She hasn't been able to stomach even a sip of alcohol since starting her treatments. "Are you sure you're choosing a dance class because you think it will be fun, and not to make voters believe you think it's fun?"

I take a sip of my sangria, relieved I can hold the plastic cup with steady hands. Sloane's skepticism is valid, but having a plan is my favorite form of fun, even if no one else appreciates it.

"It's for me. Promise." I ignore the nerves churning in my gut at what I'm about to share, and focus my gaze on Sloane.

"When I was eight, we lived in Albuquerque for six months. I had a best friend for the first time, and eventually, her mom enrolled me in a dance class with all the other girls from our grade. She felt bad that I was being left out." A smile plays at the corners of my mouth. "I loved everything about it. The leotards and tights and special shoes, even though all my stuff was hand-me-down or from the lost and found bin. Most of all, I just loved dancing."

"Okay, that's adorable," Sadie says. "I can totally picture little Iris twirling."

"Twirling was my favorite," I confirm with a grin that falters as I continue. "Mom thought it was stupid because, in her mind, dancing—fun in general—was mutually exclusive to structure. Why did I need lessons when I could move to music in any old way?"

"But she didn't stop you from taking lessons, did she?" Avah asks.

"Not exactly." I lower my gaze and pick an invisible speck of lint off my black sweater. "In retrospect, I don't think she liked that another mother was doing something for me. Mom might have been lax in parenting, but she didn't want anyone involved in our business. I guess I understand." I tried to back then anyway.

Sloane lets out a disdainful huff of breath. "Then she should have stepped up and taken an active role in your life."

Sloane's parents weren't like my mom. They're both archeologists and professors, but from what I gather, they always —and still—placed work and their own needs above taking care of their kids. I know she understands how that neglect can eat away at a child's soul.

"A week before the recital, Mom decided we were moving to Texas. She'd met some guy on Myspace and was convinced she'd found the love of her life. Spoiler alert: he wasn't."

"What about your recital?" Taylor asks.

"I didn't get to dance in it." I shrug. "I kept the leotard and other stuff and danced my heart out alone in my room. But after that, I stopped participating in extracurricular activities. I didn't want to let anyone else down." I swallow around the ball of emotion lodged in my throat and smile. "If you need verification, I still have the leotard."

"Oh, honey, that's so sweet." Molly gets up and comes around the table to hug me. "You're going to be a ballerina."

The lightness that fills my chest at her words surprises me. Maybe I have an ulterior motive for enrolling in Gloria's dance class, but it could help me discover what fun means. The fact that my potential political mentor also loves to dance is a happy coincidence, and I need something happy to end this day.

My gaze meets Sloane's, her eyes shimmering with tears. "You're doing it," she says. "You're taking my challenge seriously."

"Of course I am, you bald nut. I'd do anything for you."

"We all would," Molly says as she returns to her seat.

"Thank you," my friend tells the group. "It means the world to me. Especially because..." She trails off and swipes under her eyes. "All these stupid tears."

"You can cry all you want," I tell her, and my voice comes out a little fiercer than I meant. "There's nothing wrong with crying," I say in a gentler tone.

Sloane smiles because she knows I don't cry. But that rule only applies to me.

"What is it?" Sadie asks, and it's obvious by the look on the faces around the table that we're all worried and trying not to show it.

"I went to Nashville for a follow-up last week."

"Without telling anyone?" I demand.

Sadie takes her hand. "One of us could have driven you to the airport or gone with you. You're not alone."

Sloane laughs, but it sounds hollow. "I didn't want to worry anyone. But I wasn't alone. Jeremy picked me up in his company plane."

Sloane's brother, Jeremy, is some sort of tech genius billionaire. He lives in California, and they hadn't been close until her diagnosis. In fact, from everything she's said about him or I've read online, Jeremy Winslow is an asshole. Yet, he stepped up for Sloane, taking her to Vanderbilt in Nashville, where he has connections in the oncology unit.

We know he wants her to move to California, where he can be more closely involved in her treatment, but like Sadie said, Skylark is a home that people choose. Sloane isn't leaving. At least not yet. For that, I'm grateful.

"My body needs a break, but they want me to start a more aggressive course of chemo at the end of the month. Six weeks of it." She grimaces. "I'll have to be in Nashville for most of that time."

Avah blows out a long breath then asks, "This will kill the fucking cancer, right?"

"They hope so," Sloane answers, but sounds less than sure.

"What do you need?" I ask. "We'll do anything."

"You're already doing it." Her smile is soft. "Embracing the bucket list challenge. You make me feel like I'm not alone, and I love living vicariously through your adventures. Dancing is perfect, and performing at Fun Fest gives me a goal. I need to get home for your big debut."

My stomach knots at the thought of what I've just committed to, but I don't let my fear show. Compared to what Sloane's facing, my challenges are nothing.

My friends seem relieved at the chance to lighten the conversation once again.

"We'll all be at your performance," Molly assures me.

"Do they offer pole dancing?" Taylor asks, and we all go silent once again.

"Pole dancing," Avah repeats. "The librarian wants to pole dance."

"Just because I like books doesn't mean I don't have a racy side." She holds up this month's book club selection, which she chose for us. It's a dark motorcycle club romance with a beefed-up guy on the cover.

"Oh, we know." Sloane shakes her head. "I was reading this at the hospital in Nashville, and I swear the nurse was worried at how red my cheeks were. It had everything to do with your spicy book selection."

Taylor grins unabashedly. "Be honest, how many nights did it take you all to finish it?"

"One," Sadie answers immediately. "Well, one and a half because Ian made me read certain parts aloud. He was inspired."

Molly grins. "I'm happy for you and also insanely jealous."

"Samesies," Taylor agrees. "What about everyone else?"

Each of us holds up between one and three fingers.

"That's right," our favorite librarian says. "People might bad mouth romance, but they suck you in, in the best way possible."

"*Suck* being one of the more G-rated words," Avah murmurs.

"I'm adding pole dancing to my bucket list activity," I tell the group, "and you're all taking part."

Taylor suddenly looks terrified. "As long as we don't have to do it on stage." She suffers from intense stage fright and has trouble even reading out loud during the weekly programs she hosts for local kids at the library. Molly, who brings her kids to the library on the regular, has admitted it's painful to watch.

"A private class," I assure her.

"I'm in," Sadie agrees.

"If you get good," Sloane tells her with a wink, "Ian's going to install a pole in your new bedroom."

When I first met Sadie, that comment would have sent her into a fit of anxiety, but now a smile plays along the corner of her mouth.

"It's not the worst idea I've ever heard," she says, and we all laugh.

The lightness I felt a few minutes ago when I chose dancing as my challenge has expanded. I take a deep breath, feeling like I can salvage not only my chance of being elected mayor, but also my bid to have Gloria Johnson help me with the next step in my career.

The bucket list changed Sadie's life in countless ways, so maybe my dance classes will have the same positive effect on me. I could definitely use it.

7

JAKE

"ARE you sure I can't head straight to the office like a regular employee? I'm certain you're plenty capable of getting yourself to your dance class, Gramps."

He cackles—literally cackles—from the passenger side of the truck. "There's nothing regular about you, Jakey."

He pats the dashboard with gnarled fingers. Although Gilbert Byrne still has a thick head of shockingly white hair, he's plagued by arthritis and various other issues that have aged his body, but not his mind. "I know you're going to love Char, short for Charlotte—she's our instructor—and the others, just like I knew I needed to keep this old girl running for when you came back."

"Can we at least talk about your visions for the future on the way to your dance class?" I can hardly believe my grandfather is taking dance lessons, let alone enjoying them so much. I suppose moving is good for him, but dancing?

"*Our* dance class," he clarifies.

A knot forms in my stomach. "Uh...I don't think so. I'm dropping you off and then heading to the nearest coffee shop to get some work done."

"The hell you are." Grandpa sits back against the seat. "There's a new gal starting today who'll need a partner, so you're joining the class. I already talked to Char and got you enrolled. Char's the best. She spent years dancing on cruise ships and man, can she move."

My jaw drops. "You aren't serious. I don't have time for—"

"You can make time for this. It's an hour twice a week. Although you and the new gal might need some extra practice. We can't have you embarrassing us before the big show."

"Whoa! Big show? Let's pump the plié brakes," I tell him.

"It's not ballet, Jakey. It's couples dancing—ballroom. Like on those reality competition shows. It's real popular. You're going to love it."

"Grandpa, if I'm going to show you I'm the right guy to take the reins of the Byrne Family Foundation, I think my attention should be on that."

"I disagree." The amusement has drained from his voice, and I glance over, trying to mask my frustration and panic.

"You disagree that I'm the right person to take over the foundation?" Sure, most people think I'm a trustafarian slacker, but I thought my grandfather saw more. I wanted to believe he saw the me I could be if given the chance. "Why did you invite me here to discuss the opportunity? Why not just make the announcement that Dad's your successor?"

"Pump the jumping to conclusions brakes, kid. I'm not ready to make an announcement on who will take the reins, and I won't be rushed on my decision. I disagree about where your attention should be while you're here. Don't get your britches in a twist."

Grandpa means business when he starts talking britches, so even though it's killing me, I keep my mouth shut.

"We have your reputation to consider if you truly want to be thought of as a viable candidate." His voice is gentle even though the words land like a lead weight. "Your lifestyle is public knowledge."

I know my reputation. I'm the one who cultivated it, even

MICHELLE MAJOR

after I outgrew that version of myself. "What does me being a slacker have to do with dance class?"

"I'm happy you're interested in our family's legacy, but the foundation is about commitment to the communities we serve in Colorado and Texas. You don't stick with things."

"I can stick," I tell him. In the past decade, I've written and published eight bestselling mysteries and learned a metric shit ton about dedication, time, effort, and hard work. But I've also kept my career a massive secret from the world. Not even my grandfather knows about that part of my life, and even though the secret is coming back to bite me in the ass, I don't plan to share that information with anyone.

But, seriously? I can't stick? All I do is stick—for my readers, my publisher, and my brother's memory. Using a pen name started so I wouldn't have to explain that I was, in essence, stealing my dead brother's dream. It's allowed me to honor his memory on my own terms, preserving control and keeping the focus on the books.

I made a vow when I started writing, and I won't go back on it now. I have to find another way to convince my grandfather I'm not the silver-spoon slacker everyone thinks I am.

"How many sports did you play growing up?"

I tap my thumb on the steering wheel. "Plenty of kids are multi-sport athletes."

"How many full seasons did you make it through on a team?"

"I don't like being told what to do." I also didn't appreciate being compared to my older brother and coming up short every time. It seemed easier to go in a different direction than Mike, which happened to be quitting.

"How many schools did you attend?"

"I get your point."

"What about college?"

"It wasn't the right fit."

"Three semesters at Yale. Three."

"Who cares? All I ever heard from Dad was that Yale isn't Harvard."

According to the GPS, we've almost made it to the dance studio, and I want nothing more than to drop the old man off and keep driving. Every sideways glance from him just confirms what I already know—he still sees me as that irresponsible teenager, not someone worthy of carrying on his legacy.

Grandpa pats my arm, and even though I'm still frustrated, the blame lies with me for not giving him a reason to believe I've changed. The worst part? How much it stings. Like I'm seventeen again and desperate for his approval

"I need to know you're committed and not just looking for an opportunity to beat your father. The foundation means the world to me. The staff and the people we serve are family, Jake. Family matters."

My life has been devoted to honoring Mike's dream of writing books, but it's become even bigger than either of us could have imagined. Family matters most, but I've let the past overshadow everything.

I pull into the parking lot and turn off the truck's engine. The breeze whips a few bright yellow leaves across the windshield, and I feel like I'm swirling the same way, unsure of my path and where I'll land.

I could so easily reveal my identity as NYT bestseller Spencer Charles, but that feels like selling out on my brother. I wrote that first book as a way to finally deal with my grief from losing him, and I never intended to take credit for a career that should have been his if he'd lived.

My grandpa, like everyone else, thinks I've spent the better part of ten years partying and surfing and squandering my life. If a dance class is going to help him think I can commit to something, what the hell will it hurt? Probably a lot less than receiving kudos for success that doesn't truly feel like it belongs to me.

"Do you know why I signed up for this dancing class?"

"An excuse to wear tight pants and get a spray tan like the reality show dancers?"

"I did it for a woman."

An answer I hadn't expected. "What woman?"

"Gloria Johnson."

"Former U.S. Senator Johnson?"

"The very one. She's a force to be reckoned with. I haven't met a woman with her character since...since your grandmother passed away fifteen years ago."

"Good for you, Gramps. It's about time you climbed back on that horse."

He shakes his head. "This isn't about climbing or horses. It's about putting yourself out there and sticking with something. I started dancing because of Gloria, but I've stayed with it for me. The connection and collaboration invigorate me, just like running the foundation did for so many years. I want to share that with you. Dance is more than just moving better—it teaches you how to live better."

"Deep thoughts with Gilbert Byrne," I mutter.

"I also get my hands on Gloria twice a week," he adds with a mischievous laugh.

"My corneas are burning at the mental image." I mock shudder, then meet his gaze. "Why not just ask her out?"

"She said no," he answers simply. "But I'm not giving up. I'm—"

"Sticking," I say with an eye roll. "Fine. I'll partner up with your new gal. I'm sticking, too, Grandpa. And I'm going to prove it to you in whatever way works."

If a few weeks of dancing with one of Skylark's fleet-footed geriatrics gets me closer to my goal, then it'll be worth it. If I can prove to both my grandfather and the people around here that I'm not the same person some of them remember from that wild and regrettable summer after my brother died, even better.

Grandpa squeezes my shoulder as we enter the studio's lobby. "You won't regret this, kid."

Several couples are gathered inside a large studio. Framed photos of dancers line the far wall, while the one closest to us is mirrored floor to ceiling.

A woman who looks to be in her late thirties, wearing a fitted top and flowing skirt, steps out of a small office to greet us. "Hello, Gilbert. And you must be Jake."

"Yup." I hold out my hand to shake hers. "Based on your impeccable posture, I'm guessing you're Charlotte, my new dance instructor."

She carries herself with poise and grace, her dark hair tied back in a low bun. Her features are striking but approachable, and her dark red lips curve into a smile as she takes my hand. "Call me Char. I recognize the devilish twinkle in your eyes. Just like your grandfather."

"This one's trouble," Grandpa confirms, and my stomach tightens. I've always been the troublesome brother.

Char must sense that the joke falls flat with me because she squeezes my hand a little tighter. "We're happy to have you join us. Come in and meet everyone. What size shoe do you wear, Jake?"

"Thirteen," I answer, eliciting a throaty laugh.

"I like big feet in a man," she says, linking her arm with mine. Maybe this dance class is going to get spicier than I anticipated.

She leads me into the studio with Grandpa following. The floors are the same light wood as the lobby area, and a wide bank of windows lets in the morning light.

"Everyone, help me welcome our newest student."

I recognize Gloria Johnson as the members of the class approach. Her smile is warm, and her eyes bright as she gives Grandpa a little wave.

"Are you my partner?" I ask the woman standing next to Gloria. Both of their faces are lined with soft wrinkles, but the former senator is taller, her hair styled in a classic bob. She exudes confidence and looks elegant in her cashmere sweater and dark pants.

The woman I assume to be my partner could be a stand-in for Mrs. Claus. Her eyes twinkle and her posture is slightly stooped, but her smile is bright and welcoming.

"Not so fast, kid." A tall, balding man with a slight paunch steps forward and shoots me a glare. "Janie is mine." He puts a protective arm around Mrs. Claus's shoulder. "In dance class and life."

"Fifty-five years last week," Janie confirms, holding up her left hand. "We're glad you're here, Jake. Your grandfather said you're a great dancer."

Grandpa elbows me and says, "Jake's got all the right moves."

I'd like to move right on out of this place.

"Here she is now," Char announces before I can make an escape. "Our other new student."

I turn with the rest of the group, and suddenly I'm not going anywhere.

8

JAKE

Iris Dixon is wearing black leggings and a long-sleeve athletic top under a fleece vest. She's braided her hair, and twin spots of pink color her cheeks.

Based on how her gaze darts around the room, she looks about as excited to be here as I feel. But I was coerced. What's her reason?

"Cheeky monkey," Gloria whispers under her breath, and my mind immediately tries to connect the dots between the retired senator and Skylark's current mayor.

"Iris, come and join us." Char motions her forward. "We were just talking about the dancing prowess of your new partner. Have you met Jake Byrne? He's Gilbert's grandson and in town for..."

"A while," I supply.

"We know each other." Iris flicks a glance at me that has daggers shooting from it, her posture ramrod straight.

Grandpa clears his throat and grins. "Welcome to the class, Mayor Dixon. I guess surprises are the spice of life. That's what I always say."

"I've never heard you say that," I tell him.

"I'm saying it now."

Iris steps forward and offers Grandpa and the other members

of the class a stiff smile. She avoids looking at me again. "Thanks for letting me join. This is going to be fun." She nearly shouts that last word, and I think about what she said on the street about not being fun.

What the hell is her deal? One thing I know for sure is that partnering with me isn't Iris Dixon's version of fun. And while I don't owe her a thing, some long-dormant spark of chivalry flares in my heart at whatever private struggle she's clearly facing.

"Maybe this isn't a great idea," I say to Char. "I'm sure there's somebody else with more experience who could join the class as Iris's partner."

My grandfather nudges me with his elbow. "You quitting already?"

"I'm not quitting. I'm being respectful of Iris's feelings toward me."

Iris chokes out a laugh. "I don't have feelings for you. But feel free to quit."

"I'm not quitting," I repeat through gritted teeth.

A few more couples have entered the studio, and the back of my neck burns at the attention we're drawing. This wasn't how I planned my return to Colorado.

It's too much—Iris glaring at me. Grandpa putting me through the paces of proving myself— and my stomach churns like it used to when Mike and I would sneak into the kitchen to stuff our faces with the leftover desserts from Dad's fancy parties. I stand perfectly still and try to will away the nausea.

"Of course not." Gloria's voice is gentle but firm as she takes my arm. "Iris is here to have fun." She raises a delicate brow at the mayor. "From what your grandfather says, Jake, you're the life of the party everywhere you go. You two will be great together."

I'm unsure if that last sentence is a wish or a command, but she continues, "The past should be left in the past," and I definitely see Iris flinch.

Something's going on, and I want to know what it is. Iris

might be part of my past, but she's never truly left me. Hell, I based Ellie Spaulding, the amateur sleuth in my bestselling series, on her. She's with me every day, not that I plan to admit it.

"Then let's get started," Char says, clapping her hands. "Everyone to your places."

The other students disperse until only Iris and I are left. Her hands squeeze into tight fists at her sides, and she looks like she's about to bolt. Relatable.

If Char notices how awkward this moment is, she ignores it like a professional.

"How tall are you, Iris?"

"Five-nine," she mumbles.

"And you, Jake?"

"Six-two?"

"That's a perfect height differential for a balanced aesthetic. Of course, executing moves and the connection between the partners matters most in ballroom dance. That won't be a problem, right?"

"Not one bit," Iris lies.

"Works for me." I offer a wide smile and a thumbs up, earning an eye-roll from my new partner.

"Great." Char takes our arms and positions us in the center of the first row of dancers. "Remember, we're all about having fun."

Iris swallows, and for a moment, I wonder if she's about to hurl. "I'm all about having fun too." She sounds like a schoolgirl repeating a lesson, but elbows me in the ribs when I chuckle in response.

"Hey, now." I lift my hands. "Everyone knows fun and I go hand in hand. I'm Fred Astaire to fun's Ginger Rogers."

Iris doesn't look convinced, but at this point, there's nothing she can do about having me as her partner.

Char curls her long fingers around my wrist. "Jake, would you help me demonstrate the steps we'll focus on today? I'm sure you and Iris will catch on quickly."

I'm sure of no such thing, and Iris looks like she might be grinding her teeth to nubs behind that placid smile she's wearing.

For as much time as I've spent over the years courting attention —mostly from ill-advised rebellion, pranks, and random hijinks— having everyone's eyes on me, particularly Iris's dark gaze, makes me weirdly self-conscious. No one who knows me would guess I have a self-conscious bone in my body, and I'm not about to give away that fact now.

Char positions me where she wants me, which feels like being manhandled in a not unpleasant way. The dance instructor is gorgeous, and when she fits her body inside the arc of my arms, I expect mine to react. I like women of all shapes and sizes, but I'm about as turned on by Charlotte as I would be by my ancient housekeeper.

She demonstrates a few easy turns, then moves us into something a little more complicated, giving me soft words of encouragement and praise as I follow along.

I never took formal dance lessons, but my grandmother insisted on teaching both Mike and me some basic moves. I'm coordinated, and my body seems to know the steps better than my brain. I'm also used to ignoring my brain, so letting myself go is not a stretch. I can tell Char is surprised at how easily I follow while making it look like I'm the one leading, which is her intent.

We continue for a few minutes, and when we stop, there's an enthusiastic round of applause from the rest of the students.

"My grandson's a natural," Gilbert calls out.

Char offers a deep curtsy. "I concur," she says. "Now, everyone get with your partners, and let's work on those steps as a group."

She resets the music, but Iris continues to stand a few feet away, not coming any closer. I walk to her instead.

"How did you do that?" she demands, her arms ramrod straight.

"I didn't do anything other than follow Char's lead. I told you I've got moves." I wink. "My moves have moves."

"I want a different partner," she tells Char when the instructor comes to see why we're not starting. Everyone else is practicing the steps.

Char looks as confused as I feel. I know Iris doesn't like me, but the woman is a perfectionist, and I just proved I'm not going to embarrass her.

"Trade me out," she continues, pointing across the room. "I'll take that guy."

The man in question is possibly a hundred and fifty years old, and he's shuffling through the dance with a woman wearing brightly colored scrubs who looks to be in her mid-fifties.

"That's Louis Johnson," Char says. "He takes the class with his home health care aide."

"Great, just my speed. Give him to me and let the aide dance with John Travolta here."

"Is that John Travolta circa *Saturday Night Fever* or *Pulp Fiction*? Because either one is a compliment." I add a wink for good measure

Iris looks like she wants to kick me in the shin.

"I'm a beginner," Iris says when Char shakes her head. "I need somebody who's also a beginner."

"If you don't count clubbing in Vegas as everybody's favorite groomsman and coordinator of bachelor parties, I'm also a dancing newbie."

"You'll be fine." Char reaches out to pat Iris's shoulder, but pulls back when Iris makes a sound that clearly resembles a growl low in her throat.

"Char, can you answer a question about the step ball change?" Janie calls from across the studio.

"Of course. Jake's got you, Iris." She glides toward Tom and Janie, graceful even when walking.

The words of encouragement she left in her wake aren't going to convince Iris. But when I assume the starting position with my arms out, she steps into my embrace.

Ah, shit. I might not have reacted to the dance instructor, but my senses go haywire with Iris this close. Not a good sign.

"Relax," I tell her. Both of us, really.

She only stiffens more. "Do not tell me what to do."

"Iris, relax," Char calls out. "Your shoulders are grazing your earlobes. Okay, people, let's take it from the top."

The music starts over, and I begin the steps. It only takes a few seconds for me to realize why Iris seemed so discombobulated by my ability to pick up the rhythm of the dance so quickly. Skylark's dedicated mayor has two Sasquatch-sized left feet. Perfect Iris Dixon has zero rhythm.

She wants fun?

Oh, this is going to be fun.

9

IRIS

"IT WAS AWFUL. The opposite of fun. I'm incapable of having fun."

I lower my head to my hands and lean forward on the park bench under the shade of the bright yellow leaves of a sycamore tree in Skylark's town square. Sloane, who's taken her lunch hour to meet with me after my disastrous dance class, rubs her hand along my back in soothing circles.

"You're out of practice with fun. This morning was the start of something new. Give yourself time. It's going to be great."

I straighten and point to my chest, feeling defeated on every level. "I'm actually where fun comes to die. I suck at fun. The *fun sucker.*"

Sloane taps a finger on her chin as she considers that. "We could get you a bubble machine."

I groan. "This is serious."

"Serious *fun*," she clarifies.

"Seriously, I'm not at all fun."

She frowns when my words come out snappish, which I don't mean. "I'm sorry," I say immediately. "This isn't on you. I'm the one who should be supporting you. I'm not fun *and* I'm a bad friend, which is still about me." I slap a palm against my forehead. "Shit. I'm a narcissist on top of everything else."

She covers her face with her hands, and my heart lurches, launching me straight into recovery mode. "I'm sorry, I didn't mean to snap or swear. I take it all back. I love the dance class. I'm having *so* much fun, the time of my life."

Sloane's shoulders are shaking now, and I feel like the biggest asshole who ever lived. But when she finally raises her gaze to mine, her eyes shimmering, I realize they aren't sad tears or angry or accusatory tears.

She looks delighted.

"I love you, Iris." She reaches out to hug me then dashes her fingers across her cheeks. "You aren't selfish or a narcissist. Trust me. Thanks to my parents, I'm well-versed in narcissism."

"Are you actually crying from *happiness* right now?" I ask slowly. My heart still hasn't calmed to a normal speed. "I just told you I'm failing at my bucket list challenge. It's the one thing you wanted from us. I'm failing you, Sloane."

A sharp bark of laughter escapes her lips, and she presses a hand over her mouth as my eyes go wide.

"Watching you struggle with something as simple as having fun is...well, the most fun I've had in a long time."

My brain works to process her words. I'm glad I've made her smile but...

"Should I be offended?"

She hugs me again. "I love you because you treat me like a normal person, Iris. Not like I'm sick." She swallows then adds in a whisper, "Like I'm dying."

"You aren't dying." I wrap my arms tight around her thin shoulders. "Don't say that."

"We're all dying," she insists. "I happen to know what might kill me, and I can't forget it because no one lets me. Except you.

You aren't failing at the challenge. It's not supposed to be easy. It's supposed to push you out of your comfort zone into something different."

"A better version of me."

"A more *fun* version," she clarifies.

I look up at the clouds, fluffy cotton balls against a deep blue backdrop. The air carries a crisp scent of fallen foliage, and it's only a matter of time until the gorgeous October weather changes and we get our first snowstorm.

Will it be before or after Sloane leaves for Nashville again? Before or after the upcoming election? A sense of urgency bubbles up inside me, some tangible pressure to transform my life before the season changes. "It's nothing if I can't do it," I whisper.

"You can," Sloane promises, and I want to believe her. "If dancing isn't fun—"

"It is." I bite down on my lower lip and try not to cringe. "I love dancing. I dance alone in my kitchen all the time. Heck, I've danced in your kitchen."

"Is that what those spastic movements are called?" Sloane pretends to be shocked. "I thought a spider crawled up your leg."

"Very funny." My gut tightens. "I don't know why I thought joining a class would automatically change things. It's not fun to look like a fool."

Sloane shrugs. "What if part of the challenge is to learn not to care? I know you love dancing. I also love that you might have to work a little bit to make this class fun."

"What's fun about partnering with a man I hate?"

Sloane makes a hum of approval in her throat. "Ah, yes. Jake Byrne. Now we're getting to the good stuff."

"Give me a break. It's one thing to not worry about looking like a fool dancing with some old dude. Jake is *good*, and he doesn't even have to try. He never has to try. It all comes so easy to him."

"You don't know that. Maybe he said yes to the class because he's trying to get on his grandfather's good side. Come on. It has to be more fun to dance with sex-on-a-stick Jake Byrne than some shriveled up octogenarian."

"I don't think about sex when I look at Jake."

"Everybody—men, women, probably even Sadie's pack of canine clients—thinks about sex when they look at Jake," she argues. "If you want to have some real fun—"

"Hell, no. You know what he did to Nick."

"I know what Nick did to himself," she says gently. "Your brother made choices, Iris. Plenty of bad ones, all on his own. It might be time to stop blaming Jake."

"Pretty sure Gloria agrees with you." I think of the former senator's line about leaving the past in the past.

"I knew it." Sloane points a finger at me. "You *do* have an ulterior motive."

I take her hand and squeeze. "Getting to know Gloria better is a potential bonus outcome." My voice cracks slightly. "Or an extra layer of humiliation if she has a front-row seat to my failure." I huff out a laugh, trying not to show how much admitting this affects me. "Every time somebody tells me to relax, or loosen up, or live a little, I think about my mom saying those things as justifications for being a neglectful parent. I think about where Nick would be if she hadn't been."

"He made choices," Sloane repeats. "Just like you. Look at how great you turned out."

I laugh softly. "You're the only person who thinks that."

"Not for long," she assures me. "I love this challenge for you. For both of us."

Her enthusiasm is the reminder I need that I'm not giving up. If struggling to have fun doing something I love because I hate being bad at anything makes my friend smile, I'll make a fool of myself in front of the whole town. The whole world. Whatever it takes.

"I've got to go," I say when the chime on the clock tower above the town hall marks the top of the hour. "I'm meeting with Marla and George to talk about Fun Fest."

I give Sloane one final hug as we stand. "And I need to stop by the hardware store and pick up a bubble blaster on my way back to the office."

She flashes another wide grin. "Bubbles are hella fun."

10

IRIS

As the two committee members leave my office an hour later, bubble blasters in hand, a sense of accomplishment fills me, chasing away some of my earlier doubts.

Sloane's comment was meant as a joke, but my idea for including bubble artists as part of the festival lineup is a hit.

"It's going to be so *fun*." I give Jodi, who is seated at her desk, a pointed look.

"That's what it's all about." George chuckles as he points the blaster at Jodi and fires a stream of bubbles. "Your uncle would be proud of some of Iris's new ideas for adding more fun to Fun Fest."

"Who's going to pay for it?" Jodi asks sweetly, "since Iris has allocated so much of the approved budget to the library." She steeples her fingers. "Which is a worthy cause, of course. But if we try to do everything, she's going to put Skylark in terrible financial shape."

George and Marla frown as the bubbles succumb to gravity and silently pop, vanishing along with my fleeting happiness.

"I thought you said the budget was worked out," George says darkly.

"I said it's getting worked out, and it is." Look at me matching Jodi's syrupy sweetness and trying not to notice the bitter aftertaste. "I'm exploring new avenues for funding and sponsorship so we can expand the event and still support the literacy program."

"You suggested selling tickets for Fun Fest." Jodi tilts her head and shrugs, cloaking the malice hidden in her words.

Marla gasps. "Oh no, this is our gift to the town. We can't charge them. That takes away the fun. This needs to be free fun."

I nod and will away the heat I feel rising to my face. "I understand that."

"There's always your idea of defunding the fire department," Jodi offers like she's sharing a weather report.

"The fire department," George bellows. "What are you thinking, Iris?"

"We're not defunding the fire department," I assure him and place my blaster on the corner of Jodi's desk. The urge to use it as an actual weapon is just too strong at the moment. "No essential services they provide will be impacted by this event."

"You *did* mention it," Jodi insists, her deceptively honeyed tone making my teeth ache.

I sarcastically suggested both options in the midst of racking my brain to come up with ideas of how to make everyone happy. I wasn't serious, and Jodi damn well knows it. I should have had my guard up after she ambushed me at the start of the week, but she insisted sabotage wasn't her intention.

And, like a fool, I believed her.

"It's going to be great," I promise the two committee members. "So fun. The most fun this town has ever seen."

Marla grips my wrist. "Our budget is locked in, right?"

"Of course."

They both nod, although neither looks convinced.

As soon as George and Marla are out the door of the main office, I shut it and round on Jodi.

She wrinkles her nose. "I think our door needs to remain open so the residents of this town know they're always welcome in the mayor's office, even if *you* choose to keep your inner sanctum shut most of the time."

"As you well know, my door is shut because I can't concentrate when you play music."

"I need music to work. It helps with my anxiety."

"It's making me anxious that you seem hellbent on throwing me under every passing bus." But I open the door again.

"It's not my problem you overpromise and underdeliver." She reaches for the bubble blaster. "No one is going to be fooled by a cheap plastic prop. You aren't fun, Iris. You're a stick in the mud who wouldn't know fun if the definition was plastered on the side of a bus."

"Why do you hate me?" I force my voice to remain calm. "I didn't do anything to—"

"Your mom did plenty." Her voice is low and spiteful.

"Along with *your* father," I can't help but point out. "I was a kid."

"*I* was a kid," she counters, pointing to her own chest. "*You* were in high school."

"Don't you think I would have stopped her if I could? I'm just as embarrassed by their affair as you."

"It did more than embarrass my family." She comes around her desk until we're toe to toe. "The scandal ripped us apart, ruined my dad's career and broke my mom's heart. It destroyed her standing in this community while you and your mom got to leave town."

A whirlwind of emotions—shock, guilt, and defensiveness—tangle together inside me, making my knees go weak.

"I didn't want to leave." I say the words like they should matter, when I know they won't. I might not have caused the scandal that destroyed her family, but I'm tethered to it, nonetheless.

Her brows draw together as she studies me, and I feel a deep empathy for the woman standing before me—a person whose family was shattered by choices neither of us asked for.

"Fine, the scandal wasn't your fault. And I guess I shouldn't punish you for your mom being a slut."

"That's not exactly how I'd describe her," I say but don't argue too much.

I haven't seen my mom in five years. We talk twice a year, on Christmas and on her birthday—never mine. She's still dating, and I've stopped asking if her boyfriends are married or not. I don't want to know. It's way easier that way.

"Why did you come back now?" Her tone is curious not angry, which surprises me after all the animosity she's displayed.

I shrug. "Even though we only lived here a few months, it felt like home."

"This isn't your home."

Ouch. Still spoken gently, but that stings.

"And we all know you'll be leaving again soon enough."

I think about Sadie's comment at our book club meeting. About me putting Skylark in my rearview mirror.

"What if I don't want to leave? What if I told you things are changing? I'm changing."

Am I? Am I capable of the kind of change I want in my life?

Part of me wants to believe it. I've never been a big fan of the person my childhood turned me into.

"Just like trying to convince people you signed up for dance class because you think it would be a lol."

"I do think it could be a *lol*."

I hate using slang. My mom was beyond casual in how she spoke and acted, so I tend to be formal and stuffy. Some people might even say I have a stick up my ass. Jodi is one of those people. But I'm going to prove her wrong. I'm going to prove all of us wrong.

"Come on, Iris, I know why you're in that class."

"Fine." I blow out a shaky breath, hating that she can see through me so easily. "Just because Glo—"

"You still have the hots for Jake Byrne."

Whoa, did not see that coming.

"Trust me, Jodi," I sputter out a laugh, "I didn't know Jake was going to be part of the class when I signed up."

"I don't believe you." She returns to her chair, once again glaring at me. "I saw him on his first day back in town, you know. We were at the grocery store at the same time. We reached for the same head of broccoli."

Okay, this is getting weird. "What do Jake Byrne's vegetable-buying habits have to do with you being out to get me at every turn?"

"We had a moment, Jake and I, in the produce department. Maybe it could lead to something, but not if you go after him."

"I'm *not* going after him."

"Then drop out of the class."

"I can't. I won't. I'm not in it for him. He doesn't even like me."

"He always liked you," she argues. "Why do you think he became friends with your brother? It was to get close to you."

"Or because they were both wild party animals."

"It was to get close to you," she repeats. "Despite dressing like you're auditioning for the new season of *Suits* most of the time, I know how you Dixon women are with your feminine wiles."

"I don't have wiles." I laugh, trying not to sound as self-conscious as I feel. "I have whatever the opposite of wiles is."

"I've seen the way half the men who come through this office look at you."

The comment takes me aback. I've never wanted wiles because my mom used hers so recklessly. But I must admit, the thought of having them where Jake is concerned does have some appeal.

"I'm not in the class for Jake." I cross my arms over my chest and glance toward the door to make sure no one is close enough to overhear. "I'm trying to convince Gloria to mentor me. If she sees I'm not the stick in the mud you've led everyone to believe, maybe she will."

"But you *are* that stick in the mud."

"I am *not*." I resist the urge to stomp my foot in protest. "I'm fun, and I'm not after Jake Byrne."

She studies me for a long moment. "Promise?" she eventually asks.

I think about the way it felt to be in Jake's embrace during the class, even though I couldn't relax. The fact that most of why I couldn't relax was being in his embrace.

"I promise."

"Okay, but..." Her lips twist into an almost apologetic grimace. "You won't need a mentor if you aren't elected."

Alarm bells go off in my head. "I'm running unopposed."

The members of the town council had called me in about a month after my appointment to voice their support if I'd consider a full term in office. Despite my lack of formal experience in the position, they cited my adaptability and willingness to collaborate, plus my focus on progressive initiatives and sustainability as proof that I was a promising leader. The word fun hadn't been mentioned once.

Their confidence bolstered me in a way I desperately needed after how things imploded in Minnesota. Not that anyone—even Sloane—knows the details of that shit show. I agreed to the council's request because I want a chance to make a difference and a foundation on which to rebuild my life and career. They also assured me that with the council's backing, the election will be more of a formality than a real race.

"Not as of later today," Jodi explains. The throbbing in my head worsens with each word she speaks. "My cousin, Joey, is going to announce that he's running against you," she says out of the blue.

Her statement blindsides me. This isn't how things were

supposed to go. I have a plan, and this is just one more twist that's blowing it all to hell.

Pacing to the window so she can't read the doubt on my face, I work to control my breathing. "Joey runs the auto body shop north of town, right?"

"Third generation mechanic," she confirms.

"Which means he has even less political experience than me. I can—"

"You can't beat him."

"You might not think I'm fun, but I'm dedicated to this town. It's my home, even if the mayor's office is a stepping stone for something more. That only means I'm going to try harder. I have goals, Jodi, and—"

"He's going to use the scandal against you."

I slowly turn to face her. I've never given much thought to having a Spidey-sense, but my whole body is tingling, and not in the way it did earlier watching Jake move across the dance floor.

No one knows about *my* scandal. A wave of shame washes over me as I imagine the gossip and judgment, my reputation unraveling before my eyes. There are worse things to be known as than a stick in the mud. And given my mom's history, the "other woman" label is devastating to me, even if I deserve it.

"Why?" I croak out. "How?" I grip the edge of the window like the wood trim can keep me from falling.

She lets out a long sigh. "I get that it's unfair, and most people in Skylark don't hold you responsible for how your mom behaved, but my family still does." She shrugs. "Me included, as we both know. Joey is going to lean into the whole family values platform. Tradition, since the Moores have a long history around here. You haven't done anything to deserve it, but he's going for the whole complicit by association angle. I think it has a good shot of tilting things in his favor."

"Oh." I move to a nearby chair on shaky legs and lower myself into it. "This is about my mom."

"Your brother's kind of a train wreck, too," Jodi adds. "I'm honestly sorry, Iris. You aren't the villain here."

Not here. But I am a villain.

I cross my arms over my chest, feeling exposed and conflicted. What now?

"I could help you with a campaign," Jodi offers, making me realize I voiced the question out loud.

A laugh bubbles up in my throat. "Is this some kind of Trojan Horse deal, or like when Regina and The Plastics got their revenge in *Mean Girls*? Why would you help me when you hate me?"

"I don't hate you," she says quietly. "And I guess I understand I'm not the only one still dealing with the fallout of a scandal that wasn't my fault." She taps her shiny nails on the desk. "Plus, I'm hoping if I help you that you'll help me with Jake."

Whoa. The shock waves just keep on reverberating through me.

I don't know what to say, but I do know I made a promise to Sloane and a commitment to myself. Maybe I can finally prove to the world—myself included—that I'm not only fun, I'm also fierce.

It's time for a self-reckoning. There's a lot involved in navigating the potential fallout, but also the possibility of rebuilding my sense of self. And that's enough of a potential win to convince me not to turn away from this fight. No matter what I have to do to win.

11

IRIS

Tony's, the diviest—and my favorite—of Skylark's modest bar scene, is crowded for a Thursday, primarily because of the ever-popular karaoke night they host each week.

See what I mean about this town and fun? Even the dive bars host events that everyone from bikers to cowboys to the elementary school principal enjoy.

I'm nestled in a corner booth with two shot glasses in front of me—I should clarify, two empty shot glasses. Because the so-called fun I'm about to engage in will be easier with a smidge of liquid courage.

"Are you ready for this?" Avah demands as she and Molly slide in across from me.

A petite waitress with jet black hair arrives a moment later. "Can I get anything for you ladies?"

"Another round," I tell her, lifting a finger. Or maybe two fingers. It's a little fuzzy at the moment.

Molly leans forward to sniff one of the empty shot glasses then grimaces. "It smells like you're drinking lighter fluid." She smiles at the waitress. "I'll have a margarita."

"Two margaritas," Avah adds.

"Three margaritas *and* the shots," I insist. "Like the song. Three margaritas, Imma put it—"

"TMI, girl." Avah grabs my hand and squeezes hard.

"No shots," Molly tells the waitress. "A round of waters."

"You can't tell me what to do." I tug at my hand, but Avah's got one hell of a grip for a wisp of a thing. "I'm the mayor." At least for now.

"The mayor of Can't Hold Your Liquor Town," Avah says, her nails digging into my palm.

The waitress cracks a smile. "Well, Ms. Mayor, you have good friends. Three margaritas and three large waters coming up."

"Hey, that's not fun," I complain to my friends as the waitress turns away. "We're supposed to be having fun."

Avah finally releases me. "Karaoke is the fun part, and it's going to be a lot less fun if you're slurring the song lyrics."

"I think that's the only way it's going to be fun," I argue. "I sing better than I dance, but it's a low bar."

"I can't carry a tune to save my life." Molly cringes. "Even the twins beg me to stop."

"I have the voice of an angel," Avah assures us with a grin, "but I'm just here for moral support."

"I don't need moral support." I press two fingers to my temple, which is already starting to pound. Total lightweight. "I need a group. Harmonies. Camaraderie. Someone to hide behind."

The waitress returns with our drinks. I gulp down half the water and then push away the margarita. Turns out those shots of liquid courage might have been slightly ill-advised. "I can't go up there by myself. That's no fun."

Molly laughs. "It'll be fun from here. Just getting out of the house without my kids, who I love to death, as you know, is fun for me."

"You can't force fun." Avah licks the salt off her rim. "That isn't how fun works."

"That's the problem," I remind them. "I suck at fun." I gesture

71

to the patrons crowding the bar's interior. "Which is why I'm adding more attempts at fun to my bucket list."

Both women take long sips of their drinks.

"Leave it to you to be an overachiever," Avah says after a moment.

Heat floods my cheeks. "What's wrong with that?"

"Nothing," Molly assures me. "You're doing great, sweetie. But no more shots."

"No more shots," I agree. At least I'm not feeling quite as fuzzy as a few minutes ago. Nerves—mixed with a healthy dose of residual shame, guilt, and regret—are a real buzz kill.

"You've got this." Avah doesn't sound convinced, but I appreciate the words of encouragement. "Besides, alcohol can tighten your vocal cords. We want you to be loosey-goosey tonight."

Great. Another reminder that I need to loosen up. One more thing I suck at.

"By the way." Molly wiggles her eyebrows. "I found a company in Denver that has a mobile pole dancing—"

"Pole dancing," a deep voice echoes, followed by the sound of rumbly laughter. "Iris, are you two-timing your dance partner with a pole?"

I promptly spit the water I just drank across the table. Avah grabs a napkin and wipes her cheeks, her disgusted glare softened by the smile that plays at the corners of her mouth. "Was that necessary?"

"You're legit cut off," Molly tells me then points at Jake. "You're trouble."

"My reputation precedes me." He offers my redheaded friend a lazy smile. "Tell me more about Iris and the pole."

A blush crawls up my throat at the way his mouth caresses that word. And Jesus, take the wheel, because thinking about caressing and Jake Byrne's mouth is not a good combination for my brain.

My body is a whole other story.

"You need to get your mind out of the gutter." I sound bored and dismissive. I love that for me.

"Are you sure you don't want to join me?" he asks. "You said you wanted to have more fun, and I know fun. The dirty kind is my favorite."

"Introduce us to your friend," Molly squeaks, doing a fine impression of a kid who just sucked down half a helium balloon.

"He's not my friend."

"Iris and I aren't friends."

Jake and I speak the words at the same time. That he's willing to admit it irritates me, crazy as that sounds.

Molly glances between the two of us. "I definitely heard the word partners."

"Me, too." Avah finishes her margarita and then grabs mine.

"We're in the same dance class," I reluctantly admit. I still haven't introduced Jake by name, so neither realizes he's the guy from the street and my past. I want to keep it that way. "I wouldn't have picked that class if I'd known he was part of it."

"I wouldn't have to be part of it, if you didn't need a partner."

"Hmmm..." Molly's hum is soft and drawn out. Clearly, she's intrigued. I don't want intrigue where Jake is concerned, especially after the pseudo-agreement Jodi and I came to this afternoon.

"So you're a bonus," Avah says, making a show of looking Jake up and down. She likes to do that—to use her boldness to unbalance people. I could have told her Jake isn't easily rattled.

"I'm a lot of things," he says, taking a swig of his beer. Why do I find his Adam's apple bobbing when he swallows weirdly sexy? "But a bonus isn't one of them. Is this pole dancing something new? And are spectators invited to the classes? Because I'd pay for—"

"You aren't invited," I tell him before he can finish. "Why are you even here?"

"Same as everyone else." Another wink for Molly. "I'm here to channel my inner songstress."

"You don't have an inner songstress, Jake. You have an inner annoy-the-crap-out-of-me-ness. Did you hear me talking to Char after class today?"

"You think I'm here because I knew you were going to be here?"

"I hope so," Molly says.

"Me too," Avah agrees. "Wait... Jake? As in the guy who ran you down on Main Street?"

"Almost," he corrects. "Almost ran her down on Main Street. And only because she jumped in front of my truck."

"I did not."

"Did too." He leans in. "No take backs."

Avah chokes out a laugh as Molly offers another throaty hum. They both have elbows on the table, chins cradled in their hands like they are avidly watching a fascinating play unfold.

"Can I get you two some popcorn?" I narrow my eyes at my traitor friends and ignore the fact that I might be slurring my words just a little.

"This is so good, I don't even need a snack," Molly answers. "Would you like to join us, Jake?"

"Who is not from State Farm," Avah adds with a wink.

Jake grins at the lame joke, and Molly offers him a wide smile. "I'm Molly and this is Avah. We're part of Iris's book club. We've heard a lot about you."

Avah throws me some wicked side-eye. "But apparently not everything."

Jake heaves a beleaguered sigh. "Don't believe a word."

He shifts closer, and I scooch toward the end of the seat. "Do not sit down. You're not invited."

"What kind of books do you ladies read?" Jake asks as he folds his long frame into the booth next to me, ignoring my protest.

"All kinds. Anything from personal development to mystery to spicy romance," Molly answers.

"Spicy romance." Jake makes a satisfied sound low in his throat. "Is that where the pole dancing came from?"

"Taylor, our shy librarian, picked the spice," Avah tells him. "Pole dancing is book-club adjacent and Iris's idea. Which is weird, come to think of it. The last time she picked a book, we read a biography of John Adams. No one except her made it through it. It was boring as hell."

"John Adams led a fascinating life," I argue. "He was the first president to live in the White House."

"And wrote thousands of love letters to his wife," Jake adds.

I turn to gape at him. "How do you know that?"

"I was a history major."

"Where did you go to college?" Molly asks.

"A couple of semesters at Yale," he answers. "It wasn't the right fit."

That long ago summer, Jake talked about how his father had wanted him and his brother to go to Harvard. At the time, I laughed. Jake didn't take anything seriously, other than drinking. I couldn't imagine him getting into a school like Harvard or Yale. When you have the money and influence the Byrnes do, you can buy your way into an Ivy-league education, but still...

"Yale was a huge disappointment to my dad," he says, as if it meant nothing to him.

"It's an amazing school," I answer automatically.

"It's not Harvard," he counters. Something in his gray-green gaze makes my breath catch in my throat. A vulnerability I don't expect, and it rattles me.

After a few long moments, Avah clears her throat. "Can you sing, Jake?"

"Like a canary." His gaze doesn't leave mine.

"Then you and Iris can duet."

"Hell, no." I rotate my hand in a circle between Avah, Molly and me. "The three of us are together in this."

"I'm not singing," Avah reminds me.

"Me neither." Molly makes a face. "People would run screaming."

"No," I repeat.

"It's fine." Jake gives an exaggerated sigh. "I think I understand the problem here, ladies." He leans in like he's sharing a secret, and even my curiosity is piqued. "Iris doesn't think she can keep her hands off me...just like in dance class."

Ugh. I smack his shoulder. "I'm not supposed to keep my hands off you, dummy. I'm supposed to put my hands on you. That's the whole point of being partners."

"We both know there were a few times your hands strayed a little lower than appropriate."

"They did not."

"Iris copped a feel?" Avah sounds delighted.

"I need to get a babysitter more often." Molly is grinning wildly. "This is the most fun I've had in years. I mean, other than the fun I have with my kids. I really do love my kids."

Jake nods, the picture of innocence. "I'm sure you're a wonderful mother, and I'm having buckets of fun getting to know you ladies. Just like I plan to have fun singing karaoke. I'm trying to decide between *Ring of Fire* or *Mr. Brightside*."

"Johnny Cash, for sure. His energy fits you," Avah says.

Jake wiggles his thick brows. "Unless Iris agrees to a duet, in which case I'll let her pick the song. I'm all about keeping the ladies happy."

"I bet you are," Avah purrs.

"You don't make me happy," I snap. "And I'm not having fun!"

I didn't mean to shout that last, but I did, and because of my recent luck, a hush falls over the crowd at the precise moment my words ring out.

"Did you hear that, everybody?" Jake calls out when the other patrons turn to stare at our table. "The mayor just said she wants to have fun. What's more fun than getting the ball rolling with karaoke?"

"I'm going to kill you," I say under my breath.

"Oh, no, you're not." Avah shakes her head. "He's saving your bacon right now, girl."

She's right, even though I'm loath to admit it. I swallow a groan and follow Jake out of the booth and toward the small stage set up at the far end of the bar's main room.

"Pick your poison." His arm grazes mine, and all I can think about is the heat of his touch and how he smells like spice and clean laundry.

I swear to all that is holy I didn't purposely stumble during our routine this morning just so I could push my face into his shirt and take a big whiff of all that delectable manliness.

Then I realize the eyes of almost everyone in the bar are following us, and I pull away.

"I don't know if I can—" I start, honestly nervous.

He looks at me and inclines his head. "I thought you always had a plan."

"Not tonight." I'm talking about more than whatever song we're going to sing. We both know it. But Jake's poker face is as good as mine, and he swings his arm wide to the crowd.

"We'll let your friends and neighbors decide. Hey y'all, what do you want to hear tonight?"

Several people shout out song titles, but one voice rings louder than the rest.

"*Islands in the Stream*!"

I freeze, then turn to the booth where my friends are sitting. Sloane has joined them, and she gives me two enthusiastic thumbs up. Sloane is a huge Dolly Parton fan.

"She's got to be kidding," I mutter, but the crowd has already taken up the bandwagon with cheers and applause. Jake nods to the floppy-haired dude working the karaoke machine.

"Good choice," he hollers to Sloane. "You can't go wrong with Dolly."

I can think of a thousand things that could go wrong right now, and they have nothing to do with Dolly.

"I can't do this," I whisper. "I drank too much. I didn't drink enough."

"Hey." Jake squeezes my hand. "We're having fun, Dixon."

"If you tell me to loosen up, I'm going to kick your balls into your throat."

"You stay as tight as you want, but here we go." He hands me a microphone off the stand in front of us. The first notes begin, and my friends shout their encouragement.

I'd like to run away, because standing in front of a crowd of people who I'm pretty sure expect me to make a complete ass of myself is not anyone's idea of fun.

"We've got this," Jake says, and I remember the way he spoke those words to me that summer we spent together before everything went to shit.

We were about to jump off the cliff out at the local reservoir, and thanks to my fear of heights, that didn't seem any more fun than this. But with Jake holding my hand, I jumped anyway, and the free fall before we hit the water was one of the most exhilarating experiences of my life.

Maybe karaoke can't be compared to that, but as the words to the first verse appear on the screen with a little ball guiding me, I lift the microphone to my lips and start to sing.

My voice is shaky at first, and I hear a couple of groans, but I can actually carry a tune. At least in the shower.

Suddenly, the lights and the music and the energy of the crowd grab hold of me. It's not like I think I'm Dolly Parton—I wouldn't be fool enough to compare myself to the queen in any way, shape, or form—but I'm going to do my best to make her proud.

When Jake comes in on the Kenny Rogers verse with a smooth

baritone that shocks the hell out of me, I realize there might actually be nothing this guy can't do well.

And I have to admit, I'm having fun.

He takes my hand again, and we sing to each other, then get the crowd in on it, encouraging them to clap and join in the chorus.

To my utter surprise, they do—not just my friends, but people I don't even know. People who only know me as their stick-in-the-mud mayor. They're singing and laughing, and I'm laughing with them. It doesn't matter that my dance moves make me look like I'm having a seizure, or that I lose track of the words at one point. I'm having fun.

And when Jake spins me in his arms and sings directly to me that we rely on each other, uh-huh, I believe it.

We're relying on each other, one lover to another.

And the shocking truth hits me with the force of a sucker punch: my ultimate version of fun might be knowing what it feels like to take Jake Byrne as a lover.

Even Dolly can't save me now.

12

JAKE

WHAT THE HELL am I still doing here?

I should be home in the apartment above my grandfather's garage, alone and focused on both my looming book deadline and the next move to convince him I'm serious about being a responsible adult.

Even if he doesn't pick up my movements on his camera doorbell, I have no doubt he'll know what time I get in and guess that I was at a bar. It's not like I have a curfew, but I do have trust to rebuild.

Instead I'm on my third pint of water and watching Iris in all her dive bar glory.

Skylark's mayor has fully embraced her fun era. At the moment, she's holding court near the pool tables, and I bite back a groan as she tosses her hair over one shoulder and smiles at the two guys vying for her attention.

There was a moment during our duet when she grinned at me so openly, and it was like basking in sunlight on an early spring day. Or how I used to feel catching a buzz. The lights seemed brighter, the music richer, and the whole world more vivid as my worries faded into the background.

Only I couldn't ever stop at a buzz, and the repercussions of a blackout or fierce hangover weren't worth that first wave of pleasure.

Right now, I'm sober, just like I've been for the past twelve years. While I might nurse a beer in public to avoid questions about why I'm not drinking, I've learned the hard way that alcohol and I do not mix.

Iris's friends left thirty minutes ago, but she got pulled back to the stage with a group of middle-aged women who kept referring to themselves as the Bunko Babes, whatever that means. They needed backup for the Stevie Nicks song that would close out the karaoke portion of the night.

Hard to say whether it's the music or the margaritas, but Iris managed to shrug off her usual uptight manner—the one I find ridiculously appealing. She sang, shook the tambourine someone handed her, and twirled her heart out. It's a wonder she didn't knock one of the other ladies off the stage. She has a sweet little singing voice, but my girl has zero coordination.

My girl? What the hell am I thinking?

I'm so lost in thought, I don't notice Iris making her way to the exit until I see her duck out the front door.

"Hey, Byrne, you want another round?" somebody calls out.

"Nope. I'll catch you later." I wave and scoot past people, following the woman I've been trying to watch over all night into the darkness.

The quiet is almost jarring after the raucous noise of the bar, and crisp evening air stings my lungs. Iris is halfway down the street, and I jog to catch up with her. When I'm three feet away, she spins and holds up her hand. That's when I notice the mini canister clutched in her grip.

I stop in my tracks, hands up, palms out. "Seriously? You're going to pepper spray me?"

She seems to consider that for a moment, and I'm a little offended it takes her so long to come up with an answer.

"I'm being careful." She tucks the Mace back in her crossbody bag. "Why are you following me?"

"Where's your car? You shouldn't be driving."

"I don't need you to drive me home."

"Come on, Iris. The town's mayor can't have a scandal like a DUI before the election, even if you are running unopposed."

For a split second, wide-eyed disbelief seems to swirl in her dark gaze, like she's a deer caught in headlights. It's gone just as quickly, and maybe it was a trick of the dim evening light because she laughs and rolls those big eyes toward the starry sky.

"Are you joking? If I'd known what a few hours at Tony's could do for my reputation, I might have become a karaoke-night regular before now. It's embarrassing the number of people who were happy to admit they misjudged me." She frowns and tilts her head like she's revisiting those conversations. "I should have paid more attention to how I'm perceived before now."

"You're fine just the way you are, and you gave the fun naysayers a quick uppercut tonight. The belle of the karaoke bar." I hold out my hand, palm facing up. "But hand over the keys because you still shouldn't drive."

"I'm supposed to believe you're sober?"

"Scout's honor."

She gives a throaty laugh. "You were never a Boy Scout, Jake."

"Maybe not, but I am sober. I had half a beer at the beginning of the night, which is my limit these days."

She opens her mouth, and I know she's curious and doubtful. I was the king of beer pong the summer we spent together. Instead, she shakes her head, almost like she's trying to rid herself of any desire to know the man I am now.

It's a shame, because this version of Iris consumes me, and I don't have time for that right now.

"I walked to the bar," she says. "I live a few blocks from downtown."

I glance up at the street signs under the streetlight's glow, realizing the direction she's headed. "Did you buy the Maple Avenue house?" I ask, and she stumbles back a step.

"How do you remember the Maple Avenue house?" Even though we're alone on the street, her voice is just above a whisper.

"I remember everything about that summer," I tell her.

"Me too." Her delicate brows furrow. "Mostly I remember how it ended, especially for my brother."

She holds up a hand to prevent me from answering the implied accusation and begins walking again. "It doesn't matter anymore. What's done is done. Water under the bridge."

A smile tugs at the corner of my mouth. How many clichés can she throw at me, and which one of us is she trying to convince?

"I didn't buy the Maple Avenue house," she says. "I rent a duplex a block from that house, and I'm walking home, so you don't have to worry about me getting behind the wheel. Thanks for singing the duet with me, Jake. It was..." She almost grudgingly continues, "Fun."

"I'll walk you home." I fall into step with her. If Iris can't see how obvious it is that I'll use any excuse to spend time with her, I won't reveal myself. Not yet.

"You'll have the money for that house someday," I offer. She loved that Denver Square—the epitome of charm and practicality, perfect for a first-time homebuyer looking for character and comfort. Its classic brick façade and a welcoming front porch, framed by sturdy columns, invited teenage Iris to picture long afternoons reading on the outdoor swing. "You'll be able to scoop it up when it comes on the market."

She shakes her head. "It went up for sale right when I moved back. But I used my savings on something more important than the dream of home ownership. And renting means I'm not so tied down."

The words make it sound like a good thing, but Iris wanted roots the way kids who feel the hard tug of them crave freedom. I can't imagine anything that would be more important to her except...

"It was Nick, wasn't it? He needed to be bailed out of something."

Her step falters, and I instinctively place a steadying hand on her lower back. We were close and flirty while singing the duet, but this moment feels more intimate than anything we've shared, even that long-ago kiss.

"He owed some people money," she admits, like it's not a big deal.

Maybe it's the darkness, or the fact that she doesn't have to pretend with me, but I'm still surprised she shares the truth. Surprised and satisfied. It isn't only my grandfather's trust I'd like to regain.

"You used your house fund to bail him out?"

"And to send him to rehab. That was part of the agreement. He claims he went once before, but I don't believe it. Where would he get the money?"

I clear my throat. Although my gaze remains straight ahead, I feel deep in my bones the moment she realizes it. A shiver passes through her.

"You and my brother keep in touch?" There's a hint of condemnation in her voice.

"It's been a couple of years, but the last time I saw him, he asked for help. I gave it to him."

"I guess we're both idiots."

"You're not an idiot, Iris. You want to take care of your brother. I wanted to help, too."

"Then you shouldn't have let him take the fall for something you did. That's how it all started. He wouldn't have gone to that camp and been subjected to the abuse he suffered. Maybe he wouldn't have gotten so messed up."

I want to argue that Nick was troubled before I came into his life, but I don't disagree with her about where the blame lies. It might not be factually accurate, but if the false narrative gives her some hope and comfort, I'm okay with being painted as the villain.

"I'm sorry for what happened to him, which is why I paid for rehab. I also offered to pay for school if he could stay clean."

"Right. It's so easy for your family to throw around money. Being rich solves everything for the Byrnes." Her voice trembles.

"Hardly," I whisper. I follow her to a brick duplex's front door and reach for her, frustration pounding through me at seeing her earlier exuberance so dimmed. "Come on, Iris. You know—"

She rounds on me, swatting my hand away. "I don't give a crap about some house I imagined myself living in when I was a kid. I'm not setting down roots in Skylark. I have bigger plans, Jake. I'm not the same girl I used to be."

She bites down on her lower lip, and I hate the pain I imagine she's causing herself. I hate the pain I've caused her.

"I know. You're a thousand times smarter and stronger. I was a dick back then, and I'm sorry for what happened to Nick. For not protecting him. And for letting you down."

"Am I supposed to believe you're not a dick anymore?"

The question is posed so matter-of-factly, I nearly laugh. "Not as much of one."

Her shoulders relax at my answer, which feels like a win at this point. She unlocks the door and steps inside, gesturing for me to follow. Given that I half expected her to slam it in my face, I don't have to be asked twice. Or even once.

A lamp glows on an end table in a modest living room with art prints on the wall and a stylish gray sofa with a couple of mismatched throw pillows. There's a lived-in warmth to the uncluttered space, which seems fitting for Iris, who turns to face me.

"What are you doing here, Jake?"

"I didn't want you to walk—"

"Why are you in Skylark vying to take over your grandfather's foundation?"

My back is to the front door I've just closed. A draft seeps through, the whisper of cold air that sneaks through my thick flannel somehow unsettling. It makes me feel exposed, a reminder that I can't let my guard down. Only, I want to with Iris. She doesn't let just anyone in, figuratively or literally I'd guess. I want to see her softer side and entrust my secrets with her.

"It's a family foundation," I remind her. "I've gotten involved with some of the charities we support out of the satellite office in Austin. The work is...gratifying, to say the least. Mikey would have loved it. He would have been the obvious successor. Maybe I'm doing this as a way to honor his memory."

Maybe I've lived half my life trying to assuage the guilt of not being able to save him.

I wait for her to laugh in my face like my mother did when I told her about my plan. Like most everyone who's known me for any length of time would. I haven't given the world much reason to believe I've grown up from the smart-mouthed kid trying to shirk responsibility at every turn.

I feel raw under her scrutiny even as the urge to sway toward her hits me like a wave. I don't know how anyone resists her pull, fun or not.

"You can't know what your brother would have done with his life," she says. "From what you told me years ago, he wanted to write books."

I shift and look away, not wanting her to guess the truth of what I really do these days. She always saw me way too clearly. "He loved reading and storytelling. Escaping with books until he found other ways to escape. Ways that caused a lot more harm than good."

She draws in a sharp breath. "Just like Nick."

"You understand why I need to do this, Iris. I have a plan." Excitement courses through me as I think about the possibilities. "I want to develop the property the foundation owns in the foothills into a camp and retreat center. A place that could really help people, not the wilderness camp hellhole where Nick and I ended up."

"Have you told your grandfather?"

I make a noncommittal sound in my throat.

"How will he know you're serious if you don't share your plan?"

"Would he believe me given my history?"

"I believe you," she says softly.

Christ, this woman is going to bring me to my knees.

My smile catches us both off guard. It's not the usual one I toss around to make people feel at ease. This is different. It's me showing her...well,...me. I want her to know this moment—this smile—is just for her.

"I still need to prove he can trust me. It's the same with you. Which is why whether you try karaoke or dancing or painting yourself blue and streaking through the town square, I'll have your back."

She stares at me, and her eyes fall to my mouth. Yeah, whatever kind of fun she wants to have, including that kind, is good with me.

"Tell me what you want, Iris, and I'll give it to you."

Her pupils dilate until I can barely make out the golden rim around her dark eyes. She moves toward me, or maybe I lean into her. Either way, we're so close, I feel her warm breath on my chin. I'm dying to claim her mouth, but I need her to say the words. I need to know we both want this.

"I want you to ask out Jodi Moore," she says on a rush of breath.

13

JAKE

APPROXIMATELY NINETY-NINE PERCENT of my brain cells are having a party in the tip of my dick at the moment, so it takes me a minute to register the meaning of her words.

What. The. Hell.

"Who is Jodi Moore?" The words come out raspy as I struggle to regain control of my body. A task that's nearly impossible when she's still standing so close.

"My assistant. I mean, the mayor's assistant. You might remember her from that summer."

"I only remember you, Iris."

She closes her eyes for a moment as if she's absorbing those words. Like they're a blow more than a caress.

"Are we talking about some kind of menage-a-whatever deal?" I run a hand through my hair and surreptitiously adjust my crotch with the other one, hoping she doesn't notice. "I assume you have a reason for this rando request to ask out a woman I wouldn't know if I bumped into her."

"You *did* bump into her. You reached for broccoli at the same time in Cy's Market. You had a moment."

"The fuck I had a moment. At least not with this Jodi person. I don't even like broccoli."

She smiles, and I swear relief flashes in her gaze.

"Okay, I'm trying to get my grandpa to eat more vegetables. Maybe I bought broccoli. I buy loads of produce, most of which is destined to become science experiments in his refrigerator."

"Jodi accused me of trying to steal you."

Her voice has gone soft again, and she's not making eye contact. I'm not imagining that Iris wants me, so why is she pawning me off?

"Is this an 'I saw him first' deal? Because we have history, Dixon. You have dibs."

"I don't want dibs."

"The hell you don't."

She sighs. "Jodi's father was the town's mayor the summer we lived here. After you and Nick were sent away, I started senior year on my own." She nods like she's reassuring herself. "Sloane and I were friends, and I felt like this place could be different for me. I liked it here. I wanted to stay."

She inhales then releases a shaky breath. "Then my mom fell in love. Or lust." Her smile wobbles. "It's hard to tell the difference with her. Always was."

I refrain from admitting that's relatable at the moment. I'm not looking to get the family jewels kicked into my throat.

I brush my fingers over the back of her hand when she draws in a shaky breath, like the memory isn't one she wants to revisit. But I need to know. "Keep talking."

"Mom chose Jodi's father as the object of her affection that time around. An admired, married family man beloved by the entire town."

"That's unfortunate," I murmur. "But he was the one who cheated. Your mom didn't do what she did by herself."

"That didn't matter. We had no history here, other than the trouble Nick got into with you. And my mom was never good at female friendships, so she had no one—literally not one person—to take her side."

"Which meant you didn't either," I say and my gut twists. Because Iris should have had someone. Her brother. Or me. Definitely me, but I'd let Nick drag us both into trouble and—no—I can't blame him. I was reeling after losing Mike, and my appetite for self-destruction eclipsed what I felt for Iris. Guilt and grief blotted out everything good in my life for far too long. I hate knowing Iris was part of the collateral damage.

"Sloane stuck by my side, and I'll always be grateful for that." Her chin tips higher. "There was also a video. A sex tape, before those were a thing. His wife found it and subsequently showed several members of the town council. Jodi's dad was forced to resign, so it wasn't like he didn't deal with consequences. But the scandal consumed the community, and instead of owning up to her role or trying to make some kind of amends, Mom did her usual and exited stage left."

"Taking you with her."

"And my connection to a place that finally felt like home."

As much as I want to reach for her, I hold back. It looks like the slightest touch will shatter her into a million pieces. That's the last thing I want, but it doesn't explain her random request. "What does any of that have to do with me?"

"Jodi's cousin has decided to run against me in the upcoming election. Scandal aside, the Moores have a long history in this town. Jodi's uncle was universally loved. I'm not and my history here is shady at best. I'm going to need Jodi's help to win the election. She likes you."

"She doesn't know me."

Iris shrugs off that little fact. "She wants to. She promised to stop messing with my reputation if I promise not to mess with her chances with you."

"Would it be rude to bring up the fact that she has a snowball's chance in hell with me?"

"You might like her. She's fun. You're fun."

"I like your kind of fun."

"I'm not your speed, Jake. We both know it."

"How do you know my speed?"

"It's fast."

"I can take things slow when slow is what gets the job done. How do you like it, Iris? Fast or slow, hard or soft. Or my favorite selection, all of the above."

She snorts, but an adorable blush rises to her cheeks. "I like staying focused on the goal."

"Which is?"

"Showing people I'm not the grim reaper of fun and Skylark's reputation as one of the happiest towns in the country is safe with me."

"You're good for this town."

"You don't know that."

"I know you." I give in to temptation and trace one finger along the edge of her jaw.

She shivers but then rolls her eyes so hard it's a wonder they don't hit the ceiling. "Go out with Jodi. You said you'd do anything." She swats away my hand. "*Anything*, Jake."

Damn it. I did say that. And I'm a man of my word. Or at least I'm trying to be. Grandpa is putting me through the paces at the foundation, but I'm going to show him I can stick for the people who matter. I want to prove it to Iris, too.

"Fine. I'll ask out your friend."

"She's not my friend. She's my...frenemy."

My turn for an eye roll. "Call her whatever you want. But I have a condition."

"You didn't say anything about conditions." She's always ready for a fight, and it makes me want to be the one who breaks through her walls—just enough to let her behind mine. Everything she does makes me want her more. But it's more than physical need. It's the way she somehow makes me feel steady and unmoored at the same time.

"I want you to kiss me."

She finally takes a step away, but it's too late. I've spent too long hiding, letting what I feel sit heavy in my chest. I'm not letting her go this time. Not without a fight.

"That's ridiculous. I'm trying to set you up with my coworker. Why would I kiss you?"

"Because you might *want* me to take out this Jodi person, but you *need* to kiss me. Just like I need my mouth on yours. All over your body, if I'm being honest."

Her eyes flame—disbelief and vulnerability swirling—and I realize she's scared too. Scared of what this might mean. Of what it already does.

"Are we being honest?"

"Yes." No need for witty banter right now. The air between us is practically shimmering with desire. Beneath it is something quieter. A truth I've been circling without saying–this woman might undo me—in all the best ways.

"Honestly, you're the most irritating person I've ever known." Her voice is low, husky. "One kiss and you'll take her out." She holds out a hand to shake on it, her fingers trembling. "That's the deal."

"When did you become such a master negotiator?"

"When I learned it was the quickest path to getting what I want."

I envelop her small hand in mine and nod. "One kiss. Deal."

She tugs that lower lip between her teeth again and then says what I need to hear. "Kiss me, Jake."

The words might be spoken gently, but there's no denying the command in them. I release her hand, and she lifts her palms to my chest.

I know she can feel my heart beating a mile a minute. I reach down and grasp her hips, digging my thumbs into the fleshy space in front of her pelvic bone. Not hard enough to hurt, but she lets out a little moan.

"Oh, god," she whispers.

I press forward so she can feel that it's not just my heart reacting to her. Like I said, I'm not trying to hide anything, at least not now. I watch her, savoring the yearning in her eyes and the way I can feel her body responding before our mouths even meet.

Although we're both fully clothed, and there's no way I can smell her desire, I know it's there. I know if I were to place my hand between her legs, I'd find her wet for me. And we're barely scratching the surface. I want to make her want me so badly she trembles with it.

Then I lose all semblance of thought because her lips touch mine, and they're as soft as I remember from our one kiss, which has remained seared into my soul all these years.

Despite the fact that the restraint nearly kills me, I don't push her for more than she can give, not yet.

As she has since the moment I met her, Iris surprises me. She traces her tongue over the seam of my lips, and when I open, she takes full advantage, just like I would. Is it any wonder I've never been able to get this woman out of my mind or heart?

Shit.

I pull back, because I refuse to let my heart lead. My dad used to tell me I'm soft like my mother, and I saw what loving him did to her. If I'm anything like that, I won't risk giving anyone the power to hurt me. Even Iris.

She looks a little dazed, which is precisely how I feel. Then she blinks and offers me a bland smile. "I guess we have a deal."

"You seriously want me to ask some woman you don't even like out on a date after that?"

"What did you think I was going to do after we kissed—start practicing my Mrs. Iris Byrne signature? I'm not twelve or even seventeen anymore, Jake. I know that attraction doesn't have to mean anything more than the physical."

"Then point me in the direction of your bedroom, sweetheart, because if we're just dealing with sex, I'm an expert."

"Not with me," she corrects, and oh, how I want to prove her wrong all night long. Up against the wall, in her bed, in the shower. So loud her neighbors hear us.

But not tonight. She's already put up the walls again, and as much as I want to knock them down, I won't. Not until she begs me.

"I'll see you at our next dance class." I lean in until my mouth is inches from the delicate shell of her ear. "Sweet dreams, Iris."

She holds perfectly still but can't stop the subtle shiver that runs through her. "I don't dream."

"I bet I can change that." With a wink, I turn and walk out into the dark night.

14

IRIS

I SPEND the night tossing and turning as I dream of Jake's mouth all over my body. Whether he issued the words as a promise or a threat remains unclear.

Either way, my body aches with a yearning I'm not ready to name. I pull myself out of bed for a six a.m. run, then shower and head to the office.

Yeah, I know. Running at that hour is ridiculous unless a bear is after you, but it's one of the few methods I've found—legally anyway—to quiet the voices in my head. Exhausted as I am from the aforementioned lack of sleep, the mental chatterboxes are having a field day with Jake being back in my life.

With a kiss that left me wanting more.

I've spent years building walls that kept me safe, that kept me from becoming the kind of reckless, impulsive mess my mom was. Jake makes it hard to remember all the reasons why I shouldn't want more.

I make coffee once I get to the office. Jodi did it when her uncle was mayor, but the moment I was appointed, she informed me it was no longer her responsibility. I don't deserve her hostility, but whatever she needs to get through the day. The truth is, I make a damn fine pot. So much so, staff from other floors come to our reception area to refill their cups all day long.

Acts of service have always been my love language, but until now I listened to the muffled voices of town employees enjoying my coffee skills through the closed door of my office. I've been under the apparently misguided perception that they understand Skylark means something to me, even if I'm not great at casual conversation. But I'm a quick study and determined to win people over, even one cup of coffee at a time.

By the time Jodi rolls in just after nine—she always stops at the local coffee shop for her morning brew—a small crowd has gathered around the coffee station.

"Hey, there." I offer her a smile. "I know you've already got your caffeine fix, but let me know if you need a refill. We're doing a Friday Funday coffee bar."

"That's not a thing," she says, wrinkling her nose like I just offered her a dog turd.

I wink. "It is now."

"Did you know the mayor put herself through college as a barista?" Heidi from the parks department asks. "She can do foam art. I got a tree."

"Because you take such good care of the trees around town," I confirm.

"I have work to do," Jodi grinds out. "We can't have people loitering like we're a coffee klatch."

I smile wider, ignoring her attitude. "That's a great idea. What do you guys think? Once a month, let's move the Friday Funday coffee bar into the conference room." The half dozen people *loitering* in the office nod enthusiastically. "I'll bring donuts and we can talk about..."

What are we going to talk about?

"Our weekend plans," Heidi suggests. "There's always something fun going on in Skylark."

"That's a perfect idea. So much *fun*." I begin cleaning up the remnants of my impromptu coffee bar and incline my head toward Jodi. "You're welcome to join us. Give your budget a break from those expensive coffees."

"I didn't buy my own coffee this morning." Her smile is self-satisfied. "Someone bought it for me."

I wait until everyone files out before asking, "So your coffee's from a secret admirer?"

"No secret. Jake was in line and we started talking. He remembered me from the produce section."

I force my hand to loosen the Hulk-style grip I have on the vanilla syrup bottle and return her smile. "Broccoli brings the world together."

"Whatever works," she answers, hanging her vest on the coat tree in the corner. "The Bistro Boys Band is playing this weekend after the rodeo. He asked me to go with him. On a date."

"Sounds fun." At the moment, I hate that word with the passion of a thousand burning suns.

She studies me for a long minute. "Are you jealous?"

Hell, yes.

"Of course not. Like I told you, Jake and I are dance partners because we're both getting something from it. Actually, we ran into each other last night at Tony's."

She gives me a look like I just told her I climbed Mt. Everest since we last spoke. "What were you doing at Tony's?"

"Karaoke. Isn't that why everybody goes to Tony's on a Thursday night?"

"You're not everybody."

Fair, but I don't appreciate having it pointed out to me again. "Let's focus. I mentioned you to Jake, and he seemed open to the idea of a date."

"Wait, you were the one who suggested he ask me out?"

I shrug. "Just living up to my end of the bargain. I might have also mentioned that you frequent Skylark Roasters most mornings." Okay, that's not true, but if I'm going to take credit for the match, I might as well go all in.

"You're really not interested in him?" she asks.

Don't lie, my lady bits command. They are very interested in Jake. Especially after that kiss and feeling his hard length pressed against my body. His impressive length.

"We've already covered that. And you can say all you want about me not being fun or fitting in around here, but I'm a woman of my word. Jake and I have history, and it's not good. We'd be a terrible match."

"Picking bad matches never stopped your mother." She crosses her arms over her chest.

"I'm not my mother."

She nods. "My cousin is going to announce his campaign tomorrow at the rodeo."

I groan. "That's a pro move."

"Everyone in town will be there, including you," she says, then rifles through the papers on her desk and hands me a sheet.

I look down at the itinerary that has me kicking off the rodeo with a horse-drawn carriage ride around the arena. "This isn't going to happen."

"You weren't at the rodeo this summer, either."

"Because I'm allergic to horses."

"On-board some allergy meds because you're part of the main event. I've already said yes on your behalf."

"You can't say yes on my behalf. I didn't know about it."

She shrugs the same way I did earlier. "I'm holding up my end of the bargain, too. Joey plans to play up the fact that this community needs a mayor who supports local events."

"I support the local community. There's a line item in the budget for the Cows for Kids program."

"Iris, you can't just throw money at things. That isn't enough. People around here want you involved."

I think about all the hugs and back slaps I got after karaoke.

"Fine. I'll stop by the pharmacy store this afternoon."

"That's the spirit." She gives me a thumbs up, and it only looks a little bit like she'd rather be flipping me the bird.

I take it as a win. "Thanks for letting me know about your cousin's plans."

"As long as it doesn't get back to my mom." She takes a seat behind her desk. "She might disown me."

I won't argue whether it's right for her mom to take out her bitterness on me. Even after so many years of watching it happen, I'm still not sure why my mother gravitated toward married men.

Elena Moore wasn't the only wife to detest her. It didn't matter that the men she cheated with were the ones in committed relationships, and I'm not going to pretend that made it right. Mom knew what she was doing.

I also don't bother to explain to Jodi that much of my where-fun-comes-to-die vibe is actually anxiety. The uncertainty of never knowing how long we were going to stay in one place or who my mom was going to make an enemy out of in her quest for a good time.

That chaos taught me that love–or lust–are fleeting, conditional, and dangerous, but I built order out of that mess. But given the self-made mess that brought me back to Skylark, I have to wonder if that wild part of her lives in me, too, waiting to wreck everything I'm trying to hold together.

I turn for my office then whirl back around. "Can I ask you a question?"

She glances up from her computer screen. "You just did."

"One more, then."

"Can I stop you?"

That almost makes me smile. Almost. "Would your cousin be a good mayor?"

"I think so," she admits after thinking it over a few seconds. "He's a bit of a lone wolf but seems decent enough now. He was a dick as a kid...used to rip the heads off my dolls when my parents hosted Christmas."

"Sounds like my brother," I say with a laugh.

"Joey's mom took off when he was around five, and his dad never got over it. They seemed to resent our family and Uncle Homer's happy marriage, but it wasn't like we got any closer after the scandal and my dad's death."

"But your mom supports him in the election?"

Jodi wrinkles her nose. "She supports you not being mayor. He hasn't contacted me, so I don't know why he's doing this." She flashes an awkward smile. "But I support you, and not just because of Jake. You do okay as mayor."

"A ringing endorsement," I murmur.

"Are you thinking of backing out of the election?"

Jodi sounds oddly bothered by the idea.

"No," I lie. I'm thinking exactly that, as imposter syndrome and the fear of failure dance the cha-cha across my nerve endings. "In fact, I have a strategy meeting with Gloria before dance class this afternoon."

Jodi nods. "She can help you."

I hope so.

"But right now, I need your help," she says, gesturing me forward.

Is hell freezing over or are Jodi and I becoming friends...or at least friendly?

She points to her computer screen. "What do you think of this dress?"

I always wonder what she's working on so intently as she sits at her desk glaring at me. I've never asked or tried to get a peek since I wanted to respect her privacy. And not give myself a migraine thinking about how much work she *isn't* doing.

Most of my suspicions about how she spends her day are confirmed by the number of open tabs—a mix of online shopping and social media sites. The dress she's considering is a pale blue gingham with a deep-V neckline. It's also short enough to function as a T-shirt, and Jodi has great legs.

"I'm thinking of this with my sparkly cowboy boots for the date with Jake. Is it too much?"

I can imagine his reaction to the dress, except the thought of it makes me feel mildly nauseous. Like I've made a terrible mistake encouraging this match. "You'll look like a rodeo queen."

She startles, and I immediately straighten. "Is that bad?"

"Not necessarily," she answers with a sharp laugh. "I was supposed to be Skylark County Rodeo Queen the summer I turned sixteen. But my mom made me pull out of the competition. I was Lil Miss Skylark when I was ten and part of the princess court every year after that."

"Why weren't you the queen?" I ask the question even though I'm pretty sure I know the answer.

"Too many people were talking about our family. Mom thought laying low was the best idea. There was no question of me putting myself out there."

"I'm sorry. I wish I could have stopped my mom."

"Like I said, I spent a long time hating you for what she did," she tells me. "My mom tried to rationalize things by saying your mom targeted my dad because she wanted a good man to be a father figure for her kids."

"I wish my mom had considered Nick and me," I admit, stepping back. "Having her cheat with a married man would have been the last thing either of us wanted."

"I get that now." She nods. "But back to the dress. It's in stock at a shop in Fort Collins. Would it be okay if I take a long lunch to run up and get it?"

Since Jodi has set her own schedule I took office, I recognize her question as an olive branch and gladly take it.

"There's not much on the calendar, and I'll be back after my dance class. After you pick up the dress, take the rest of the day off."

She beams at me. "Thanks. You'll do great tomorrow."

"I hope so." I try not to look as panicked as I feel.

"Hey, Iris," she calls out as I head toward my office.

"Yeah?"

"A little advice. Those shiny cowboy boots you wear whenever you think you need to look the part of a Coloradan? Bang them up a bit. You'll look more like a local with scuffed boots than ones you keep in a box on your closet shelf."

"Pro-tip." I offer a genuine smile. "Thanks."

15

IRIS

As I drive to Gloria's house on the outskirts of town a few hours later, my body feels as numb as I've tried to make my heart.

A loud bark greets my knock, and when Gloria opens the door, an animal resembling a giant white wolf leaps out of the house and prances around me on the flagstone tile.

The sun is warm on my back—and maybe that's why sweat is pooling under my arms. I know from reading interviews she considers this home her sanctuary.

The quaint farmhouse is nestled in a grove of aspens. The side yard has been converted into a large garden with raised beds of tomatoes and sunflowers, and there are several Adirondack chairs on a wide patio that boasts an impressive view of the Flatirons in the distance.

"Iris, this is a surprise. Winston, with me." She gives a sharp whistle and the dog pads to her side. In a cardigan sweater and trousers with a crisp pleat down the legs, she looks more put together than most people on their best days. Her poise makes me hyper-aware of the chaos I feel inside. Not intimidating at all.

"I needed to speak to you. I'm sorry for not calling first."

"I assume if you drove all the way out here, it's something that can't wait until class this afternoon?"

I shake my head. "I don't think I can do it."

"Do what, dear?" She gestures to the chairs, and I take a seat. Winston, who I now realize is more husky than wolf, stretches out at Gloria's feet when she sits. "The salsa or the tango? Or simply performing in public?"

I clear my throat. "I don't think I can run for mayor. I'm not built for a life in the political spotlight. My past is too much."

She raises a brow. "Are you referring to your mother's behavior or the scandal that caused you to lose your job?"

My heart plummets to my feet as heat explodes in my cheeks. Despite my shock and mortification, I force myself to meet her steady gaze. "No one knows about that."

Gloria waves a dismissive hand. "I'm seventy-five, Iris, and I spent most of my adult life working in or around D.C. I have friends everywhere. Even Minnesota. I know why you left your position."

Shame washes over me. Not even Sloane knows the details of the scandal that brought me back to Skylark. "As humiliating as that is, it's not the reason I can't continue."

"Would you like a glass of water or a cup of tea?" How can she sound so calm when I'm baring my soul?

"Jodi Moore signed me up to participate in the opening ceremony of the rodeo tomorrow night."

"That's lovely. I wondered why I didn't see you at the summer rodeo series. Usually, the mayor—"

"I'm allergic to horses." My voice sounds desperate and pathetic, even to my own ears.

She and the dog incline their heads in unison like they can't quite figure me out. "They have medicine for that."

"I think I'm allergic to fun," I blurt.

"No one is allergic to fun."

"I'm allergic to the type of fun it takes to be a small-town mayor."

She lets out an incredulous sniff. Winston averts his gaze like he's embarrassed on my behalf. "What kind of talk is that? You're going to have a great time at the rodeo. You don't have to ride a horse. They'll settle you in the wagon, and you'll wave to the crowd, smile and admire some rodeo cowboys. It will be fun."

That word again.

I shake my head. "It sounds like torture. And another chance for people to see that I don't belong. I don't belong anywhere. I'm terrible at being fun. I have cowboy boots that I thought I was supposed to keep nice in a box."

"Honey, you're supposed to wear cowboy boots."

"I'm not western enough for the cowboys and ranchers. I'm not cool enough for the hipsters who love it here. I'm not even outdoorsy enough for the sporty crowd."

"I've seen you running around town, and nothing is chasing you. You're outdoorsy enough."

"I run next to the woods, not in the woods. And I don't know how to have fun or let loose." I think about the night before at Tony's and how relaxed I felt after a couple of drinks. "Unless I'm liquored up. What kind of a politician spends their time in office liquored up?"

"I assume that's a rhetorical question."

"I belong behind the scenes. I don't have your gift with people. I'm awkward, and I make things uncomfortable. I'm too direct and don't pick up on social cues. What kind of a politician doesn't pick up on social cues?"

Gloria laughs. "Another rhetorical question, given the state of politics in this country. Is working behind the scenes what you want? I thought you wanted to make a real difference because you love this town."

"I do."

"You think Joey Moore's a better person to lead it?"

My eyes widen. "Do you?"

She holds up a hand. "If I thought Joey was the man to lead this town, I would have told you before now. But I didn't, because I think you're the right person for the mayor's position. Even if it's a stepping stone. There's nothing wrong with having goals and aspirations, Iris, but you've got to play the game."

When emotions clog my throat, I look away. The view from the house stretches wide, the mountains jagged against a sky streaked with soft blue and faint wisps of clouds. From this angle, the mountains appear both imposing and inviting—a reminder of nature's permanence and the endless possibilities just beyond the horizon. I want to fill my life with possibilities, but change is so damn hard.

"Another thing I was never good at. I take winning too seriously."

"Are you telling me all this as an excuse to quit dancing?"

"Why would I want to quit dancing?"

"Because you're terrible," Gloria says matter-of-factly.

"Fair point," I answer, trying not to take offense. "But I like dancing, and I don't care that I suck. Well, I do care, but I'm getting better. I've been watching endless YouTube tutorials."

"That's what I'm talking about." Gloria pats my arm. "You don't have to be the life of the party or the belle of every ball to be a good mayor."

"I don't think I can be those things even if I wanted to, which I don't. My mom was the life of every party. More than anything else in my life, I want to not be like her." I cringe and tighten my hands into fists. "Then I did exactly what she would have done and fell for a married man."

"I'm guessing it wasn't the same thing," Gloria says, and I wonder if she believes it.

"I hurt an innocent woman, and I might care about that in a way my mom never did, but it doesn't change the outcome." The words taste bitter in my mouth.

I wasn't like her—I've told myself that so many times. *He was practically separated*, I'd rationalized. *The divorce papers were being drawn up.* Those justifications crumbled under the weight of the devastation on his wife's face when she confronted me. Despite how I'd tried to separate my situation from my mother's affairs, I became the villain in someone else's story. The fact that I cried myself to sleep for weeks while my mother never showed a flicker of remorse didn't erase what I'd done. The apple fell from the tree and rolled right into the same damn gutter.

"Scuff your boots and down some allergy meds, Madam Mayor. Keep letting people get to know you." She laughs when Winston stands and nudges his fluffy head against my leg. "My boy is a great judge of character. You might be an acquired taste, but you're a good person, Iris. That counts for a lot."

"Thanks, Gloria," I whisper and will myself to believe it's enough. That if I try hard enough, I'll be enough. That someone will want to acquire me.

16

IRIS

I OFFER Gloria a ride to dance class, and to my surprise, she accepts. I don't know why it always comes as a shock when people willingly spend time with me. I've always held people at arm's length, even my book club friends. Even Sloane to some extent.

I can't help but believe if they knew the real me—the parts I inherited from my mother, the capacity for selfishness I try so hard to suppress—they'd walk away.

My mother collected people and discarded them when they were no longer useful. In my determination to be nothing like her, I somehow decided I didn't deserve meaningful connections at all.

As much as we moved, I learned early on that being useful was the quickest way to make friends. Whether that was letting someone copy my homework or cleaning a new friend's room when I went over to hang out—because I couldn't invite anyone back to our crappy apartments—my combination of a need for acceptance, social anxiety, and lack of confidence made me a doormat.

By contrast, Nick found his stride with his fists. In every new school, my twin brother spent the first day quietly observing the kids and then challenging the toughest, meanest, and most arrogant boy in the class to a playground fight.

Neither of our methods was healthy. And based on the scab above my brother's eye the last time I saw him, and the fact that I still have trouble relaxing in most situations, those early habits stuck with us.

Like Sloane, Gloria doesn't seem bothered that I'm uptight. I've only encountered a few people who are so utterly comfortable in their own skin that they don't take on the energy of the people around them. Gloria and Sloane both fit that mold.

I wish I could be like that.

Gloria tells stories about the good old days in Skylark as we return to town on the tree-lined roads, the bright gold leaves nearly at their peak. Hearing about the area through her experience makes me feel even closer to it. Makes me want to stick it out long enough to become the acquired taste Gloria seems to believe I am.

There's very little you can't learn by watching YouTube tutorials. Maybe becoming socially adept is one of those things.

We're both smiling as we enter the dance studio, but mine fades as we approach our fellow class members. All eyes are watching Jake and Charlotte twirl and spin across the wood floor. The frozen emotions that had thawed out in Gloria's company come roaring back like mountain runoff in the spring. It's a reminder of what I might never have or feel for myself. My stomach knots as I watch him, all smooth confidence and easy charm. No wonder people gravitate toward him. I wish I didn't want to.

How can I be jealous of two people who embody the confidence I wish for in my own life?

He pulls her in close and says something that makes the beautiful dance teacher laugh. The sound is like an angel chorus. I tend to bust out in a cackle when I forget myself enough to laugh out loud.

The music stops, and Gloria and I join the rest of the class in applauding for the show these two celestial beings just put on for us.

"Well, now, that was some show." Tom Baker shuffles toward Char. "Janie is having a bit of a migraine today. I figured I could dance with you, Miss Charlotte. But after that display..."

"I'd be honored to be your partner during the class," Char tells the old man, bestowing on him the same sweet smile she gave Jake during their dance.

"I could dance with Tom." The offer is out of my mouth before I think better of it.

Char gives me a funny look. "You and Jake are partners."

"Sure, but the two of you give us something to aspire to in a way I never could."

"Come on, Dixon." Jake kicks out a foot. "I wore my steel-toe boots today in anticipation of dancing with you."

The rest of the class laughs, and I pretend to join in because I'm seriously that bad. But I don't like being that bad at anything. Or having it pointed out publicly. I've spent my whole life trying to be perfect at everything I touch, as if excellence could somehow make up for my fundamental flaws. Being laughed at, even good-naturedly, makes me feel exposed. Like everyone can suddenly see through the competent façade to the fraud underneath.

"You dance with Jake," Char tells me, placing a soft hand on my arm. "You'll need all the practice you can get since you two will be doing the featured dance during the Fun Fest showcase."

My mouth drops open, and I quickly snap it shut. "Excuse me, what now?"

"Come on, Iris, it'll be fun." Gloria pats me on the shoulder. "We needed somebody to be our principal couple, and no one wants to look at us old fogies up there."

"Speak for yourself, woman," Gilbert says, running a hand through his hair like he's well aware of how rare it is to have such thick strands at his age, and he's not above a bit of pride in that fact.

Jake walks over to me. "The steel-toe boots were a joke. Sorry if I took things too far."

Am I that easy to read? That's annoying AF. "Did you know about this featured dance?"

"I volunteered us." He offers the charming smile I'm sure has gotten him out of all sorts of trouble over the years. The one that won't work on me because...been there, done that. And I was left with the souvenir broken heart to prove it. "I got here early, and Char mentioned it."

At least, that's what I tell myself. Loudly and often.

"We aren't doing that."

"Iris, you love dancing."

"I also love not making a fool of myself in public. I assumed you and I would be hiding in the back."

"Nobody puts Baby in the corner," he says with a wink.

"You are no Patrick Swayze."

"You wound me, Dixon. Cut right to the heart."

It's also not true. He's just as sexy and cool as any A-list actor or Hollywood heartthrob.

The strong jawline, high cheekbones, and the slightly scruffy beard he's grown since returning to Colorado add to his outdoorsy, everyman appeal. And don't get me started on those deep-set, soulful eyes. Or the quiet intensity that draws people to him. That draws me in.

But I'm not the right partner for him. I'm not the awkward ingénue duckling who just needs a floaty dress and a show-stopping dance lift to turn me into a swan. And I wouldn't become a princess even if I kissed a million frogs. That life isn't for me. Even though I want a place to belong—somewhere to truly call home. For the briefest moment, wrapped in his arms, I almost believe it could be.

The irony isn't lost on me that I chose a career in politics—a world of spotlights and scrutiny—while desperately avoiding the kind of attention that comes with relationships. But in politics,

I'm playing a role, advocating for others, hiding behind policies and platforms. It's different from being truly seen.

Char claps her hands and class begins.

I take my position with Jake's arms around me, and my body isn't at all convinced I wouldn't love to be a princess if this man was my charming prince.

Class goes on, and I do my best to focus on the here and now. Am I any better from all those YouTube hours? It's doubtful. To his credit, Jake does his best to make me look like I know what I'm doing—a nearly impossible task.

"Can you two stay for a few minutes?" Char asks at the end of class.

I immediately shake my head. "I gave Gloria a ride so I need to take her home."

"I'll drive her and Gilbert," Tom offers. "Janie needs quiet after a migraine so I was going to give her some time anyway."

"Works for me," Gloria agrees.

"I'll take any extra time I can get with you," Gilbert tells her.

She rolls her eyes but also blushes slightly. The way the older man is so upfront about his crush makes me smile.

"I know the feeling," Jake says so quietly only I can hear. Shivers erupt across my skin, and a dangerous need pools low in my belly.

"I should get back to the mayor's office," I tell Char. "Jodi took the rest of the day off. She's getting ready for a big date tomorrow night." I say the last part for Jake's benefit, but he doesn't react.

"A few minutes," Char promises.

I can feel Jake watching me, and I don't want to seem scared to be alone with him. Which I definitely am. Terrified I might be tempted to climb him like a spider monkey, which is simply a reaction to being dance partners and the heat of his body pressed against mine.

It's a simpler explanation than admitting I'm reacting to him in particular. It would likely be this way with anybody, even Tom Baker.

Yeah, right.

The studio empties of everyone except the three of us. Char approaches and hands me a slip of paper.

"What's this?"

"The name of my favorite dance club in Denver." She smiles. "I want the two of you to check it out. Tonight."

Friday night in a club with Jake like we're a real couple. "I don't think that's the best idea."

I try to return the paper with the address to her, but she refuses to take it. "It's a necessary idea," the dance instructor assures me. "We have a month until the showcase, and you two are going to be the headliners. You need more practice and a bit of time outside of the studio setting to get more comfortable with each other."

She looks at me when she says that last bit. Yep, it's me. I'm the problem. But still...

"Jake and I can't go dancing in Denver," I insist.

"Why?" they ask in unison.

"Because that seems like a date, and he and I can't go on a date."

The smile playing around Jake's lips fades.

"Do you want it to be a date?" Char asks, one delicate brow arched, curiosity clear on her features.

"Of course not," I snap. "That's why I don't want to do it."

"Then consider it homework. I'm giving you homework, Iris. This is important."

She reaches out and takes my hand. "I'm new to Skylark." Something like defiance sparks in her soft eyes. "It's a great place to start over, and that's what I'm trying to do. Right now, most people drive to one of the neighboring towns for dance classes because they don't know me. My best way to advertise to the community is through the community seeing the success of my students."

"But you're great. You're a fabulous teacher. A natural," I assure her.

She laughs softly. "I appreciate your confidence, but I want to show I can do more than toddler or mommy-and-me classes. I need people to trust me. And if the two of you look like you're having fun—like you could win the hometown version of the DWTS mirrorball trophy—it's going to attract new students."

She places the folded piece of paper in my hand and closes my fingers around it. "If you won't go dancing just because I guarantee you'll have fun, which should be reason enough, do it to help me."

And that's how she gets me. Because acts of service are my love language, and helping people in my community is a big part of that.

"What time should we get there?" I hold the slip of paper between two fingers like it might catch on fire at any moment.

"The doors open at eight, but things really heat up around nine. You'll be salsa dancing...all kinds of dancing," Char says. "It will be good for both of you."

That's debatable, but I nod and glance at Jake. "Pick me up at seven thirty."

"Did I hear a please in that request?" he deadpans.

"You did not."

If Charlotte recognizes the tension crackling between us, she ignores it. "I promise it will be fun."

Sure. Like one of the Hemsworth brothers giving you a root canal. "I've got to get back to the office."

"Have fun tonight, you two." Char blows out what looks like a relieved breath as she rubs her hands together. "Thank you, Iris."

Like I have a choice, but I don't say that. I smile and head out the door.

There's a chill to the air this afternoon, as if we might be in for our first taste of winter weather, but it does nothing to temper the heat coursing through me. It's a strange, contradictory feeling—

part mortification at having my incompetence laid bare in front of everyone, and part something else entirely. Something sparked by Jake's nearness. The casual confidence in his movements. And the thought of spending even one night in his orbit.

"I can pick you up at six thirty and we can grab dinner first," Jake says as he follows me to the small parking lot behind the dance studio.

"This isn't a date, Jake. It's homework."

"Why can't we have both?"

"You know why. I let Jodi have the afternoon off to buy a dress to wear to the rodeo tomorrow night."

"I'm sure she'll look lovely."

"She will, and you're going to fall for her."

He takes a quick step forward then encircles my wrist with his big hand.

"No."

I pull my hand away and plant both hands on my hips. "You told me you'd do anything. You haven't—"

"I told you I'd take her out, and I am. I can't force myself to fall for somebody any more than she can. I'm not going to lie or pretend. Not even for you."

"Why not?" I snap. "You're good at it."

He flinches, then searches my gaze as if I've uncovered some deep, dark secret I'm about to call him out on. I've been so busy with my own problems, I haven't looked more closely at Jake or considered what's really going on with him. If there's more to him now than I know.

Something shifts in my perception, like when you've been staring at a puzzle piece and suddenly realize you've been holding it upside down. I've been so consumed with keeping my own walls intact that I never considered he might have defenses of his own. The easy charm, the casual flirtation—what if they're just as much a shield as my professional detachment? What other layers have I missed while I was busy making sure he couldn't see mine?

"That's a low blow, Dixon."

He's right, even if he is hiding something. But I can't bring myself to apologize. Not when I'm so spun up with no outlet for my overactive imagination or overburdened anxiety.

"You might like Jodi," I say, deciding to focus on the issue at hand while I think about what he could be hiding.

"If so, it won't be because you commanded it. I need you to understand that. I'm willing to do a lot to make up for the past. Being a man whore isn't on my resume."

"Nobody's asking you for that, but don't deny you're good with women."

"Why would I want to deny it?" He gives me that easy smile again, but it's tight around the edges this time. "I like women. I like you. God knows why sometimes."

"How lovely, the patented Jake Byrne charm on full display."

"Why are you so hell-bent on pushing me away?" The question is spoken softly, making it hit even harder.

Do I tell him it feels easier to push before he runs in the other direction? We're at a standoff now, and I wish I had my cowboy boots on because it feels like this setup fits the old-west Skylark history Gloria shared earlier. This town ain't big enough for the both of us and all that.

Of course, as much as I want to throttle him, I also want to grab his shirt and pull him closer. Give both of us a reason to quit arguing, at least out loud. Use our mouths and bodies to decide who comes out on top. Or on the bottom. With Jake, I have a feeling any way would be good. It might only take one touch to shatter me.

A horn beeps, and we break apart.

Saved by the Subaru, I think, as my friend Molly pulls up. She rolls down her window and grins. I smile and wave at the two tow-headed kids sitting in the back seat.

"Another exciting beginner hip hop class coming up," she says, then glances between Jake and me. "You doing okay, Iris?"

"Always," I lie, but just as Molly is about to question me further, there's a shriek from the back seat.

"Mommy," a girl shouts, "Luke hit me."

"No hitting," Molly calls over her shoulder.

"Laurel called me a butthead," comes the impassioned response.

"No name-calling," she hollers back before focusing on Jake and me again. "They are my pride and joy," she says through a tight smile.

"Are you okay?" I ask gently.

"Always." She sounds only mildly on the verge of a breakdown. "I'll call you later," she says, then pulls forward to park closer to the studio's back door.

"No one is pushing anyone," I tell Jake. "In fact, you can skip tonight, and I'll drive to Denver by myself. I'm the one who needs practice."

"I'm your partner," he says, his voice low and gravelly.

I hit the key fob to unlock my car. "I'm sure I can find somebody to dance with me," I tell him over my shoulder.

"The fuck you will."

Those crass words shouldn't thrill me, but they do. "Have it your way." I give a jaunty wave. "See you tonight, partner." Then I duck into my car and pretend to check my phone until Jake turns and heads toward the ancient truck parked a few spaces away.

I'm going to need the rest of the day to tie my libido down. Shove it into the dark dungeon where I keep all the things I've ever wanted to do but didn't because they were bad for me.

There's no doubt in my mind Jake Byrne would be the absolute worst. And the best.

17

JAKE

Seven-thirty on the dot, and I'm at the curb in front of Iris' house, planning to walk up to the porch and ring the doorbell. Despite what she says about this not being a date, I want to treat her like she means something special. Because she does.

More than I care to admit to either of us. If I'm being honest, no woman has ever elicited the kind of visceral response in me that Skylark's prickly mayor does.

But before I step out of the car, she's bounding down the front steps, and damn if she doesn't take my breath away in a flowy skirt and body-hugging black top, her hair falling in glossy waves past her shoulders. She doesn't look like the mayor tonight. She looks like the heroine in every story I ever read or wrote.

She slips into the passenger seat and motions with her hands. "Let's get going before anybody sees us. Hopefully, they won't recognize you driving this fancy urban assault vehicle." Patting the dash of the G-Wagon, she offers a bland smile. "I didn't know you needed a car that could climb Mt. Everest to go dancing. Where's the truck?"

Her citrusy scent winds around my senses, sweet with a tangy undertone, just like Iris. Her sharpness is more in your face, but the sometimes surprising bursts of sweetness balance things quite nicely. And, let's face it, I like her sharp edges. I want to soothe them, preferably with my tongue until she's screaming my name. To bury my face in the curve of her neck and forget everything that ever hurt.

"You'll take any opportunity to give me shit, huh? Driving down to the city isn't exactly a vintage truck outing. And we both know the G-Wagon is the epitome of luxury meeting rugged capability." I wink at her as I pull away from the curb. "Just like me."

"You're trying to be inconspicuous around town?"

"I don't want to come across like a douche," I admit with a shrug.

She barks out a laugh. "Spoken like someone steeped in generational wealth."

That's not meant as a compliment.

She leans back in her seat as I accelerate onto the interstate. "So tell me, how is a luxurious and ruggedly capable guy spending his days in Skylark? Where does he spend his days? Will you be leaving a job if you take over the foundation?"

I shrug. "How do most trustafarians spend their days?"

"Doing blow," she suggests. "And looking for financing for the documentary film they believe to be a passion project."

I laugh even though I'm not sure she meant it as a joke. "I gave up blow before I gave up the alcohol." Obviously, I'm not mentioning my work on adapting the book series for film. "But I manage to keep myself occupied."

I stretch out my arm and then flex for her. "These muscles don't come easy, you know."

"You want me to believe you're a gym rat?"

"In Austin? No way. There's too much outdoor goodness to enjoy—hiking, paddle boarding, mountain bike trails."

Her lips thin, and I realize I'm playing into every stereotype she has about me. I don't like it, but it's safer than letting her in on the truth. Not that she'd believe me. No one other than my literary agent and editor knows my true identity.

I wrote that first book after dropping out of college and moving to Austin. I'd decided to go clean and stop relying on my family's money to fund my self-indulgent lifestyle. No one who knew me then would believe I had the talent and discipline to write one book, let alone a series.

And at that point, I didn't trust it myself. It felt too personal. There was too much at stake in honoring my brother's memory and dreams to risk failing publicly.

Now, I want to go clean in all areas of my life, but can't quite find the courage to do it.

"You can't spend all your time paddle boarding," Iris tells me.

I tap a finger against the steering wheel like I'm considering my answer. "Not all my time. Beauty rest is important, too."

"The foundation has an office in Austin, right? Do you do any work there?"

"Grandpa put me on the board of directors a few years ago, so I'm an expert at ribbon cutting and awarding checks. I keep my visits to the office limited to the days when lunch is catered."

"You always had an appetite," she says with an indulgent smile and then falls silent, staring out the window at the darkening sky. The silence stretches comfortably between us as shades of purple and orange streak above us.

I've actually taken on a more significant role in the foundation's activities in Texas in the past couple of years, partnering with grant seekers to understand and champion their work. It took a bit of time to gain the trust of the staff, especially since I've requested that my growing role be kept out of the spotlight—and off my grandfather's radar—as much as possible.

Why do I insist on letting the people I care about think the worst about me?

I can tell myself a story about wanting to ensure my actions are genuinely about helping others rather than seeking validation.

How keeping my efforts private helps me separate my ego from my work. But I'm also processing ongoing survivor's guilt, and the feeling of not deserving recognition for doing the right thing now when I spent so many years feeling like I was always doing the wrong thing.

They say the best defense is a good offense, or maybe that's backwards, but I'm going with it either way. I don't like having the spotlight pointed in my direction, and I want to know more about Iris. Who she is now and what truly makes her tick under the defenses she so faithfully maintains—something we have in common, even though I'm not dumb enough to mention that to her.

"Tell me what brought you back to Skylark."

"A position in the mayor's office." The answer is generic and doesn't even begin to satisfy my curiosity. I'm pretty sure I'm not the only one who isn't telling the whole truth.

"Why a small town in Colorado? You went to school and started your political career in Minnesota, right?"

"Mom had a friend in St. Paul, so when things went bad so quickly after that summer, she moved us to Minnesota." She wrinkles her nose. "Isn't everyone's dream for their senior year to spend the winter with months of snow, ice, and freezing temps?"

"Seems like you made the most of it," I answer. "You were awarded an Academic Excellence Scholarship for undergrad."

Her eyes widen. "Did you Google me?"

"Of course. You have an impressive LinkedIn profile."

She groans.

"Don't be humble, Dixon. Lots of university honors. A job after graduation working for the governor as a youth policy advisor and community engagement manager. Quite the overachiever."

Her voice is quiet when she explains, "Given everything Nick and I faced, creating better opportunities for kids like us is important to me."

Her hands are clasped tightly in her lap, her knuckles white. What isn't she saying about Minnesota?

"Is your mom still in St. Paul?"

She frowns and turns her face back to the window. "She moved to Florida when I was in college. Other than our awkward holiday conversations, we don't talk."

"I'm still having trouble understanding why you left your role in the governor's office." I scratch a hand across my jaw. "The opportunity for advancement there seems—"

"I wanted to come back and implement some of those same programs here. We never stayed in one place long growing up, but Skylark felt like home." She draws in a long breath. "In a mostly affluent community, with people who have been here for generations, families who might need help or interventions can fall through the cracks. I don't want any kids to fall through the cracks. Skylark is more than our reputation for fun. We're a place where all families should be able to access the healthcare and education services they need."

"Okay." I reach over to squeeze her hand, but she quickly pulls it away and crosses her arms over her chest.

I can't stop prodding for what she's not telling me. "From what I hear on the news, Robert Wilhelm is a contender for the party's presidential nomination in the next election cycle."

"Governor Wilhelm has done an amazing job for the people of Minnesota," she says, tension radiating off her like a wave. "I'm sure he'll do the same if elected on a national level."

"You don't want to be a part of that? It seems like a lot of opportunities would have come your way if he's successful in his bid."

"I want to be here," she insists, and I wonder which one of us she's trying to convince. "There's nothing wrong with starting small and building my resume the old-fashioned way. Gloria is also here, and she was the first politician who inspired me toward a career in public service. I wanted a chance to be mentored by her."

Her answers sound rehearsed, podium ready, and with every syllable, I'm more convinced I'm not getting the whole story. She's hiding something. But then, so am I.

You could cut the tension between us with a machete and I don't want that. I want tonight to be easy and fun, so move on to a less charged topic.

"Tell me about the book club that has you signing up for dance classes and belting out karaoke favorites. Is everyone taking part in this bucket list challenge?"

"Yes," she says, her shoulders visibly relaxing. "We take turns picking something personal to us. It was inspired by the book *The Year of Losing It* by an author named Kristen Quinn. Sloane had us read it last spring, right before she told us about the cancer diagnosis."

"I saw Sloane at the bookstore the other day. She's as sweet as ever. Told me she's getting ready to head to Nashville for another round of treatment."

"What were you doing in a bookstore?" Iris taps an elegant finger against her lips, pretending to study me.

"I can read. Picture books are about my speed."

She frowns. "Why don't you defend yourself against the jabs I throw your way? As much as I hate to admit it, we both know there's more to you than you let people see."

"People see what they want to," I tell her, knowing how true that is.

She shakes her head. "Sometimes. But it feels like this whole bucket list challenge has made me come face to face with parts of myself that have been easier to ignore. For example, I'm prickly."

Rather than agree, I point out, "You have friends who care about you."

"Because of Sloane. She's the reason I'm part of the book club. She chose us. We're not the most obvious choice on paper for a friend group, but somehow it works. She made it work."

"Who isn't giving herself enough credit now?" I ask, changing lanes to take the exit onto I-25 toward downtown Denver, the lights of the skyline welcoming us into the city.

"Nick was the social twin," she says instead of answering. "My brother could charm his way out of almost any situation."

"Charm his way into the heart of anyone he meets," I add.

Her smile holds a trace of sadness. "He was different the last time I saw him. More subdued."

"That might not be a bad thing in Nick's case."

I don't want this night to get derailed by talk of her troubled brother, my wayward friend. But I can't escape the fact that Nick is as much the impetus behind so much of what I've done and want to do as Mikey is.

"Tell me about some of the other bucket list activities."

"I'm only the second person to take the challenge," she says. "Sadie Hart, a Skylark native, was the first. Her mom died when she was in college, so she came home to raise her little sister."

"Let me guess. She wanted more adventure in her life."

"In a manner of speaking. Her bucket list item was losing her virginity."

"Wow. That's a big deal."

"I'm not a virgin," she says when I raise a brow.

"Duly noted." I choke out a laugh. "How do you pick the books?"

"We take turns. Usually, we meet at the bookstore, but whoever picks the book is the unofficial host. It's me this month."

"Another dead president biography on tap?"

"We're reading the latest by Spencer Charles."

I jerk on the steering wheel, and Iris lets out a little gasp. "What's the matter?"

"Debris on the highway," I say, forcing my voice to be steady. What the hell am I supposed to say to that? "Why Spencer Charles?"

"Have you read any of his books?"

"I'm familiar."

"Then you know how good he is. I'm fascinated by how he puts together these complicated plots. His books are like puzzles, and my mind tends to work on overdrive. Having something to solve helps relax me. His books—and, by extension, the author himself—have had a major impact on me.

"From the chat on the book club text group, everyone loves my pick. It's pretty gratifying, you know? A lot of people look down on commercial fiction, but Spencer Charles writes good books, full stop. Sloane even contacted his publisher to get him to join our book club meeting via Zoom. We've had some authors do that, although not Kristen Quinn. She was hiking some crazy peak in the Swiss Alps the month we read her book."

I'm floored by the idea that Iris is such a fan, but my editor and agent know to reject any requests for an appearance. No one knows me in that way.

I clear my throat. "I thought Spencer Charles was some kind of reclusive hermit."

She inclines her head. "That's a little dramatic. Historically, he doesn't do interviews. Sloane figured that might be more his reluctance to meet with the press than real fans."

"You're like a super fan," I murmur, and she gives me a funny look.

"I'm not going to deny it, and there's nothing wrong with being a super fan. Why are you being so weird about this?"

"I assumed you'd only read pretentious books."

She immediately shoots me the middle finger. "I read good books," she insists. "You should try not being such a snob."

A snob. That's laughable.

Writing the story that my brother and I had come up with as children, based on the movies and comic book heroes we idolized, meant more to me than anything except Mike. It was my connection to him. I knew if our father found out, he'd find a way to ruin it. My father's judgment had tainted everything in my life I cared about, I wasn't giving him the satisfaction of tarnishing this too. Keeping my identity a secret was a no-brainer.

I never expected it to be the bestseller it became, but the more successful the sales were, the more I knew I didn't want anyone to realize I was the author of the Ellie Spaulding mysteries. And I've never regretted that decision as much as I do at this moment.

Because more than almost anything, I want Iris to know the real me, the me that isn't hidden behind a pen name.

No one can know, I remind myself. And I'm not even sure Iris can be trusted. Not with how uber-focused she is on her own goals. Goals that likely don't align with mine.

"It sounds like you might have a little author crush," I say instead and have the pleasure of seeing her blush.

She might not know I'm Spencer Charles, but I do. If she likes him, that means she likes me—well, at least a part of me—and that feels like a win for now.

"I don't have an author crush." She rolls her eyes. "I don't even know him. Although I have a lot of respect for his talent, and he's obviously a good guy."

If only she knew.

That catches my interest. "Why 'obviously' when you don't know him?"

"I've read all his books, some of them twice, and I can tell the kind of man he is. No one could write such a strong female character like Ellie Spaulding if he doesn't respect women. Something you might not be able to understand, because womanizing is different than caring."

"Ah, yes, back to my lack of character. Let me ask you something, Iris. Are you the same person you were at seventeen?"

"Of course not," she replies.

"And have you ever done anything you regret?" I keep my eyes on the road as I take the exit for the club. "Made a whopper of a mistake in your life?"

She glances away, and I know I've hit a soft spot. "Of course I have. I'm not perfect, Jake. Besides, is there anyone who hasn't made mistakes?"

"Do you want to continue being judged on that decision, or the worst moment of your life?"

She brushes her hair away from her cheek. "No."

"Then perhaps you can acknowledge that whether or not I deserve forgiveness, I do want it. I do regret what happened. Not just to Nick, but to all of us. You have no idea how much."

"Fine. Let's pretend like the past didn't happen. Is that what you want?"

I shake my head. "I wish it was that easy. I don't want to pretend with you. Is it so wrong to want to move forward?"

It takes her so long to answer, I wonder if she's going to argue with me about that. Finally, she shakes her head. "It's not so wrong," she concedes, "and I appreciate you going out with Jodi."

"One time," I remind her. "You can't force me into a relationship with a woman I don't want to date."

She laughs. "No one can force you to do anything you don't want to. I know that better than most people."

I don't like the certainty in her voice any more than the words she's saying, but I'm sick of arguing.

"You're going to have fun tonight, Iris."

"You can't force me to have fun."

"No, but you will."

"There's the cocky Jake Byrne I know."

"Self-confidence is sexy. Isn't that what your man Spencer Charles says about Ellie Spaulding? Her self-confidence makes her sexy."

"You are no Ellie Spaulding."

No, I'm not, but so much of my inspiration for Ellie came from the woman beside me—at least at the beginning. Nine books in, and Ellie has taken on her own personality, but she started with Iris.

"I'll tell you what. I'm so confident you're going to have a good time tonight, that if you don't, I'll extend our agreement and ask Jodi out again at the end of our date tomorrow. But if you have fun with me, then you and I have a real night out."

"I'm not dating you, Jake."

"I didn't say a date. I just said we'd go out and have fun, only *I* pick the activity. My version of fun." I lean over and wink. "We both know I'm a guaranteed good time."

"We also both know I could easily lie."

"That's not who you are, Iris. If you give your word, it's golden. You are the most honorable person I know."

Her mouth thins, and she shakes her head. "All that confidence is going to get you into trouble, Byrne. Because you might be a good time to most people, but I'm immune to your charm."

God, I hope not.

"Challenge accepted, Dixon. Challenge accepted."

18

IRIS

I was lying through my teeth when I told Jake he isn't my idea of a good time. I'm guessing we both know it, but the moment we walk into the club, I realize it doesn't matter. Because I could actually win our silly wager.

I'm so far out of my league, I might as well be Rose at the below-deck party on the Titanic. But the idea of winning feels less important than just getting to be here with him.

I pictured something like one of the ubiquitous dance club interiors you see in movies—flashing lights, a mass of drunken, sweaty bodies, and a crowd big enough to blend into without being noticed.

This club isn't that.

It's way more.

The lighting is low, and the dance floor—clearly the heart of the club—is polished and surrounded by cozy seating areas with plush cushions. Couples of all ages, shapes, sizes, and sexualities wend and sway together on the dance floor. The energy is raw and real, the sensuality in the air palpable. I relied on liquid courage for karaoke, but I might need a full-on psychedelic trip to relax in this place.

A few people turn as we make our way through the crowd. While Jake gets welcoming smiles, I receive cool stares, like they know someone called the anti-fun SWAT team to wreck the vibe.

Jake places a hand on the small of my back. "Do you need a brown paper bag to breathe into?" The warmth of his touch zips up my spine like the first crack of lightning before a summer storm —startling and impossible to ignore.

I'd snap back with a sharp retort, but I'm hurtling toward a full-blown panic attack. Forming words is way beyond me when I can't even seem to suck air into my lungs

"Seriously, Dixon, are you okay?" He leads me toward a booth in the corner, saying something to the waitress we pass that I can't make out because of the ringing in my ears. I'm not sure my knees will bend to sit down, but Jake practically shoves me onto the red velvet seat and slides in next to me, his muscular thigh pressing against my now trembling leg. Even as my world narrows to a panic-filled tunnel, his voice is an anchor pulling me back to safety.

"What the hell is going on?" He waves a hand in front of my face.

"I can't do this."

"You don't have to do anything except follow my lead."

"They'll know I'm terrible."

"Iris, it's just dancing. Everybody's doing it. No one gives a shit about you and me joining in."

"I can't."

"Let's have a drink, and then we'll reassess."

"We could chug a bottle of Everclear, and I'm still not going to do this. This is *not* fun for me."

"What's going on?" he repeats, his tone softening, coaxing.

How do I explain my reaction without reliving the humiliation all over again? I bite my lip and stare out at the club, the music pounding in my chest like a second heartbeat.

"I took that one dance class as a kid, but moving wasn't the real reason I missed the recital. We were supposed to, but I pitched the only fit of my entire childhood and begged my mom to stay so I could dance."

I wave a hand toward the club's dance floor but snatch it back, embarrassed that my fingers are shaking. "We were performing to 'What a Wonderful World,' and I was so excited. I finally felt like I belonged somewhere and had friends and I loved dancing."

Jake grins. "I wish I could see little Iris in all her glory."

"The costumes were atrocious," I say with a laugh that dies as I remember that time with more clarity. "Mom was pissed that I'd taken a stand. She was champing at the bit to meet her new online love in person."

I swallow hard. My throat feels coated in sawdust. "Thinking back on it, I'm pretty sure she got caught with the husband of one of our neighbors in the apartment complex where we lived. There were a lot of slamming doors and hushed arguments that week, but Nick had also gotten into a fight so she blamed the tension on him."

"Maybe your brother went looking for trouble to deflect attention from her," Jake suggests evenly.

The idea throws me for a loop. I've never connected my mother's behavior with Nick's trouble, but it makes sense. It's a sad, terrible insight, but one that resonates.

"I don't know," I say honestly, but the pit in my stomach would say otherwise. "Parents weren't allowed to watch class or attend rehearsals, but my mom came anyway. She pulled me from the recital as soon as she saw me dance. There was a huge blow-up between her and the instructor, with Mom screaming about how I was going to humiliate myself and her."

"That doesn't make sense," he says, shaking his head.

"I was terrible, Jake." I lick my dry lips and try to detach from how I felt then. I'm a grown-ass adult, I remind myself. Not that little girl with silent tears running down her face. "She knew people would laugh at me if I got up on stage. For once in her life, my mother was trying to protect me."

"What are you talking about?" He sounds both confused and irritated, but gently takes my hand like he knows I need something —someone—to ground me in the present moment so I don't lose myself in the past. "Iris, I've seen enough viral reels to know the cringey kids are the ones people love to watch. It doesn't matter if you're bad. It matters that you're bad with enthusiasm."

I choke out a laugh. "You've seen me dance. All the enthusiasm in the world isn't going to make someone with two left feet look good."

"We're not talking about now, are we?"

He brushes a strand of hair away from my face, tucking it behind my ear. The touch is both soothing and electrifying. It makes me want to lean into him. Find comfort in him. But Jake isn't my person. The tenderness of the gesture short-circuits the walls I've spent years constructing.

"What did your mother tell you?"

"She was protecting me," I say again, then roll my lips together because it still hurts.

"What exactly did she say, Iris?"

"I told you already. That I was going to embarrass myself. People were laughing at me."

He continues to stare, and I shrug. "They were laughing at *her*. My mom, who loved being the center of attention and never cared what anyone said about her. She was embarrassed by me. Nick could get into all kinds of trouble, but everybody knew he was cool. She could sleep with a string of married men, but she was beautiful and funny. I was the embarrassment because I wasn't good at something, even though I loved it."

"You were a good kid," he says. Not that I need the reassurance at this point. Okay, I totally need it. "You would have gotten better if you'd stayed with the lessons."

"It doesn't matter. I never danced in public again." I look out toward the crowded dance floor. "Until this class. Until I tried to let myself have fun."

"Tonight is no different than when we're at the studio."

I snort. "There's a big fat difference."

"Do you honestly think a bunch of strangers will care about your skill?"

"I think I'm not going to give anyone a chance to laugh at me again."

"Did you see them laughing when you were a kid?"

"What does that matter?"

He links our fingers together and squeezes. "Your mother wasn't a saint, and it's likely she was being run out of another town for having a relationship with another married man. You said it was the only time in your life your mother ever protected you. Is there a chance that, once again, she was protecting herself? This time at your expense?"

The breath leaves my lungs in a whoosh, and I feel like I'm watching a missing puzzle piece fall into place. "You think she pulled me out because of an affair?"

His smile is so sweet my heart flings itself against my ribcage like it wants to take refuge in Jake's arms. I know the feeling.

He traces a finger down my cheek. "I've seen the joy on your face when you forget to worry whether you're hitting a step or moving your hips the right way. If a good mother had recognized that joy in her child, she would have given you a standing ovation at that recital. Maybe you weren't going to embarrass yourself. Maybe your mother was going to be publicly humiliated for something she did, and chose to take care of herself instead of you."

All these years I thought I was the failure, but maybe it wasn't about me at all.

The waitress arrives at the table with two glasses of sparkling liquid and sets them down in front of us.

"You okay, hon?" she asks.

I take a mental inventory and find the panic has ebbed slightly.

But I could still use a healthy dose of courage—liquid or otherwise —to handle tonight.

"I am," I answer, and Jake gives her a thumbs up.

When she turns away, I lift the drink to my lips, not caring what type of alcohol he's ordered. I'll take anything right now.

"Why does that taste like lemon-lime soda?"

He winks. "Because that's what I ordered."

"Tell me there's a shot being delivered to the table next."

He shakes his head. "If you want to order a drink, Iris, be my guest. But I know what happens when a person focuses more on numbing their feelings than acknowledging them. It's not a solution. At least not long-term."

"If you're looking for fun Iris, she's more likely to show up with a buzz than when I'm sober."

The waitress catches my eye as if she knows I was expecting something stronger, but I give a small shake of my head. As much as I don't want to live in fear, I don't want to be numb either.

"I'm looking for you to have fun, and not because you're drunk. That's fake fun. I want the real you. All of it."

Damn it. How am I supposed to keep the wall around my heart fortified when Jake keeps being so damn sweet?

Not only is there more to him, but he also makes me believe I'm more than I give myself credit for. I feel something crack inside me, a hairline fracture in the armor I've worn for so long. I know what flirting with Jake feels like. I can handle that. But this? This genuine interest in the real me? It's terrifying. I don't know how to be vulnerable. My mom used her vulnerability as a weapon—it's all I've ever known.

This feels like... an invitation. And I'm not sure if I'm ready for that level of exposure. Or if I even remember how to let someone in after keeping everyone at a safe distance for so long.

"Even if my mom did what she did for the reasons you're implying, it doesn't make her wrong about me potentially embarrassing myself. The people here, it's like natural rhythm is part of the requirement. I don't have that, Jake. Like I said, it's one thing when I'm in a class with the AARP set, but I'm not looking to publicly humiliate myself."

"Have a little faith in both of us. Charlotte sent us here for a reason. We can learn the moves and the counts in her classroom, but until you start trusting me and yourself, it won't change. If we concentrate on having a good time, then—"

"You won't have to ask Jodi out again, and she goes back to undermining me. Then who knows what happens to my chances of being elected."

He releases a noise that sounds suspiciously like a growl. "Or maybe you stop trying to backdoor your way into being elected and believe you're the best candidate for the job."

"I *want* to believe," I answer honestly.

"Start acting like it."

"Fine." I grab his hand and basically push him out of the booth then onto the dance floor. "For the record, I can already feel people looking at us."

"Of course they're looking. We're the hottest couple in the place."

As tense as I am, that tossed-off bit of cockiness elicits a real laugh. "Do you ever take anything seriously?"

"You have no idea."

19

IRIS

JAKE PULLS ME CLOSE, and instead of our practiced steps, he simply holds me. His breath fans over my neck, sending shivers cascading down my spine.

"I know you have better moves than this." My voice is shaky. "You don't need to pretend for my benefit."

"No pretending." His lips graze my earlobe. "Not tonight. We don't have to prove anything to anyone right now. It's just you and me, Dixon."

His hand is warm on my back, and he draws the other one up my body, stopping just below the swell of my breast. My breathing is unsteady once again, but it has nothing to do with nerves, and everything to do with need and the heat pooling between my legs.

Jake takes my hand and curls it toward him, pressing his lips to each of my knuckles. From the outside, I'm sure what we're doing here looks innocent enough. It's not overtly sexual or suggestive, but I feel like my body is changing as we sway to the music. It's like someone is pouring warm honey over me, and all I can think about is Jake Byrne licking it off every inch of my body.

When he moves, I move with him, and for once I'm not worried about the steps, count, or whether I'm treading on his toes. For the first time in forever, my brain quiets. I'm not overthinking, just responding to his energy from someplace deep inside. He twirls me away from him, and I keep my eyes closed because I know he'll pull me back and keep me safe. At least for now.

I'm not kidding myself into thinking I look like I know what I'm doing, I just don't care. This is the joy and reckless abandon I remember from when I danced as a kid. It's what it still does for me in the privacy of my own home.

Dancing alone allows me to be me, without worrying what other people think.

Jake touches me low on my back, pressing his hips into me so I can feel how hard he is behind the zipper of his dark jeans. And I'm not thinking of anyone else but the two of us.

I'm having fun.

The song comes to an end, and I blink open my eyes, glancing around as my mind revs up again. Only, nobody's staring at me. It hits me suddenly—people are too wrapped up in their own lives to scrutinize mine the way I've always feared. How much of my life have I spent performing for an audience that doesn't actually exist?

Even though I don't have proof, and it truly shouldn't matter, I understand he was likely right about my mom. The humiliation of the recital wasn't going to be mine. But she let me take the fall. She ruined the thing she knew I loved the most because she couldn't stop being who she was. The weight of imagined scrutiny begins to lighten as I accept that maybe I've been the harshest judge of myself all along.

"Stay with me," he says, squeezing my hand.

The next song that comes on is faster-paced. It's the perfect tempo for the salsa we're supposed to be performing at the Fun Fest Showcase. And suddenly, I am Rose on the Titanic. And the man smiling and laughing as he twirls me is my version of Jack— only a whole lot sexier than Leo, even in his *Titanic* heyday.

In fact, Jake is sexier than anybody I've ever seen. I want him more than is smart for either of us, especially when I promised Jodi I'd stay away. Need crackles between us, and I'm tired of pretending I don't feel it.

I'm a woman of my word, but this is an assignment from our dance instructor.

I push my promise to Jodi to the back of my mind, tucking it away in that mental drawer where I store all the uncomfortable truths I don't want to face. Tonight isn't about politics or my complicated past. I've spent so long being responsible, maybe I deserve one night to just feel good without worrying about consequences. I'm still not sure how this is going to make a difference in my ability to follow the steps during the showcase. But it's done miraculous things for my heart. It's about finally choosing something—someone—that feels like joy.

We dance to a few more songs, the music smoothing out all the sharp edges between us.

As we leave the club, one of the couples we met invites us for a late-night—or early morning, as the case may be—meal at a nearby twenty-four-hour diner.

Jake looks to me for an answer. "It might be fun," he tells me with a wink.

Why is it so easy to have fun when I'm with this man?

"Totally," I agree, and we spend the next hour talking and laughing with our new friends, Margo and Andrew.

We plow through breakfast burritos served with crispy hash browns, a mountain of fluffy pancakes drenched in butter and syrup, and a homemade cinnamon roll topped with cream cheese icing that melts in my mouth. The conversation is easy and natural, and I forget about worrying if they're judging me or if I need to act a certain way to be liked. I'm just me, and that seems to be enough.

We hear about their upcoming wedding plans and I invite them to come to Skylark for the Fun Fest weekend. Margo assures me we'll do amazing in the showcase, and the confidence of a woman I've just met makes me want to believe. I'm stuffed and exhausted and more relaxed than I've felt in forever when we hug goodbye and head to where the G Wagon is parked a block away.

Jake takes my hand as we walk down the nearly empty city sidewalk, his thumb tracing circles on the inside of my palm. "So much for your claim about being an acquired taste. Those two picked up on how amazing you are in a matter of hours."

I want to believe him, but it's not that easy. "I'm pretty sure the me they saw was the one basking in the glow you put off. Anyone would seem appealing if they're standing next to Jake Byrne."

"Don't sell yourself short, Iris." All hint of teasing has disappeared from his voice. "You're perfect just the way you are." His words undo me, because a part of me—maybe the most broken part—wants to believe them.

"This night has been perfect," I tell him, unable to respond directly to his words. They mean too much.

"And fun?" We're at his vehicle now, and he links our fingers and pulls me close.

"You know it was."

The temperature has dropped, and I can almost see his breath in the cold air. We're inches apart. All I have to do is lean in and brush my lips across his. There's no doubt he wants me. I can see it in the sparks that flicker in his gray-green eyes. Feel the desire radiating from him like an electrical current. I want him so much my body practically trembles with it. The two of us together could be so right. I know that deep in my bones. But also...

"You're going on a date with Jodi tomorrow," I remind both of us as I force myself to step away from him, out of the magnetic pull that sucks me in like a black hole.

His thick brows furrow. "I could cancel and—"

"No. You promised." I shake my head. "I promised."

Promised to keep my distance.

Promised myself I wouldn't fall for the wrong guy after my last disaster. That I wouldn't make the same mistakes my mother did. Not again.

With our history, Jake can't be right for me. No matter how much my body and heart want to convince me otherwise.

"One date, Iris." I hear the frustration in his voice. "But you owe me a date, too. A real one."

"Wasn't tonight enough?"

He barks out a sharp laugh and opens the passenger door. "Not even close." The need in his voice is matched by the heat in his eyes. One touch and I'll unravel.

The emotion in his tone steals my breath. But I climb into the seat like I'm not affected. Like I can ignore the connection between us. Like it's not killing me to think of him out with another woman.

"It has to be," I whisper, wondering which of us I'm trying to convince.

20

JAKE

THE LIGHTS from the arena cast a glow against the backdrop of the Colorado mountains, the peaks dark silhouettes under a sky streaked with the last hues of sunset.

Jodi and I find seats near the edge of the action, the wood bleachers rough beneath us. There's a chill to the October air, and the smell of hay and leather mixes with the scent of barbecue from a nearby food truck.

Damn my stupid promise to Iris. After last night, holding her in my arms on the dance floor and watching her come to life in the club where no one knew either of us, all I want is more time with her.

She's made it clear in a thousand different ways that I'm not for her, but the reality doesn't stop my body from rebelling at the thought of spending time with someone else. It doesn't stop me from wanting her.

"Do you ride?" Jodi asks and my attention snaps back to her—where it should have been this entire time.

Instead, my gaze has been locked on the barrel racers, my mind consumed with thoughts of Iris. It's not fair to my date for the evening, and I owe her at least that courtesy, even if I'm here so she stops sabotaging Iris.

"Enough not to embarrass myself," I say. "My grandfather made sure both my brother and I could handle ourselves in the saddle." The crowd erupts in cheers as the last competitor crosses the finish line. "But this is a level I can't even comprehend."

"Yeah," Jodi agrees, pointing to the final rider exiting the arena on her horse. "Maddie James was the favorite tonight, but her turns weren't tight enough to clinch the victory."

"Did you compete?"

Jodi seems comfortable at the event, and the cowboy boots she's paired with a short gingham dress are embellished with rhinestones, but look authentic. Still, she doesn't strike me as the horse-crazy type.

She barks out a laugh. "Only enough to win the rodeo pageants. Horsemanship was part of the deal, but I was always more interested in the dresses and makeup. And being an ambassador for the events." She winks. "I thrived on the attention."

That part doesn't surprise me. Most of our conversation tonight has revolved around Jodi, which is fine with me. She's nice enough and pretty enough, but she isn't Iris. And let's face it, I've been secretly hung up on Skylark's interim mayor for far too long to have my head turned by a minidress and bright pink lip gloss.

The announcer's voice booms across the speakers, wrapping up this event and introducing the slate of bull riders, the final competition of the evening.

I discreetly scan the crowd again.

"You're going to get a crick in your neck working hard so I don't notice you searching for Iris." Jodi elbows me gently. "You're a terrible date, Jake Byrne. Spending our evening together pining after my boss."

"I'm so sorry," I stammer, heat rising to my cheeks. What the hell is wrong with me? I'm going to be in big trouble for this. I turn to face my date. "I've been rude, Jodi. You deserve something better."

She wrinkles her nose. "I think you mean *someone* better."

"A hundred percent," I agree. "But I can make it up to you. I think you're great, it's just—"

"I think you're boring as hell," she interrupts, then pats me on the cheek the way my grandmother used to do when I gape at her.

Okay, maybe the conversation hasn't flowed the way it does with Iris, but I'm not boring. Iris didn't seem to think so anyway.

"She's going to kill me for screwing this up." I take Jodi's hand and squeeze. "I really am sorry."

"It's okay." She grins. "You paid for dinner and the rodeo and concert tickets. Plus, you're easy on the eyes."

"Are you going to tell Iris I screwed this up?"

"You like her."

I blow out a breath. "Since I was seventeen."

Her smile widens, then turns into a grimace. "No offense, but why? She's about as cuddly as a porcupine."

"A cruel irony," I answer. "For the record, porcupines are actually known to be sweet and affectionate. You just have to know how to pet them."

"I'll take your word on that." She holds up a hand. "But I'm done torturing her, and I'm not going to throw you under the bus either. Turns out Iris is actually a decent human, and I get that she has the town's best interest at heart. I wanted to hate her because of her mother, but I just can't."

"Also for the record..." I lift Jodi's hand to my mouth and brush a kiss across her knuckles. "I have a feeling you could have any guy you set your mind to."

She laughs. "Except you."

"You don't want me."

"True," she agrees, pushing out an audible breath.

"That sigh means something," I tell her and she tugs her hand from my grasp. "What's his name?"

"It doesn't matter." She turns to face the arena, wincing when the first bull rider is thrown. "He's definitely not interested, and it isn't because of Iris."

I hope to hell not.

"You want to tell me more?" I ask. "Maybe over a funnel cake?"

"Not sure about bearing my soul to you," she answers, "but I do adore funnel cake."

As the crowd cheers for the next rider, we walk down the bleacher steps. The sky is growing dark above us, but the midway lights glow brightly. Couples and families wander down the aisles of vendors selling various kinds of merchandise and all sorts of snack foods.

"Hey, Jodi," a man says as we find our place in line at the funnel cake booth.

I see her startle before regaining her composure. Hey, Daniel," she answers with a bland smile.

Daniel, several inches taller than my six feet, runs a hand through his floppy brown hair. In his crisp white button-down and dark jeans with Converse sneakers, he looks like he belongs at the rodeo even less than I do.

"Did you get the hummingbird feeder I brought back from Hawaii for you? I left it with your mom."

Twin spots of color bloom on Jodi's cheeks.

Interesting.

"Yes," she tells him. "Thank you. It's real pretty. Nice of you to think of me."

The dude beams like she's just promised him her firstborn child.

"Hey, I'm Jake Byrne," I say, stretching out a hand.

"Daniel Pearson," he replies. "I actually work—"

"As the senior program officer at the foundation," I interrupt, recognizing his name. "My grandfather says great things about you. How was your vacation?"

"A week in paradise," he answers. "My sister got married on the Big Island, so we had a mini family reunion. I'm the only single pringle left out of five siblings." He swallows like he's just admitted something scandalous.

"No pressure," I tell him with a laugh.

"No kidding," he mutters, then glances at Jodi, who is suddenly very interested in the ground beneath her boots.

The plot thickens.

"I'd love to grab lunch next week if you have time?" I'm trying to make a point of spending time with all the key employees of the foundation. I bet money my dad doesn't even know one of their names.

"I'd like that," Daniel says. "Jodi, don't forget we're going to grab coffee sometime. Vanilla iced latte with oat milk and extra foam."

A man with that kind of girlie order memorized is more than just a little interested in a woman. I wonder if Jodi realizes this.

Her voice is tight when she answers, "I'll look at my schedule."

"Sounds great." A lock of hair falls across Daniel's forehead as his head bobs. Jodi lifts a hand, almost like she wants to brush it back into place, but then she pulls it tight against her waist. "One part sugar to four parts water is the best ratio for hummers."

"Got it." She points to the booth. "We're up to order. I'll talk to you later, Daniel."

"Nice to meet you," I say when she turns away.

"Yeah. You too." The guy looks like he's just been kicked in the stomach as he walks back toward the arena.

We order the funnel cake and sit on a nearby bench to share it.

"What's the deal with you and Daniel?"

She lets out a powdered sugar-dusted scoff. "No deal. We're just friends."

"He brought you a gift from his sister's wedding and has your drink order memorized. The dude likes you."

She frowns and adjusts the strap of her gingham dress. "He'll never ask me out."

"Why not?"

"I don't know." She tears off a piece of funnel cake and pops it in her mouth, chewing like the pastry did her dirty. "But I do know there's only so many times a woman can throw out hints that she'd like a man to ask her out before she gives up."

"Don't give up on Daniel." I wipe my fingers on a paper napkin. "Coffee is a good sign, right?"

"Well, you asked me out over coffee," she counters, "and we know how this date is going."

"I'm seriously so so—"

"Do not apologize again." She rolls her eyes. "Maybe you can point out some of these guys you think are so into me at the concert. Because I don't want you, and Daniel Pearson doesn't want me."

"I'm pretty sure you're wrong," I say gently.

"I hope you're right." She snags the final bite of funnel cake and grabs my hand. "Let's get back to our seats. I just heard them announce Chase Calhoun as the next rider."

The way the excitement has ramped up inside the arena is palpable as we climb to our seats once more. This evening isn't what I expected, but that doesn't bother me any longer. I'm quickly learning I have the choice to make any moment count.

"Chase grew up in Skylark." Jodi points to the cowboy currently mounting a giant, stomping creature in the stall on the far side of the arena. "He won the PBR World Finals last year and is a legend around here."

"Do you know him personally?"

She leans into me. "Remember, I grew up in Skylark. I know almost everyone. Plus, I've been friends with his sister since third grade. In fact, I had a little crush on him in junior high."

"I hope he wins."

"Our hometown guy always wins. Eight seconds to prove he's

got what it takes." She grabs my hand again and moves a little closer as the air begins to buzz with anticipation.

A few people around us stand to get a better look at Chase Calhoun. He looks like the hero of an old Western movie, all grit and swagger, but his eyes are laser-focused on the massive animal beneath him.

I feel a tingle of awareness between my shoulder blades and look up to see Iris staring at me from across the arena. I recognize her friend Sloane next to her, and that must be Sadie, the dog trainer, on her other side because Ian Barlowe is sitting two people away.

There might be a former NFL MVP in the stands, but I can only truly focus on Iris and the fact that she's giving off kicked-puppy vibes from across the arena. Which is ridiculous considering I'm only with Jodi to make Iris happy. But she doesn't look happy.

"Ladies and gentlemen, riding Black Tornado, let's hear it for Chase Calhoun."

The audience goes wild as Chase nods and the gate opens. The bull explodes forward like a coiled spring, and Chase clings to the rope with one hand while his other waves high in the air. I've lived in Austin for years but never attended an event like this. Cowboy culture isn't my thing, yet I'm mesmerized by the sheer power of the scene before me now.

The crowd shouts the countdown and then the buzzer blares. Chase launches into the air and lands in a tangle of limbs on the dirt floor. Rodeos clowns—bullfighters, Jodi calls them—rush forward. The bull twists, and, in the center of the ring, one giant hoof comes down on Chase with unthinkable force.

His body goes still, and an immediate hush falls over the arena. My chest tightens even as one of the bullfighters waves a colorful flag to guide Black Tornado to the chute.

Chase Calhoun is motionless on the dirt.

"Oh my God." Jodi stands as the medical team moves in. "Is he okay?"

"Nothing can hurt Chase," a boy in front of us assures her. The kid's father places a heavy hand on his son's shoulder, clearly not convinced.

The medics work quickly, loading the cowboy onto a stretcher. His face is pale and streaked with dirt as they carry him out of the ring.

Jodi shakes her head. "I need to find his sister. Ada and her mom are here somewhere."

"Of course. You want me to go with you?"

"No. His family is private. I'm going to take a rain check on the concert." She flashes a tight smile. "Maybe you and Iris and me and someone can double date next time."

"Go find your friend." I squeeze her hand. "Let me know if I can do anything." She nods and hurries away.

The announcer's voice returns, cutting through the tension. "Folks, we've got one of the toughest cowboys out there in good hands. Let's show him our support."

As the crowd cheers, I look up to where Iris and her friends are sitting, but she's gone. I stand, only to have a heavy hand fall on my shoulder.

"Fancy meeting you here," a familiar voice says.

21

JAKE

I LOOK up into a pair of chocolate-brown eyes and try to hide my shock. "Nick?"

What the hell is Nick Dixon doing in Skylark, let alone at the rodeo?

"Sit down and visit for a bit, Byrne. It's been a minute, and we have some shit to catch up on."

The announcer's voice rings out, once again assuring us that Chase Calhoun is in good hands before introducing the next competitor. Obviously, the crowd is still upset, but the fans offer a polite round of applause for the cowboy prepping for his ride.

I lower myself to the wood bleacher as Nick sits beside me. "What are you doing in town? Does Iris know you're here?"

"Not yet." He keeps his gaze on the arena. "But I saw you drop her off at a stupid hour this morning."

Irritation ripples through me. "For the record, it was five-thirty."

I haven't seen Nick in person for a couple of years—not since he showed up on my doorstep in Austin in need of a loan. It was an awkward reunion then, but this is downright strange.

"What the hell were you doing lurking around her house at

that ungodly hour? I don't remember you being a morning person."

"Maybe things change," he says tightly. "Maybe I was communing with the sunrise." He scrubs a hand over the dark scruff of his jaw and mutters, "Definitely not lurking." His eyes narrow as he glares at me. "And what the hell are you doing staying out all night with my sister?"

I easily match his temper. "None of your goddamn business, Nick. We aren't seventeen anymore." Even though she makes me feel like a stupid, infatuated boy hoping for one more chance to get it right.

"The rules we set then still apply, Jake." He places the same emphasis on my name as I did on his. "My sister is off-limits."

"I respected your wishes back then, but I'm an adult. Iris is an adult. As far as I'm concerned—"

"I don't give a shit about your concerns," he snaps back.

His shoulders rise and fall as he draws in a deep breath. The show has mostly gone on around us, and people are cheering for the cowboy who just finished a successful ride. But a couple in front of us dart speculative looks in our direction at his tone. I don't want things with Nick to escalate. Iris, who has always been overly protective of her twin brother, wouldn't want that either.

He nudges my arm with his. "I'm also wondering what you're doing on a date with another woman after being out all night with my little sister."

"Younger by two minutes," I feel compelled to point out. "She's also a ton smarter and has more common sense than the two of us put together. Do you really think she'd spend time with me if she thinks it means trouble?"

Okay, maybe that's a stupid question, because I already know she thinks I'm trouble. But her brother doesn't know that. At least not yet.

"She has a blind spot where you're concerned."

Doubtful, but a guy can dream.

"Why haven't you asked her about last night yourself?" I turn to study him. "Have you seen your sister outside of spying on her?"

The way his gaze slides to the ground, I know the answer without him saying a word.

"I wasn't spying," he insists. "But I haven't seen Iris yet. I needed to take care of some stuff today. Anyway, that's not the point. We're talking about you."

"I don't think so." My protective instincts roar to life. Iris loves her brother, which means he has the power to hurt her. That isn't going to happen on my watch. "You're at least as much trouble, if not more. You know she used the money she'd been saving for her dream house to bail you out this last time."

Shame flickers in the depths of his dark eyes as he shakes his head. "I know, and it kills me. But it was the last time, and I have a plan to pay her back. I'm sober, Jake. I have been since my last stint in rehab."

"Good for you, man. I hope it sticks this time."

"It will." He laughs softly. "Not that anyone has a reason to believe me, but I know it will."

It's hard to explain the conflicting emotions I have when it comes to Nick Dixon. He was my best friend that summer after Mikey died. Sure we got in a hell of a lot of trouble, but we also had a shit-ton of fun. The bond between us was real—a couple of messed-up kids with too much trauma in our respective pasts.

That doesn't change the fact I don't want Nick upsetting Iris. She's got enough on her plate, and I hope to hell that includes the two of us getting together. After last night, I'm convinced Iris and I are making progress. Or we will be once she accepts that Jodi is about as interested in me as I am in her.

I'm not ready to let our connection go, even if I know there's no future in it. For once, I want to stop ruminating over the past and worrying about the future. I want to enjoy the present—soak in every moment I can with Iris. Preferably a few of them with us both buck-ass naked. Even the idea of surrender doesn't feel like losing with Iris—it feels like finally coming home.

But first, I need to deal with Nick.

"Then I believe you. I don't want to argue, man." I clap a hand on his shoulder. "I swear I won't hurt Iris. Can you say the same?"

"Yes," he answers without hesitation.

I nod. "Then I'm damn glad to see you. You look good, Nick."

It's true. His hair, the same dark shade as Iris's, is neatly trimmed, and his eyes are clear. He's wearing a canvas vest over a long-sleeve Henley, and I can see he's been working out. It's been years since I've seen Nick look healthy, and despite my reservations about him being back in his sister's life, I want that for him. He's been through enough already.

"I feel good." His shoulders relax slightly. "A whole lot better than that trampled rider."

"He'll be okay," I say, even though I have no idea if that's true.

"You always were an optimist, Jake." He leans back against the empty bleacher behind us. "Let's catch up for real, man."

"Yeah," I agree. "That sounds like a plan."

22

IRIS

"ARE YOU OKAY?" Sloane asks as I pull to a stop in front of the bookstore after our night out at the rodeo and concert. Her apartment above the shop has made it easier for her to keep working—and still take breaks during the day—since she started treatment. "Tonight couldn't have been easy."

"I can't get the image of the cowboy this town adores being carted out of the ring on a stretcher."

"Bull riders are tough as nails, and he's one of the best."

"You're right."

I checked in with one of the EMTs during the lull between the end of the rodeo and the start of the concert. According to her, Chase was awake and alert at the hospital but would need surgery to repair the shattered bones in his leg. Word that he would likely make a full recovery spread quickly, so the crowd at the concert was in high spirits.

"And you know I wasn't talking about Chase," she says gently.

Sadie and Ian had gone home early, but Sloane and I stayed until the end. I tried not to make it too obvious that I spent most of the time surreptitiously searching for Jake and Jodi, but I guess I hadn't been as sly as I thought.

I close my eyes for a moment. "Being sad about two people going on a date that I helped set up feels even sillier in light of what happened tonight." But it doesn't dull the ache in my chest. Especially when I picture him with someone else.

"Emotions aren't trivial." She reaches out to squeeze my arm. "And the only way to move through them is to let yourself feel."

I cover my face with my hands. "Hearing you say that makes me feel like the worst friend on the planet. You're dealing with the big C, and I can't even manage to keep fun simple. It shouldn't be this hard."

"As simple as having fun sounds," Sloane answers, "I understand why it isn't that easy for you. The fact that you're willing to try gives me hope. I didn't start the bucket list challenge just to watch each of you easily succeed at something." She gives an unsteady laugh. "I wanted to see other people struggle. Maybe that makes me a terrible friend. Everyone believes I'm handling my diagnosis and treatment so well. The truth is, I'm scared, angry, and resentful. Sometimes I hate everyone."

"You don't—"

"I do," she insists, her voice quivering. "I hate people who are healthy. I hate people who have things worse than me because it makes me a jerk for feeling sorry for myself. I hate people who think they know what I'm going through. I hate myself for all of those things. I grew up in a house filled with anger and hate, and I swore I was going to be a happy person. I wouldn't let that hate define me. Yet here I am."

"Sloane, honey, if I'm allowed to feel emotions, so are you. Even the hard ones."

She turns to look out the window, and it breaks my heart to see tears shimmering in her eyes under the moon's silvery glow.

"People think I'm a hero. '*Sloane has such a good attitude. She's so strong.*' I don't feel strong. You flaunt your flaws, Iris. Use them as a calling card. At least you're handling the hard stuff."

"Look at my life." With what I hope is a wry—and not

pathetic—smile, I hold my fingers up one at a time. "I'm fighting for a job I don't even know if I truly want. My heart hurts watching a man I shouldn't want to go on a date I pressured him into. I'm trying to have fun but suck at dancing—"

"You love it," she interrupts.

"But I suck," I repeat. "There's a decent chance I'm going to publicly humiliate myself in front of half the town at Fun Fest. Oh, yes. Fun Fest. To prove that I'm the right candidate for the job I don't know that I want, I'm on a mission to also prove I'm fun to a community that seems to care more about karaoke than literacy. And I can't convince them otherwise."

I slap a palm to my head. "I won't bore you with the rest of the list, but it's a doozy. Trust me. I'm not handling anything. At least not well."

"That's what I mean." She swipes at the edges of her eyes and then offers a watery smile. "You're so upfront with your shit-show life that you make me feel better about mine. We're quite a pair."

I reach across the console and wrap her in a tight hug. "If it counts for anything, there's no one I'd rather be dysfunctional with than you."

"It counts for a lot," she whispers into my hair.

"You know..." I cup her too-thin face with my palms. "A brilliant person told me you can't move through emotions unless you let yourself feel them. You're allowed to be pissed about having cancer. I think it would be more concerning if you weren't."

"But what if I let the rage and hate have their way with me?" She bites down on her lower lip. "What if the hate latches on and doesn't let go, the way it did with my mom and dad? I might as well let cancer win because I'll poison everything and everyone around me."

I grab her shoulders and give her a gentle shake. "Don't you say another word about cancer winning. This world needs you, Sloane. You're a gift to the people lucky enough to have you love them."

"I could say the same about you," she says. "The outcome of an election and some festival dance routine don't determine your value as a person. Nothing outside of you can. I've seen the soft parts beneath your prickly exterior. You deserve a lot more than you're giving yourself credit for."

"Maybe," I say, even though it's still hard for me to believe. "We might just have to agree to disagree on which one of us is more awesome."

"Uhhhhh..." Sloane mock scoffs. "It's me. I'm the more awesome one." She taps on the cotton beanie she's wearing. "There's no way you could rock a pixie cut the way I'm going to when my bald nut grows out."

I laugh and hug her again. "Fair point. For the record, I love your bald nut and all the rest of you."

"Love you, too, Iris." She starts to open the door, glancing over her shoulder. "Call me after you talk to Jake."

"What makes you think I'm going to talk to Jake before I see Jodi on Monday?"

"Just call me," she repeats with an eye roll, then heads inside.

Driving home from downtown only takes a few minutes, and the quiet night surrounds me like a blanket. I appreciate the houses that leave the porch lights on, welcoming visitors to their door. It tugs at something deep within me—the community I never had growing up with my mother's nomadic lifestyle. In these lit doors, I see the possibility of belonging. It's what drew me to local politics in the first place—the chance to help weave together the threads of community that I'd always longed for but never experienced.

My heart skips a beat when I notice the silhouette of a man sitting on my porch swing. I smirk and secretly wonder if Sloane's treatment has made her clairvoyant. I plan to rip Jake a new one because he shouldn't be here, but I'm also ridiculously happy to see him. A ridiculous, hopeful part of me perks up at the idea that it might be Jake.

Only it isn't Jake. Disappointment stings sharper than I expect.

Worry suddenly tinges my happiness as I park in the driveway and rush toward the house.

"Hey, Sis." Nick stands to greet me as I take the front porch steps two at a time, throwing my arms around him. No matter how long it's been or what he's done, seeing my twin in person is like having a part of me come home.

"When did you get in? What are you doing here? *How* are you doing?"

"Whoa, whoa, whoa." Nick drops a kiss on the top of my head. "It's good to see you, Sis. Let's pump the brakes on the firing squad of questions."

I pull away and look into his face, searching for...what, I'm not sure. That's a lie. I know exactly what I'm looking for. Evidence that he's using again. That he's here to ask for money or hide from some shady deal he got himself into.

"I'm okay, Iris." His voice is so sincere I can't help but believe him. "I mean it." He gives me a gentle smile. "I'm in a good place. And I'm staying there."

"That's good, Nick." I release the breath I didn't realize I was holding. "Really good."

As easily as I can read my brother, the twin bond goes both ways. He's studying me in return and sees something that makes his thick brows draw together.

"Why don't you invite me inside so you can tell me what's going on with you?"

"Of course. Come in." I notice the duffel bag at his feet. "Are you staying?"

"Maybe a few days if it's okay?"

"You can stay as long as you like." I squeeze his hand and then move to unlock the front door. "But I thought you hated Skylark." No matter the mess he's bringing with him, Nick is still home to me on so many levels.

"I hated what happened to me here. To both of us."

My hand jerks as the door swings open, and the keys fall to the hardwood floor. I bend to retrieve them, willing myself to stay calm. Does he know that Jake is also back?

I know Jake told me about helping Nick with rehab, but so much of my brother's negative feelings about Skylark are tied up in the trouble he and Jake got into. The trouble I always believed wasn't my brother's fault.

Is that simply what I wanted to believe all this time? To blame that night on Jake so I didn't have to hold my twin responsible.

"It isn't the town's fault."

"Of course *the mayor* would say that." I turn to face him, and he winks as he kicks the door shut and drops his bag on the floor.

Although we text and talk a decent amount, it's been nearly a year since I've seen my brother. I visited after his last stint in rehab, when he asked me to pay off the loan shark he owed. But it's always been easy to focus on Nick and his problems, and keep him in the dark about mine. I told him I was moving back to Skylark, and he knows about me being appointed as mayor, but nothing that led up to it.

"You don't like me being here?" I ask cautiously.

"I'm happy for you. You've worked hard your whole life. You deserve all the success that comes your way."

I think about Sloane's comment that I deserve more. Based on how I've gotten to where I am now, is that really true?

My friends don't know about the affair or losing my job. Returning to Skylark with my tail between my legs and only getting the position I'm in now because of a tragedy.

Yes, I've worked hard. But where has that gotten me?

"Thanks. I appreciate the vote of confidence."

He frowns slightly, like he realizes I'm lying, but thankfully, he doesn't call me out on it. I'm not sure I could resist revealing everything if he pressed me on my secrets.

Not that my brother has any room to judge my mistakes. He's

got me beat in the screw-up-your-life department by a mile, but I don't want him worrying.

I'm the strong one, the one who takes care of things.

If I'm being honest, I don't know who I'd be without that as my identity. Without giving and doing to prove I'm worth my dreams and goals. I'm worth being loved.

"Are you hungry?" I ask, moving down the hall to the kitchen.

"You know the answer to that."

"You're always hungry," I answer over my shoulder, then flip on the overhead light in the L-shaped kitchen.

"Your house is cute, but not exactly your style."

"What do you know about my style?"

He points to the rooster-patterned valance that covers the bottom half of the window overlooking the backyard. "I know it doesn't include barnyard animals."

I chuckle. "Yeah, well, it's a rental, so no point updating things."

I grab the loaf of bread from the basket on the counter and open the fridge. I stand before it longer than I need to, letting the blast of chilled air cool my cheeks. I'm not sure if Nick knows how much that last loan I gave him cost me, and I don't plan on mentioning it.

"Speaking of updates, maybe you want to give me the 411 on you and Jake Byrne." He makes the request casually, like we're talking about the weather, as he takes a pan out of the drawer below the stove and turns on the gas range's front burner. I hand him the bread and butter and try to appear just as casual.

Despite some of her more glaring flaws, our mom was always a fantastic cook. When she was in the mood, Mom had the ability to meld spices and flavors into the most mouth-watering meals with the most basic of pantry ingredients. Even though our mother had natural talent, she had little inclination to use it for anything so mundane as feeding her children on a daily basis. As backward as it sounds, her indifference made the meals she did cook even better, at least to me.

I don't know how Nick felt about her somewhat lackadaisical commitment to raising us. But as Nick inherited our mother's cooking skills, he did most of the cooking when we were growing up. When we were young, we spent most of our time trying to survive and cope. Later, I spent way too many nights praying he'd survive his own demons.

"Are you and Jake still friends?" I ask casually. "Is that how you know he's back here?"

"Jake didn't tell me, but I know." He smears two slices of bread with butter as I cut thick slices from a block of golden yellow cheese. I don't love how this visit is starting, but appreciate having something to do with my hands if we're going to talk about Jake. There's no doubt I'd have a hard time hiding my feelings from Nick if he was looking into my eyes right now. "I saw him at the rodeo tonight."

The knife slips from my fingers and skitters across the counter before I grab it back. "What were you doing at the rodeo?"

"Hoping Chase Calhoun makes a full recovery, just like everybody else." He nudges me with his elbow. "Why is it that while we're both asking questions, I'm the only one answering them? I'm real curious about the two of you being friends."

"We're taking a dance class together."

My brother barks out a laugh. "Shut the front door."

"It's true." I focus on slicing more cheese. These sandwiches will be two inches thick by the time I'm done. "We didn't sign up together," I clarify. "I'm in the class because my political mentor is there. And while you might not remember this detail from our childhood, I love dancing. It's fun."

The magic word.

"I know you love to dance," Nick says, and my hand stills on the block of cheese. At this rate, I'm going to be lucky not to slice off a finger.

As usual, Nick sees more than he lets on. He takes the knife and slides the cutting board away from me.

"I'll handle the grilled cheese," he says. "Do you still have a thing for chamomile tea?" His memory of the smallest things is one of the things I love best about him. My brother is the best despite his demons.

"I've upgraded to lavender," I tell him.

"Even better. Lots of honey in mine, please. And while you're boiling water—which I assume you can manage without hurting yourself—you can explain why Jake is part of the dance class. Does he wear tights?"

"Don't be a dick." I grab the copper kettle from the back burner and fill it with fresh water. "Not that there's anything wrong with wearing tights, but it's ballroom dancing. His grandfather is part of the class. Jake joined as a favor to Gilbert. And he's good."

Nick laughs as he layers the cheese across the bread. "That doesn't surprise me. Jake is the most naturally coordinated person I've ever met."

I snort. "Right? He's annoyingly good at pretty much everything."

"Not everything." He glances at me while he places the second side of bread on top of the cheese, buttered side up. The scent of toasting bread fills the kitchen. "He's terrible at relationships, and I saw him dropping you off a couple blocks from here early this morning. Too damn early for a ballroom dance class. You spent the night with him, Iris." The way he says it feels like a warning, echoing the doubts in my own head and heart.

"Who I spend my nights with is none of your business." I swat his arm. "And you sound like a total creeper spying on me. Why didn't you tell me you were coming?"

"I wasn't spying." The smell of melting cheese and the sizzle of buttered bread in the pan bring me back to my childhood as much as arguing with Nick does. Only now, it's not cheap processed singles in individual wrappers, but locally-made smoked cheddar and artisan bread from the local bakery. And we're not fighting over who used the last of the hot water but things that are far more serious for both of us.

"I flew in from Savannah last night. I wanted to surprise you."

"You hate surprises," I remind him.

He glances in my direction and then flips the bread, which is perfectly crisp and golden on one side. "Okay, I didn't call or text first because I wasn't sure how you'd feel about me coming to Skylark. My flight got delayed, and we didn't touch down in Denver until nearly three a.m. I didn't want to wake you up at that god-awful hour, so I parked the rental in the neighborhood and went for a run."

The kettle begins to whistle, and I pull it off the burner and pour water over the teabags I've placed in ceramic mugs. They're a set I bought myself when I first moved here—deep blue with little white daisies, nothing like the mismatched collection our mom pilfered from restaurants and hotels.

"Since when have you become a runner?"

"Since I saw how much good it does for you mentally and emotionally." He shrugs. "My last rehab center was surrounded by nature trails. One of the counselors did ultra-marathons. I've never been a great sleeper, so I started tagging along."

"That's what you were doing yesterday morning when you saw Jake drop me off?"

"I saw him drop you two blocks from your house like he didn't want any witnesses to you getting out of his car. Like he has a problem being seen with you."

I carry the mugs to the table while Nick scoops the sandwiches onto a cutting board. "It's not Jake who has a problem with it. This is a small town. I don't want people talking about us when there's nothing to talk about."

"Yeah, well, maybe we should talk about me seeing him at the rodeo with another woman. What the hell, Iris?"

He places a plate with four perfect triangles of the grilled cheese sandwich in front of me, then turns around and opens the refrigerator to grab a bottle of Dijon mustard. My throat constricts with emotion when he sets it next to my plate. I've always loved dipping any sandwich in mustard, which most people think is gross. Maybe it is, but my brother remembered that I like it.

I squeeze a generous dollop onto my plate, dunk one corner, and then take a big bite. "God, you missed your calling," I whisper. "It still isn't any of your business, but I asked Jake to take out the woman he was with tonight."

"Why would you do that if you have feelings for him?"

My heart squeezes. "I don't have feelings for him. Like you said, Jake doesn't do relationships. I'd be a fool to fall for him."

My brother takes a sip of tea and then adds another spoonful of honey. "You aren't a fool, but I swear I'll beat the shit out of Jake Byrne if he hurts you."

"I'm not going to let him hurt me." *Liar*, my heart screams. Because it doesn't mean he couldn't. Or that I haven't already let him close enough to try.

"I hope not."

"Besides, you don't need to fight my battles, especially against your best friend."

"Jake and I aren't about to start braiding each other's hair, Sis. But speaking of battles, some tool bag at the rodeo was bragging to his loser entourage about kicking your ass in the upcoming election. You texted that the election is just a formality. You're running unopposed."

I take another bite, then lick a tendril of cheese off my finger. "You really are checking up on me. That tool is Homer Moore's nephew."

"Jesus Christ, Iris." He drops his mug to the table, dark liquid splashing over the rim. "You're a glutton for punishment. First Jake, and then you want to dredge up the scandal that ran you out of town in the first place."

"It wasn't my scandal."

"Do you think anybody cares? You're her daughter."

"I'm nothing like her." *Liar*.

"I don't want to see you get hurt or watch your perfect reputation torn to shreds in an election. You have a history here, whether you like it or not. If Homer Moore's nephew is going to the trouble of running against you, he'll use it."

I cross my arms over my chest, hating the truth in his words. But they aren't the whole truth. "Mom wasn't the only one who caused trouble here."

A muscle ticks in his jaw. "Do you want me to leave? No one but you and Jake even know I've been here. It can be one more secret to bond the two of you."

Instead of reacting, I force myself to take a slow, steadying breath and then meet his eyes, several shades darker than mine. "I don't want you to leave, and I'm sick of secrets. I want to get to know you again, Nick. Please stay. I promise I know what I'm doing."

"You always do, Iris," he says after a long moment.

I stand and walk around the table, wrapping my arms around him. "Not always. But when it comes to you and me, I know I've missed you."

"I've missed you too, Sis. Now sit down and finish your sandwich." He squeezes me tight. "The past can't be changed, Iris, but it's a hell of a teacher."

"We've both had some hard lessons. It's time for something better." I just hope I've learned enough to move on without my past defining me.

23

JAKE

THE FOLLOWING MORNING, a round of loud knocking wrenches my attention from the screen in front of me, and I open the door of the garage apartment to find Iris glaring at me from the other side.

"What a lovely Sunday surprise." My heart flings against my ribcage like an exuberant puppy begging for attention from its favorite human.

She crosses her arms over her chest as if she senses my pleasure and wants nothing to do with it. "We need to talk."

I offer a broad smile, ignoring her tight frown and the fact that she's shooting daggers at me. "Did you jog all the way here? That's six miles one way. Impressive."

"I didn't want anyone to see my car." The blue sky and bright sun overhead take the edge off the crisp air of another perfect Colorado fall morning.

Her fitted athletic top and leggings cling to the gentle curve of her hips, and there's something weirdly sexy about the sheen of sweat across her brow. I want to explore other ways to make her hot and sweaty—ways that involve tangled limbs and my mouth all over her body. And while my heart might want to cuddle up to her, my dick is begging her to turn around so I can check out her ass in those tight leggings.

Concentrate, you idiot, my brain commands. But now that I've gone down the mental road of imagining touching her—tasting her—I'm having a hell of a time focusing on anything else.

"Did I wake you?"

Her words snap me back to the present, and I lift my gaze to find her looking me up and down. I can only imagine what she's thinking based on my current appearance. I didn't bother to change the grubby gray T-shirt after spilling coffee down my front, and my baggy fleece sweatpants with a hole in the knee happen to be my lucky writing pants. I run a hand through my hair to try to smooth it down since I have a habit of pulling on the ends when I'm really thinking.

"No."

"Then what are you doing?"

She sounds suspicious, and I wish I could answer her honestly. I've been up since before dawn because the big climax of the latest Ellie Spaulding book—the one due to my editor at the end of next week—untangled itself in my brain at four in the morning.

Some people might think losing sleep over writing a few chapters is silly, but getting up when it's still dark because the words are coming fast and furious is way better than sleeping in only to stare at a blank screen for most of the day. Deadlines are more important than rest, but I can't tell Iris that. No matter how much I want to share it, Spencer Charles is my secret, and I don't trust how people will react to the revelation. Or if anyone will believe me. And Iris's opinion matters more than most.

"I'm working on the proposal I'll present to my grandpa in two weeks. Hammering out my vision for the future of the foundation."

"Hammering?" She arches a brow. "At nine o'clock on a Sunday morning?"

"Did you run all the way here to give me shit about my sleep habits?" I encircle her wrist and pull her forward. "Or are you here for my version of Sunday service?"

She stumbles into me, and I quickly take advantage, kicking the door shut with one foot.

"You don't have a version of Sunday service," she says, her mouth curving up at one end. At least she seems less angry now. I'll take a win where I can get it.

"Oh, but I do." In the three-way battle between common sense, emotions, and desire, my dick is in the lead, so I lean down and kiss the underside of her jaw, loving the taste of the salt on her skin. "It involves worshiping your body."

Her answering moan makes my fleece pants tent in front. I can't remember ever wanting anything or anyone as much as I do Iris. I reach for the hem of her shirt, but she places a hand over mine.

"What happened with Jodi?"

And rational thinking—the buzziest of buzzkills—takes over as I straighten. "I went on the date, just like I promised."

"She texted first thing this morning." Iris is back to glaring and my pants are back to normal.

I shrug and try not to let my burning curiosity show. "What did she report?"

"She said it was a one-and-done thing between you two."

"I could have told you that, Dixon." I move toward the table where I've been working, snapping my laptop shut with more force than necessary. "I tried to tell you that. Now will you give it a rest?"

"You could try again." I ignore the frustration I feel radiating from her as she follows me into the tiny kitchen area.

Other than the bedroom and attached bath, the bunkhouse floorplan is open-concept. It's a far cry from my house in the Travis Heights neighborhood in Austin, with its modern design, expansive layout, and a wall of windows that offers an absurdly breathtaking view of downtown. But I like it here. The compact space feels like home, even though it isn't.

I know she's waiting for me to say something, but the words are stuck in the void between my chest and throat. Instead, I take eggs and other ingredients out of the fridge.

"What are you doing?" Confusion laces her tone. Join the club, sweetheart.

"Making the two of us an omelet. I'm not arguing with you on an empty stomach."

"I don't want to argue."

"Then what the hell is your deal?" I crack three eggs into a mixing bowl, the familiar task calming me. "I took her on a date just like you asked. We aren't a match." I grab a whisk and point it at Iris before starting in on the eggs like I'm nursing a grudge. "Did Jodi happen to mention in her text that she's done messing with you?"

Iris snags her lower lip between her teeth and shifts her gaze from mine as she gives a reluctant nod. "Yeah."

"What the hell?" I repeat, as much to myself as to her. "You know she thinks I'm boring? Told me straight to my face."

My revelation cuts through some of the tension simmering between us.

Iris drops into one of the chairs on either side of the table, letting out a shaky laugh. "Despite a plethora of faults, you're the least boring person I know."

I season the eggs, then add a scoop of the diced pepper and sausage mixture I prepped earlier in the week. "I think her exact words were 'boring as hell.'"

"Did you mess it up on purpose?"

After pouring the egg mixture into the sizzling pan, I lean one hip against the counter, scrubbing a hand over the scruff on my jaw. "Are you listening to yourself?"

Her big eyes flare with emotion as our gazes hold. "I'm sorry."

It sounds like she means it, but I'm too pissed to let this go.

Pissed she's willing to give up on us so easily and pissed that it was my past actions that led to this distance between us in the first place.

"Why are you so damn intent on pushing me away? You had fun Friday night," I remind her. "With me. I'm not the same guy I was at seventeen. Is that so hard to believe, or are you just one hundred percent sure I'm going to mess it all up, on purpose or not?"

"It's not you," she admits in a quiet voice. "It's me. I'm scared I'm going to screw up my life, and I don't want anyone near me when it happens. My mom didn't care about the collateral damage, but I do. It's easier—safer—to keep you and everyone else at arm's length. I deserve whatever bad things happen to me, but—"

"Damn it, Iris. Take off the fucking hairshirt for a minute." I turn back to the pan to flip the omelet, adding a handful of cheese to the top before folding it in half. "The way I see it, you deserve all the gold stars in the world for how hard you work. For the person you are on the inside. You deserve your dream house and whatever white-picket-fence future you want. And you sure as hell deserve somebody who'll stick around and fight for you, even when you're being your own worst enemy."

She doesn't answer for a long moment and the air pulses with the undeniable connection we've always shared. "Are you suddenly interested in being that person, Jake?"

I want to say yes, but I can't give her that. Iris has her fears, but mine have their claws dug into me just as profoundly. I don't let myself care about people—not the way she needs someone to care about her.

"I'm saying I don't want to let go of whatever this is between us."

"Me neither." She sounds as shocked by the whispered admission as I am hearing it. Two simple words, but they're important coming from this gorgeous, infuriating, enticing enigma of a woman.

"I like you, Jake. A lot."

My hand jerks and the omelet nearly slides out of the pan onto the counter before I can transfer it to a plate. "That's a decent place to start." Especially for my heart, which is once again trying to pound its way out of my chest.

From the corner of my eye, I watch her draw in a deep breath. She has more to say, and I'm here for it. All of it.

"I spent most of my life shut down, or at least shut off. It always felt safer. But I don't want that with you. Being perfect on paper hasn't fooled anyone, and I'm sick of pretending." She pauses and frowns, staring at her hands, tightly clasped on the table in front of her. "I'm too blunt too often. I'm socially awkward and nowhere near perfect with all my prickly edges. And I'm afraid all the fun in the world isn't going to change me."

"You don't have to change, Iris. Not one damn thing. I like prickly, and the fact that not everyone gets to see your soft side." I think about Jodi's comment from the previous night. "Porcupines happen to be my favorite animal."

I place the plate and two forks in the center of the small table and slide into the chair across from her.

She smiles. "Nobody picks porcupines as their favorite animals."

"I do."

"I'm sorry I made you the punching bag for my fears."

"I can handle it," I assure her.

"And what about Nick?" She pauses with a forkful of omelet midway to her mouth. "He was waiting on my porch after the rodeo and is planning to stay a while. Can you handle him being back in town?"

I close my eyes for a moment, tamping down the tangle of affection and regret I feel for her twin, and then nod. "Yeah. Nick and I are good. But I'm going to kick the shit out of him if he hurts you again."

"What a coincidence." She rolls her eyes. "He said the same thing about you."

"Look at that." I wink, needing to lighten the mood. To lighten her emotional load in any way I can. It's what I failed to do for Mikey, and I won't make the same mistake with Iris. "Your brother and I are already on the same page."

"I'm not sure that's a good thing," she says, then sits back in her chair and sighs. "You make a damn good omelet, Byrne. It's not fair that you and Nick are amazing in the kitchen when I can't even boil water."

"Eggs aren't exactly complicated." Although how happy it makes me to take care of her, even in this small way, feels ridiculously complicated.

"Trust me, I can mess up eggs," she says.

"Your brother taught me how to make an omelet that summer. He called it the perfect hangover food."

She laughs. "He made grilled cheese last night after the rodeo. That's what I remember him claiming was the perfect hangover food."

"Nick probably has more than one cure for the common hangover."

Her lips press together, and I curse my lame attempt at humor.

"I want it to be different for him this time. I want a lot of things right now." She takes another bite and then puts down her fork. "I want a lot of things, and that isn't something I normally allow myself."

"There's nothing wrong with wanting." I lean across the table and take her hand. "These days, I mainly want you. All of you. All the time."

Her smile is one part sexy, one part shy, and completely irresistible. "I'm gross and sweaty. Dried sweat is disgusting. There's nothing sexy about that."

I shake my head. "The thought of you in my shower is sexy."

She mock pouts. "All alone?" she asks as her cheeks turn pink.

"No worries, sweetheart. I'll be with you. That's a given."

"What about your work?" She places her free hand on top of the laptop. Once again, I think about telling her my secret, until she continues, "Unless you have a different kind of hammering in mind."

Okay, so much for thinking about anything but getting her naked. "Do you like sexy-times talk, Dixon?" I grin as I stand and take the empty plate to the sink.

She covers her face with her hand but peeks through her fingers at me. "I can't believe I said that. Hammering." She laughs low in her throat, the sound pouring over me like honey. "It's so embarrassing."

Returning to the table, I hold out my hand to her. "I can't wait to hear what you scream when I make you come for the first time."

She gasps and wags a finger at me, all prim and proper. "You can't say things like that," she admonishes, but I know she likes it. And I like flirting with her, teasing her, and snaking my way past that prickly exterior. Porcupines for the win.

"That's just the tip of the iceberg, Iris." I give an exaggerated wink. "The tip? Get it."

She giggle-snorts, and I must be really far gone because it's fucking adorable. "I didn't plan for this." Her gaze drops from mine and focuses on my outstretched hand. "The plan was to say my piece then work off the inevitable frustration of you being disagreeable on my run back to the house."

"Wouldn't you rather work it off in the shower?" I crook my finger. "I promise to agree to anything you want, sweetheart."

"I want you, Jake," she whispers, and when she places her hand in mine, it feels like a victory.

The apartment's bathroom isn't large or lavish, but the shower's roomy, with subway tile covering the surround. The glass door opens out, and I reach in and flip on the water, waiting for it to run hot. I tug my shirt over my head and turn back to find Iris doing the same, leaving her standing there in a sports bra and those leggings that make her legs look a mile long.

All I can think about is having them wrapped around my hips —or even better, my shoulders, as I bury my face in her.

"Turn around," she says, and I blink.

"We're about to shower together, honey."

"Taking off a compression bra isn't sexy, and you won't convince me otherwise with the way it straps the girls down."

"Free the girls," I tell her with a grin. Is it a lascivious grin? I sure as hell hope so.

"I'm about to," she answers and then does a little spinning motion with one finger. "As soon as you turn around."

24

JAKE

I COMPLY with Iris's request, although it's ridiculous to think anything could make this woman less attractive to me at this moment. But I wasn't kidding that I'd agree to anything. I'm just grateful she's here and willing to give us another chance—like my reward for untangling that thorny plot issue. The best damn reward I've ever had. I might have been joking about Sunday service, but I'll worship at the altar of Iris Dixon as long as she'll have me.

"Okay." Her voice is little more than a squeak, which makes me grin even harder.

The breath whooshes out of my lungs because she's taken off not only her bra, but the leggings as well. Her cheeks and chest are flushed with color, and she's having trouble looking me in the eye, like it's not easy for her to stand in front of me naked.

"You're so beautiful, Iris."

"I'm so naked," she replies.

I'm not going to say out loud how much that makes her all the more beautiful to me, but I take a step closer and use one finger to trace the shallow indentation from her shoulder to the swell of her breast where the bra strap left a mark.

"These poor, imprisoned ladies. Finally earning some well-deserved freedom." I cup her breasts in my palms, and it's no surprise they're a perfect fit.

"It's better when they're not bouncing around."

I trace my thumbs across her pebbled nipples, and she draws in an unsteady breath. "Bounce away, girls."

She laughs and then hooks one finger in the waistband of my sweatpants. "You're overdressed for this occasion."

It takes me seconds to yank down my sweats and boxers and step out of them. My cock springs free and juts out like it's straining for attention. No surprise, given that it feels like I could pound nails with it.

Iris's eyes widen in—oh, yeah, that's appreciation, and my cock hardens even more, which I didn't think was even possible.

I draw her forward, and we step into the shower with the spray at her back. Iris tips up her head, giving me access to the graceful column of her neck as water cascades over us. I kiss and nibble her soft skin until she jerks away with a yelp.

"No hickeys," she commands, holding my face between her hands and looking deep into my eyes. "This isn't high school, Byrne, and I'm not a fan of turtlenecks."

"I wouldn't even think about marking you."

It's a bald-faced lie. I want to mark every inch of her skin so the whole damn world knows she's mine. I want to get her a biker jacket emblazoned with the words "Property of Jake Byrne," which is embarrassingly primitive, especially knowing that my independent woman doesn't belong to anyone but herself.

Which is one of the things I lo—

Nope, not going there. It's one of the things I *appreciate* most about her.

"No hickeys," I promise, and one corner of her mouth tips up before she fuses her mouth to mine.

We kiss for minutes or maybe hours. Finally, I grab the bar of soap and lather up my hands, then move them across her body. I could stay like this for hours, especially when I glide my hand around her hip and down to the juncture of her legs, sliding one finger through her soft folds.

She bites down on my lip in response. Not hard enough to draw blood, and in this case, the pain is pleasure. I move my hand so I can push two fingers inside her while using my thumb to press against her clit. We're still kissing, our tongues tangled together, and I'm gathering her soft, sexy moans inside my mouth like I'm lost in the desert and catching raindrops on my parched tongue.

Those moans turn into cries, and she grips my shoulders like she'd melt into a puddle on the shower floor if I weren't holding her steady. That works for me. I wrap an arm around her waist as I speed up the rhythm of my fingers. Then I pull out. She offers a whimper of protest, but it's drowned out almost immediately by a sharpened cry as I gently squeeze her clit between two fingers.

As good as it feels to make her tumble over the edge from my touch, it only makes me want more. It makes me want to bury myself inside her and stay there forever, like she's my actual home.

Despite the longing pounding through me, I'm happy to let her revel in her release all day if she needs it, so damn self-satisfied that I'm the one to give her that pleasure. Her forehead rests against my chest, and I wait until her breathing starts to return to a normal rhythm before opening the shower door.

As much as I'd love to take her right here against the wall, there's not enough room for my need to spread her out in front of me.

"Bedroom," I manage, my voice shaking. I open the shower door then still when her hand grips my arm.

She looks up at me with those big brown eyes. "We're not going anywhere yet."

25

IRIS

"Sweetheart, waiting isn't an option."

Instead of answering, I close the shower door and drop to my knees in front of him.

"Holy shit," he whispers.

I lick my tongue along the length of his hard shaft, refusing to be the only one who receives this kind of pleasure.

"Iris, you don't have to—"

He chokes to a stop as I take him deeper into my mouth, and he mutters another curse. I draw back and look up at him.

"I want to, Jake. I want all of you."

He's adjusted the shower head so it's hitting the wall, but the steam envelopes us, and his lids are at half-mast as his chest rises and falls.

"You've got me," he manages with a raspy breath.

If I'm being honest, I've never felt comfortable with this kind of intimacy. There's a level of trust in taking a man into my mouth. It makes me feel physically vulnerable, and I don't trust people easily. Especially men.

But I love the taste and feel of Jake. The way he keeps murmuring my name like a prayer. The fact that I—uptight, awkward, stick-in-the-mud, Iris Dixon—can make a man like preternaturally charming Jake Byrne wild with desire.

And there's no doubt I'm doing that to him. His hips have started pumping slightly like he can't control himself. Because of me. It's a powerful feeling, and I know enough not to take it for granted. To take this connection we have for granted.

"That's it, sweetheart," he tells me. "So good, Iris. So fucking good."

I might not have a lot of confidence in my own sexual skills, but I'm a quick learner. I revel in every moan and shudder that goes through him and adjust my rhythm in response. Then I reach up and cup his balls with one hand, massaging them gently. He rewards me with another string of cursing that's strangely gratifying.

He jerks back suddenly and reaches around me to turn off the water. Before I can protest, he yanks me to my feet and lifts me into his arms.

"I'm just getting started," I tell him, and he groans again.

"I need to finish inside you, Iris. And before I do, I'm going to make you come again. So fucking hard."

He walks the two of us, soaking wet, out of the bathroom toward the bedroom across the narrow hall.

"I don't think I have it in me to come again so soon," I say with a laugh as I kiss the underside of his jaw.

"That sounds like a challenge," he growls. "One I'm happy to accept."

I smile as he pulls back the covers and lays me across the sheets, but then I prop up on my elbows. "Jake, I'm dripping wet. I need a towel."

"You haven't seen dripping, but we're going to get you there."

"Big talk," I tell him, and his eyes flash with delight.

I've also never had this much fun in the bedroom. I'm not super experienced, but in the past, sex has felt like something serious. Not that this doesn't mean something. It means far more than I'm willing to admit. But the lightness of it—the fun—surprises me in the best way possible.

Fun.

Is there anything that isn't fun when Jake is involved?

Unbidden, the image of him walking away springs to my head.

But he's no longer seventeen-year-old Jake who I watched drive away with my brother, both of them headed for the wilderness camp. The rehabilitation center was supposed to help them grow and learn from their mistakes, but sent my brother into a downward spiral he barely survived.

Right now, I see this version of Jake leaving me. Because that's what happens when I love someone. They leave.

"Don't do it," he says as he climbs onto the bed and balances his big body over mine. For a moment, I feel like he's invaded my thoughts and read my mind. "Do not leave me, Dixon. Get out of your head. We're at this service together, and it's just getting to the best part."

He's right, I don't want to think about the past or the future. I want to enjoy the moment, the fun, and how we make each other feel.

"I'm right here," I tell him and reach out to pull him closer.

He kisses me, but instead of settling himself between my legs the way I expect, he moves down my body.

"Jake, it's too much."

"Not between us," he argues, and the next protest dies on my lips when his tongue sweeps across my center.

Despite my claim that there's no way I could come again so soon, Jake fulfills his promise to prove me wrong. Within minutes, I'm writhing on the bed from him feasting on me.

I'm so close and then...

"Wait for me, Iris," he commands, placing a gentle kiss on my mound before climbing off the bed to grab his wallet from the dresser. He takes out a condom, sheaths himself, then returns to me.

"What happened to waiting isn't an option?" I ask as he kisses his way up my body before centering himself between my outstretched legs.

"This is worth the wait," he promises and enters me in one powerful stroke.

"Yes." I'm not sure if I've thought the word or screamed it, but this is what I want...what my body has been craving.

How am I so close to losing my heart to Jake when he's been back in my life for such a short time? I feel like I've fallen for him in a way my teenage self never could have imagined.

I know it opens me up to a world of hurt, but not right now.

Right now is all about pleasure and the two of us together, which makes it easy enough to forget the rest.

I taste myself on his lips when we kiss, which somehow adds to the intimacy of it all. His movements become wilder, and my hips thrust to meet his. It's like neither of us can get enough of the other. When he reaches between us and flicks that sensitive spot at my core, my body shatters harder than it ever has before. Pretty sure I'm screaming now. Jake calls out my name and then goes still above me.

This is more than just sex, and I can't be the only one who realizes it. This kind of connection doesn't come along with everyone, right? Is it just me being silly and naive?

"Fucking hell, Dixon," he whispers, placing a gentle kiss on my forehead. "Are you trying to kill me?"

Which is funny, because to me it feels like being with Jake is bringing me to life in a way I've never imagined for myself.

I smile, my body boneless and totally relaxed, which doesn't happen often. Or at all. "That was nice."

He barks out a laugh. "That was amazing and awesome and mind-blowing."

Oh. Yeah, those things, too.

"How do you feel about frequent flyer miles? We need a regular meet-up once I'm back in Austin."

I blink. "What do you mean, 'back in Austin'? You're hoping to be named the head of your grandfather's foundation. The headquarters are based here."

He flops down next to me and stretches his muscular arms above his head. "For now. But we also have an office in Austin. That's where everything was based before my grandparents retired to Colorado. In this age of working remotely..."

He pauses and rolls on his side to face me. I can feel the weight of his gaze, but my eyes are trained to the ceiling above us.

"Did you think I was relocating to Colorado permanently?"

He reaches out and takes my hand. I'm surprised he can't sense the ice that's suddenly running through my veins. He has to feel how cold I am. Or maybe numb is the right word.

"I guess I assumed...which is my bad," I tell him.

"Do you want me to stay?" he asks softly.

"I want you to do what makes you happy."

I sit up, gathering the sheet to my chest. Well that post-double-orgasm glow faded fast. Although my body still feels heavy with contentment, my brain has short-circuited to the point that this morning's interlude never happened. So much for Sunday service.

"Tell me you aren't going to take jobs away from the people in this town."

"Oh, I get it." His gray-green eyes narrow. "You only care about the election and me not messing that up for you."

"I care about the people I represent and what it's going to mean if the foundation is based someplace else. I know how this goes, Jake. Philanthropic organizations tend to fund locally."

Damn it. How did we go from awesome and mind-blowing sex to a full-on political debate?

"That's not necessarily true, and I can guarantee that if my father takes over, he's going to have an agenda that won't make either of us happy. His idea of philanthropy is getting his name on as many hospital wings and university buildings as possible."

I nod like I understand what he's saying, and I do get it at an intellectual level, but my heart isn't exactly keeping up with the program. "You have to do what's best for you," I tell him.

"I want to do what's best for the people our foundation serves."

"That includes the residents of Skylark and the employees who are based here."

"Are we really doing this right now?" he asks, his thick brows drawing together.

I tell myself to stay in the moment.

"You're right." I squeeze his hand. "I'm grateful for this time with you, Jake."

I must be a better actor than I realize because he relaxes again like we've just overcome some huge hurdle. Maybe we have. At least now I know what he's thinking. And despite his words and my hope to the contrary, it doesn't involve sticking with me.

26

IRIS

JODI STALKS into my office on Monday morning, glaring like someone poured curdled oat milk in her morning latte, and I wonder what I've screwed up now.

"Can I offer you homemade granola?" I hold up the mason jar Nick handed me on the way out the door this morning. "My brother's in town and on a major cooking jag. Breakfast foods might be his specialty."

I'm not complaining. Compulsive cooking is a vast improvement over some of Nick's former habits.

She grabs the mason jar and unscrews the lid. "I actually want to talk about your brother. He's a liability." She pops a handful into her mouth. "But wow," she murmurs around the bite. "He makes kick-ass granola for a junkie."

Her words hit me square in the chest, and I don't hide my shock. Nick is flawed, but he's mine. "My brother isn't a junkie or a liability. Yes, he's had substance abuse issues, but he's clean, and I love him so—"

"Cy Bradshaw just donated ten thousand to my cousin's campaign." She scoops out another bite as I gasp.

"Why is the owner of the local grocery getting involved? No one spends that kind of money on an election in Skylark."

She takes a seat in front of my desk. "One of the college girls who ended up in the hospital after that drag racing accident was his granddaughter."

"No," I say, my heart plummeting to my feet. I thought I was free from having that part of the past come back to haunt me. "He can't do that."

"He's already done it."

"The accident wasn't Nick's fault."

"Excuse me?" Jodi blinks and sets the granola container back on my desk.

"The drag race was Jake's idea, and he was driving. They made Nick take the fall."

Jodi's mouth drops open, and she stares at me for what feels like an eternity. "Who told you that?"

"It's the truth," I insist.

"Who told you?" she demands through gritted teeth.

"My mom," I admit. "Nick wouldn't say anything because that was part of the deal with Lane Byrne to ensure they weren't criminally charged."

I remember the emotion of that awful night like it was yesterday, but the actual details are muddled after so many years. I confronted Jake, and he told me he and Nick shared responsibility and that his family would take care of things.

My mom ranted about the Byrnes using their money and power to force my brother to lie about being the driver, making it look like Jake's worst offense was picking the wrong friend. The near tragedy was reminiscent of the secrecy surrounding the accident that claimed the life of Jake's brother months earlier. If I'm being totally honest, I just assumed...the worst.

It suddenly feels like a portal to the truth of our shared past has opened, and I'm falling through headfirst and hurtling toward my own crash landing.

"Jake didn't deny the accusation," I tell Jodi. Like that makes a difference. Like my whole world isn't tilting on its axis with the dawning realization that something I believed to be true...wasn't.

"Did he confirm your mom's story?"

I shake my head. "No, but I didn't give him much of a chance to. I was so mad. Nick locked himself in his room until the moment they left. Things went from bad to worse at the camp, and after that he was—"

"What do you mean bad to worse?" Jodi asks quietly.

I've told no one about the hell Nick endured under the guise of rehabilitation. Even Sloane doesn't know. But maybe people should. Perhaps then they would understand why my brother has struggled so much. Why I've given him so many chances. Why I'll continue giving him chances.

"Nick was abused at the rehabilitation center."

Jodi looks horrified. "Do you mean..."

I shake my head. "Not sexually, but the methods the counselors used were barbaric, to say the least. One of them had it in for my brother, so he was a target the entire month they were there."

This much I know from what Jake told me after their release. "He was starved, beaten, and made to stand in the sun for hours for whatever minor infractions the counselors accused him of. If he complained or fought back, they threw him into some version of solitary confinement. I'm sure that's not the worst of it. Nick still won't talk about that time in any detail."

Jodi grimaces. "I've seen documentaries on those places. Why didn't someone help?"

"We had no communication with them while they were there." I shake my head. "Gilbert Byrne had the place shut down after that summer, but he didn't want any publicity about it. Jake's dad was an investor in the partnership that ran the center."

I let that sink in for a moment before I lean forward and ask,

"Are you sure about my brother's role that night? My mom was convinced he took the fall for Jake."

Jodi examines the granola jar like she doesn't want to meet my gaze. "No offense, but do you trust your mom to tell the truth?"

My heart twists. My inclination has always been to give my mom the benefit of the doubt, which is half of what made my childhood so difficult. I always believed things were going to change. To get better.

It was long before the term "gaslighting" gained popularity, but my mom was an expert at it, nonetheless. Every time she told me she cared or was doing something for the good of all of us or that I needed to lighten up and learn to have more fun, I trusted her.

I've held a grudge against Jake all these years—one he might not even deserve. And that might be the heaviest truth of all.

I struggle to take in a steady breath. It feels like the walls are closing in on me when I think about how my mother's lies—so much of her behavior—shaped my adult life in ways I can't seem to control or escape. If Jake wasn't the villain...what does that make me for believing he was?

He called after they were released because he wanted to explain what had happened to my brother, assuming Nick would suffer in the aftermath. Maybe he wanted to reconnect with me—to give us a chance at exploring the spark from that summer—but I maintained that any problems Nick had were Jake's fault, and I'd never forgive him.

I always wondered why Nick wasn't angrier with his former friend. Now I understand—he was taking responsibility, not scapegoating someone else the way I did.

Jake might not have been totally innocent, but he wasn't the villain my mom portrayed him to be. And I believed her without question, even knowing she's an unreliable narrator.

No wonder all Jake wants from me now is a temporary

relationship, some deep-meaning version of friends with benefits. He can't trust me any more than I've trusted him.

"Even if that's true..." I grasp the edge of my desk, pressing my fingers against the wood like it can ground me and my tumbling emotions. "I don't understand why Cy is doing this. My brother isn't the same person he was back then."

"Nick's in Skylark because of you," she explains slowly, like she's talking to a toddler. "Cy doesn't want him here. If Joey wins the election, the assumption is you won't stick around. And neither will Nick."

"It's not fair." I say the words out loud, but I'm speaking as much to myself as to Jodi. "I'm being punished for my brother's actions, just like I was for my mom's choices."

Then I remember my relationship with a married man. I believed him when he told me they were separated, only together on paper for political reasons. But I should have known better. I should have known not to get involved with him. So maybe I'm not being punished for my family's mistakes. This is karma kicking me in the teeth for *my* choices.

I told Jake I deserve whatever bad things happen to me, and this is the universe confirming that in no uncertain terms.

"Fair or not..." Jodi grabs the granola jar and stands. "By this afternoon, there'll be yard signs and banners with Joey's name all over this town. He's planning to host a pancake breakfast at the community center every week until the election—"

"I'm already doing donuts with the mayor on Saturday mornings at the community center," I remind her.

"He's going to sponsor the kids' carnival at Fun Fest."

"I've shifted things around in the town budget to fund almost every activity that weekend."

"Except for the kids' carnival."

"I'm a good mayor," I say weakly. "I want what's best for this community. But I don't have a campaign budget because I wasn't planning on having to campaign."

"I know." Jodi sighs. "And all is not lost. You have grassroots options. Door-to-door canvassing, bake sales, maybe a debate?"

My stomach lurches. "What are we going to debate—family values?"

"Okay, no debate, but Joey is serious." She tells me that as if I don't realize it. "You need to get your shit together, Iris. Fun is all well and good, but it's go-time, girl."

"Go time." I nod. "I'm on it."

She doesn't look convinced but gives me a thumbs up. "Let me know how I can help—signs, setting up baby-kissing events... whatever you need. You need to find opportunities to show your dedication and vision for the future."

"Got it," I assure her and flip open my laptop. "My vision."

Right now, my vision is fuzzy at the edges as panic threatens to overtake me. I'm not exactly the baby-kissing type.

Jodi leaves my office and I push back my chair and lower my head between my legs, gulping for air. I've spent most of my life trying to prove I'm different than my mom and brother—that I'm my own person. But what if this election digs up everything I've worked so hard to bury? Will they see me or just my past? And will it confirm I'm exactly what they expected—the apple fallen close to the proverbial tree.

I straighten and send a text to the book club chat, asking if anyone is available to meet me at Casa Rosa after work for emergency meltdown avoidance.

As soon as I hit the send button, I regret it. I don't like to ask anyone for help. And in my deepest, secret heart, I remain halfway convinced the only reason I'm in this group is because of Sloane. Everyone loves her, and she made it clear that we're a package deal when she started the book club.

I remind myself to breathe. It's okay if no one can make it. We all have busy lives. It doesn't have to mean anything.

But my phone pings, then pings again and again. Every single member has texted in quick succession that they'll be there.

My eyes sting. If I were a crier, this would be the moment to cue the waterworks. Maybe that would ease the weight in my chest, even a little. Instead, my body doesn't know how to let it out, so the pressure keeps building tighter and tighter.

I force myself to take a breath and then square my shoulders. The town doesn't stop simply because I feel like breaking down. I gather my things and head to a meeting with the parks department and then stop in at the senior center, where no one seems to mind my porcupine energy.

Jodi is gone by the time I return to the office in the afternoon, but there's a stack of paperwork waiting for me—permits to sign, a budget report to review, and an email from the mayor of a neighboring town asking if we'd be interested in partnering for an inter-town charity drive.

I'd like to claim I don't spend a good portion of the day thinking about Jake, but it's hard not to when every hour on the hour he sends me a new photo or meme of an adorable, if prickly, porcupine.

> Me: I'm starting to get a complex. Am I really that prickly?

His response is a picture of a sleeping kitten.

> Jake: This is how I see you.

And there goes that ache in my chest again. Reminding me that even when I'm about to break apart, the world keeps spinning on.

27

IRIS

THE FALL AIR bites at my cheeks as I leave town hall, the early scent of fallen leaves hanging in the evening breeze. The restaurant is close enough that I can walk, and just as Jodi warned me, there are yard signs placed squarely on every corner like weeds sprouting overnight.

She didn't warn me about his campaign slogan: "Joey Moore. A legacy of tradition and values."

Yikes, that hits right in the feels.

The other book club members are seated around a large table near the back when I arrive. Each of them stands to give me a hug. My friends are like a lifeline, tethering me to a version of myself that doesn't always have to be alone.

"So you've all seen Joey's signs," I say as I take the last empty seat.

"How are you doing?" Sadie asks, sympathy in her gentle eyes.

"We're going to campaign the shit out of this election," Avah adds, saving me from answering. "But let's get you a margarita first."

"Do you need a campaign manager?" Molly leans across the table. "I can do that for you."

Sadie pats the redhead's arm. "You don't have any political experience, but you do have a flower farm and high-energy twins to manage."

"I'll figure it out if Iris needs me," Molly answers without hesitation.

And that's when something cracks open inside me.

The invisible weight I've been holding for so many years is suddenly too much to keep inside any longer. My jaw clenches, and I swallow, trying to pretend the moment will pass if I ignore it. The same way I've been ignoring my fear and loneliness.

But these women are all-in, and the support—their love— wraps around me like a blanket. The understanding that it's okay to let someone else carry a little of the weight releases the tight knot of emotion inside me. And with it, comes the tears. Tears I've been holding back for years.

It's the first time I've cried since childhood, when my mom weaponized her tears to manipulate and guilt Nick and me into going along with whatever outcome she wanted. I don't see crying as a weakness in others, but I taught myself to hold it all in because I didn't want to be like her.

Just my luck that the floodgates decide to open in the middle of a Mexican restaurant, and I'm powerless to stop it. Tears roll down my face faster than I can wipe them away.

I laugh to cover up how exposed this makes me feel as Sadie hands me a napkin. "I'm sorry. I don't know what's wrong with me."

"Tears aren't wrong." Taylor loops an arm around my shoulder. "We've got you, Iris."

"You're allowed to feel," Sloane reminds me, her voice steady and warm.

The more I try to pull it together, the harder the tears fall. But Sloane isn't wrong. There's something cathartic about letting myself fall apart, no matter how much it scares me.

The other women seem to take it in stride.

Molly dips a chip in the salsa bowl. "I sometimes cry so hard I hyperventilate."

"When I cry, I get the hiccups," Taylor reveals.

"My dad didn't believe in tears," Avah tells the group. "I tried so hard to hold them back when my childhood dog died, I ended up puking all over his favorite shoes." The edge of her full mouth curves slightly. "Which made me feel a little better."

"I don't want to cry," I say, even as I continue blubbering.

"You're a pretty crier," Sadie observes.

Taylor nods. "Which is not fair at all. My entire face turns bright red."

"I've seen you cry," Sloane confirms, pointing a chip at our favorite librarian. "You also get this weird, pinched look like you're sucking on a lemon."

"That's going to be my sign." Taylor nods and squeezes my shoulder. "When I meet someone who thinks I'm adorable when I cry, I'll know I've met my soulmate."

"Girl, that's a terrible benchmark." Molly shakes her head. "Trust me. Men hate it when women cry. I was super emotional when I was pregnant with the twins, and Teddy couldn't take it."

"Ian can take it," Sadie counters. "He's a crier himself."

That comment makes me laugh through my tears. "You aren't going to convince us that Ian Barlowe is a crier."

"I'm not kidding. He was highly offended that I don't watch football, which meant I've never seen a Super Bowl commercial. We went back and watched a highlight reel of the most emotional ads, and it turned him into a blubbering mess. His brother is even worse."

"Sign me up to wipe away Felix Barlowe's tears," Molly says with a dreamy sigh.

The conversation swirls around me while Taylor keeps an arm around me and Sloane pats my thigh at regular intervals. None of the women make a big deal about my tears or push me to talk or get over whatever is bothering me. They just let me cry while they wait, like they'll wait forever. And I realize that for all my fears about them only wanting to be around me because Sloane insists, they are truly my friends, prickly edges be damned.

I don't know how long it takes before my emotions are under control again. As if by magic, the moment I wipe my last tear away, a waitress arrives at the table and places a margarita in front of me.

"Thank you."

She nods. "I'll have the nachos and quesadillas y'all ordered out in a sec. Mayor Dixon, I want to say that I honor tradition and appreciate your opponent's dedication to... well, from what I can tell so far, he's devoted to seeing his name flashed all over the town."

"No doubt," Sloane murmurs.

"I'm a single mother," Regan—based on her name tag—continues. "I have a son who struggles with reading. Well, Jonah struggles with a lot of things since his dad left. Because you support the literacy programs at the library, he's gotten the extra help he needs. It's improved his behavior in school, and homework isn't such a fight. If there's anything to be grateful for, it's not fighting with my eight-year-old every night."

"Amen, sister," Molly agrees.

Regan flashes a smile. "I just want you to know I appreciate what you've done since you took office. As far as I'm concerned, you stand for the right kind of values. Also, the churros are on the house tonight."

I return her smile. "Churros might be the best medicine after a rough day. Thank you."

She nods and heads back toward the kitchen.

"Did you all pay her?" I demand with a laugh when she's gone, grabbing a napkin to blow my nose.

"No." Taylor shakes her head. "But it would have been a heck of an idea."

"She's right, you know," Sloane tells me, "and so is Molly. We'll all pitch in to help, Iris. We can campaign Joey Moore into the ground."

I take a sip of margarita and let the cold liquid ease the burn in my throat.

"That's the thing." I keep my gaze on the salted rim of my drink. "Do I want to open myself up to that kind of scrutiny? Joey could dredge up things I've spent years trying to forget. How can I stand in front of the town and talk about integrity and trust when I come from a family that broke both? I've tried my best, but maybe it's time to cut my losses."

"Sweetheart, no." Avah shakes her head and tucks a strand of glossy hair behind one ear. "You shouldn't be held responsible for the mistakes your mom and your brother made. If we were each accountable for the wrongdoings of our family, we'd all be in jail right now."

There's a beat of stunned silence at the table, and Avah wrinkles her button nose. "Okay, maybe it's just my family that gets on the wrong side of the law at that level, but most of us would be rocking in the corner or screaming into a pillow."

Everyone nods and murmurs words of agreement, but it feels like a four-hundred-pound gorilla is sitting on my chest. He stares into my eyes, daring me to be honest with these women. As much as I appreciate their support, if they only like the do-no-wrong version, what kind of friendship is that?

As scary as it is to say the words aloud, I force myself to begin. "It's not just what my mom and brother did. I'm my own biggest liability."

The waitress returns with a plate of chicken nachos and cheese quesadillas. She places them in the middle of the table, along with six appetizer plates. Her hand is barely out of the way before Sloane grabs one, drops a triangle of quesadilla and a large scoop of guacamole on it, and places it in front of me.

"You don't need to feed me like I'm a child," I tell her.

"I know how you get when stressed," she counters. "You forget to eat. Did you eat today?"

"Does an extra dollop of vanilla creamer in my fourth cup of coffee count?"

Taylor gives my shoulder another squeeze before removing her arm. "Take a bite before you tell us whatever you're about to tell us."

Everyone else nods in agreement.

"I'd rather say it first. Otherwise, I might add public puking to my current humiliation. But please eat while I'm talking. If your mouths are full, at least your jaws will be less likely to drop at my bombshell."

"I love a bombshell," Molly says as she scoops a heap of nachos onto a plate. "Is anybody else watching the latest season of *Castle of Love*? Boris, who is supposed to be the heir to a European principality, was just revealed as a phony by the real heir, Mikhail, who showed up at the castle to win back Maria, his childhood sweetheart he lost touch with after his family was forced to flee their homeland."

"Slow the reality roll." Avah waves a hand in front of Molly's face. "I'm not knocking your TV choices, because we've all got our guilty pleasures, but our girl Iris is about to share something real, and you're blathering about fake drama."

"I don't think it's fake." Molly looks genuinely disturbed, then offers me a wan smile. "I'm also not trying to steal your thunder. I just figured in the realm of misery loves company, you might like to know there are other people dealing with bombshells."

"Eat your nachos, Mol," Avah orders.

"I appreciate hearing about Boris and Mikhail," I tell her with a soft laugh. "I wish my confession involved true love and redemption. Instead, I play the part of the villain—or at least the fool—in this story." I take a deep breath and just blurt it out. "I had an affair with a married man." The words taste bitter coming out, laced with the shame I tried to bury.

Five pairs of eyes lock on me.

"After everything that happened with your mother?" Sloane asks, sounding confused and, if I'm being honest, disappointed.

"It's not an excuse," I continue, "but he told me they were legally separated, only staying in the marriage for political reasons."

"Then he lied and deceived you, which isn't your fault," Sadie says, always wanting to give people the benefit of the doubt.

She has the kindest heart of any person I've ever met. Maybe it's because she spends most of her time with animals and not people. Is it too late to change my career path to veterinary medicine? Except I'm allergic.

"Political reasons," Sloane repeats. If anyone realizes the man I'm talking about, it's my best friend. "Who was it?" Based on her flat tone, she already knows the answer.

"Robert Wilhelm," I say quietly.

"The governor of Minnesota?" Molly practically shouts, and Avah elbows her hard.

"Not so loud."

Molly's big green eyes go even wider. "This could be an episode of *Castle of Love*. Maybe we'll call it *Politics of Love*."

"No." I shake my head and offer her a weak smile. "Not love. We're calling it Iris being a fool because Robert and his wife are not separated, legally or otherwise. I know that because—"

"She had a baby last year," Taylor says. "I remember seeing a clip of them on one of those Sunday morning news shows. The perfect political family, a potential Camelot for a new generation."

I choke out a laugh. The reference to the lore surrounding John F. Kennedy and his beautiful wife, Jackie, is ironic, given what we now know about the former president's wandering eye.

"Yes, well, good luck to her," I mutter. "I shouldn't have believed him, and it's humiliating enough to be part of something so sordid. But the worst part is knowing I'm exactly the kind of woman my mother was."

"Your mother went after married men for sport," Sloane points out. "You aren't the same."

"It doesn't feel that way." I draw in a deep breath. "After watching her sneak around with a string of boyfriends, I should have known better when Robert told me we had to keep things quiet because they were still working through the dissolution. I should never have believed him, but I did. His wife found out and confronted me with a picture of her unborn baby's sonogram, along with photos of her other two children and their happy family." I sniff and wipe under my eyes. "The one I was going to destroy if I didn't walk away. So I came here thinking I could lick my wounds and start over. I never expected Homer Moore to die, or to be appointed interim mayor when he did."

"Of course you didn't," Sadie agrees.

"I won't say I didn't appreciate the opportunity." I blow my nose again. "It felt like something good was coming from the worst moment of my life. But if Joey does any digging, he'll find out."

"He's not going to find out. This is Skylark. Nobody digs that hard," Molly assures me.

Avah nods. "Besides, you've got so much lukewarm tea thanks to your family, I doubt he's going to be looking that hard at you."

"The one benefit of your reputation of being a rigid stick-in-the-mud," Sadie tells me with a slight grimace, "is no one's going to guess you could have done anything like that."

"But I did do it," I say, devastated. I brace myself for the judgment I've been drowning in ever since Dana Wilhelm came to see me.

Instead, I feel Sloane's hand on my leg again, steady and firm. "You wouldn't have if you'd known," she insists.

I appreciate her confidence in me, and while it's true, my heart doesn't feel like it absolves me of my wrongdoing. I caused a stranger the type of pain I swore I would never be a part of, in any circumstance.

"The bottom line is, you have to decide what you want," Avah says in the silence that follows. "And know we've got your back in whatever way you need."

"I love you guys," I whisper as the tears threaten again. Just like I feared, they might never end now that they've started.

"But you have to decide fast," Sloane cautions. "If Joey gains momentum, you might not be able to stop him."

"If he discovers my secret, I definitely won't."

"You made a mistake," Molly insists, and I finally get the nerve to look around the table. But my friends aren't glaring at me with anger or disgust. Just understanding.

The fear that I'm just like my mother—that no matter how hard I try, I'll hurt someone and end up alone—finally starts to fade, maybe this time for good. Because I've shown my friends the worst parts of me—and they've stayed anyway.

I raise my margarita in a toast to this incredible group of women. "No matter what happens, I appreciate knowing I have you all in my corner. No campaign win could be more satisfying than that."

"Good speech," Avah says, holding up her glass and toasting me in return. "Hopefully, you'll give an even better one on election night."

I take another sip, feeling both weighted and free at once. I've been drowning in a shame I didn't know how to shake, and now that the secret is out and my friends are still on my side, I'm lighter. Yet, I'm still heavy because I can't take back what happened, no matter how much I want to.

The combination is disconcerting—like I can't catch my balance. But their faith in me, even knowing my shameful truth, makes me believe there's hope. Maybe I can trust myself to do more. To be more than I thought I could. And at this moment, that hope is enough.

28

JAKE

I HAVEN'T SEEN or spoken to Iris since Sunday. Our flirty texts have *almost* kept my need for her at bay. Almost, but not quite.

By the time she walks into the dance studio for the next dance class, it's all I can do not to rush forward and gather her in my arms. Sure, our physical connection is undeniable and the sex was mind-blowing, but at this point, I want to breathe her in. Drown in that sweet and citrusy scent that is uniquely hers. Revel in the way her body tenses for a quick second before she relaxes into me.

My girl doesn't let just anyone in, so the fact that I've breached her defenses at any level makes me feel ridiculously self-satisfied. It feels like the room shifts to accommodate her presence–just like my stupid heart shifted to let her in fully.

She gathers with Char, Gloria, and the other women in the class at the far end of the studio. They're clearly talking about the mayoral race, which has turned into a heated battle—or as heated as things get in Skylark—with Joey Moore's influx of cash. I understand why Cy is bankrolling him, but hate that Iris is being negatively impacted by the mistakes Nick and I made as teenagers.

I made peace years ago with the fact that she blamed me, but I want the past to stay where it belongs—behind us.

Tom Baker sidles up to me. "You've got it bad, huh?"

I cross my arms over my chest and give the old man some wicked side-eye. "No idea what you're talking about."

My grandfather appears on my other side and elbows me in the ribs. "Denial ain't just a river in Egypt, Jakey." He turns to Tom. "I wasted three summers pretending I didn't notice my Sylvia at summer camp. Finally pulled the ol' head out of my arse when Bobby Park put his arm around her at one of the bonfires. It takes a minute for us Byrne boys to sort out matters of the heart."

I turn to face my grandpa. "I thought you and Gram were high school sweethearts."

"We were summer camp sweethearts." His smile is wistful. "Why do you think we came back here and bought the camp when I retired?"

"But you've never done anything with it," I say.

"It's part of the foundation's land trust," he answers with a shrug. "That's something."

"Damn shame it's not being used," Tom says. "We had a lot of fun times out on Echoveil Lake."

"It's where I asked your grandmother to marry me," Grandpa says. "Have you been up there since you came home?"

I smile at his use of the word home. Other than the summer after Mikey's accident, I never lived in Colorado. Even now, I'm only here temporarily. He still doesn't know that, though.

"Not yet."

He pats my shoulder. "You should get up there before the first snowfall. The roads get nasty with the ice."

I can't help that my gaze drifts to Iris.

"It's pretty this time of year." Tom gives me a pointed look. "Romantic, if you know what I mean."

"I do, but it's not like that."

Tom snorts. "A man of your age and good looks should have more game, Jake, but we'll get you straightened out."

"Somebody needs to," Grandpa mutters.

"Iris and I are just friends," I tell the two octogenarian matchmakers. Friends who have sex, I add silently.

"I've seen the way you two move." Tom shimmies his hips, and I try not to cringe outright. "Based on how it started and how it's going, I'd say a trip to Echoveil Lake might be just the thing to seal the deal."

I'm saved from responding when Char claps her hands and indicates class is starting. "The Fun Fest showcase will be here before we know it," she reminds us. "I want to see you all giving it everything you have during each dance."

Grandpa winks at me. "Give her everything you have, son."

"Why are your grandfather and Tom giggling like a couple of schoolgirls?" Iris asks as she takes her place next to me.

"Probably laced their Metamucil with something," I answer.

It's clear my grandpa hears, because he laughs harder.

He takes Gloria's hand and bends over it in a gallant bow, kissing her knuckles and making her laugh softly. "See how it's done?" he calls out.

Iris stares wide-eyed at me. "What's going on?"

"I have no idea," I lie as Char starts the music.

We begin the steps of our first dance, a waltz. "I missed you," I whisper into her hair.

"We were together a few days ago."

"It's not enough," I say, letting my hand drift lower on her hip.

"Jake, position, please," Char admonishes me, her voice laced with humor, and I raise my hand to the small of Iris's back.

"That's another thing I haven't been able to stop thinking about," I say against her ear as we take our first turn. "All the different positions I want you in."

She misses a step, but I twirl her so no one in the class notices. If she falters, I want to be the one who catches her.

"You have to stop. I'm barely holding it together as it is."

"Let me do the holding, Iris. Have dinner with me tonight."

"Jake, you've seen the signs Joey put around town. If I'm going to have a chance, I need to dedicate myself to work."

"We'll strategize while we eat," I tell her. "You owe me a date."

"Your version of fun is dinner and campaign strategies?"

"I'd prefer you and me in bed, but I'll take what I can get."

The song comes to an end, and Char gives us a few tips for the salsa, which is up next.

Only three couples are part of this number: Iris and me, my grandfather and Gloria, and Louis and his aide.

I glance down at Iris, expecting to see her exasperated by my teasing—instead, her bottom lip trembles.

"Oh, shit. Are you crying?"

"I don't cry," she insists, even as her dark eyes shimmer with tears. "At least I didn't before Monday night. But I'm not going to cry in the middle of dance class." Her voice catches on the last word, and one plump tear streaks down her cheek before she can wipe it away.

"We need five minutes," I call as I take Iris's elbow and lead her toward the back of the studio. "I've got a cramp, and Iris is going to help me work it out."

"That's a good one," Tom shouts with a hearty laugh. "The ole 'I need you to rub my—"

"Hush, Thomas," Janie commands.

"We're good." Iris raises her hand, but the fact that she doesn't argue or pull away tells me everything I need to know.

I lead her to Charlotte's tiny office and close the door behind us. "What's going on?"

Her eyes are brimming with tears that she's trying hard to blink back.

"I really am not a crier."

"Iris, you can cry all damn day if you need to. Just tell me what's wrong."

She draws in a shaky breath. "You don't mind my tears?"

I run a hand through my hair. "I hate that you're upset, but tears don't bother me. How much of a jackass do you think I am?"

She gives a shaky laugh, then grabs a tissue from the box on Char's desk and swipes it under her eyes.

"I'll be fine. Really. We should head back and—"

"Tell me what's going on." I place my hands on her shoulders and crouch so we're at eye level. "Is it the bullshit with the election?"

"It's you," she whispers.

Shit. I draw back like she's slapped me. How did I screw this up so quickly? "What did I do?"

"Not what I thought." She swallows hard. "Jake, I owe you an apology."

That's a shocker. Definitely filing that under things I never expected to hear. Her delicate brows draw together, and I can't help but reach out to smooth the furrow that appears between them.

"I blamed you for the accident," she continues, voice steady, eyes fixed on mine. "But I know Nick was driving that night. It wasn't your fault."

Every muscle in my body tenses, her words hitting harder than I could have imagined. "Don't paint me as a hero, Iris."

I've been carrying the weight of that summer for so long. And it's more than just everything that happened with Nick. Losing Mikey in the boating accident and then the wreck months later—two things I couldn't control, but I still believe are my fault.

"I shouldn't have let him get behind the wheel and—"

She places a finger over my lips.

"I painted you as the villain for so long. Why didn't you call out my mom on her lie?"

The question hangs in the air between us. I look away, unsure how to answer without revealing too much—more than I've ever let anyone see. "You were going through enough already. There was no reason for me to deny what you thought of me when I deserved it. Nick and I were both responsible. It could have just as easily been me."

"But it wasn't." She takes my hand, her eyes filled with a forgiveness I didn't ask for but somehow need like my next breath. I don't know if I deserve her, but I want to try to be the man who does. "You also weren't driving the boat the night your brother died."

"That doesn't change anything." She's peeling back the layers I've spent years building, walls that keep the guilt contained, leaving me raw. "I should have done something. Been stronger or faster. I should have saved—"

"No." She cuts me off, cupping my face between her soft hands. "You couldn't have stopped either accident, Jake."

I don't pull away even though I want to. The intimacy of this moment is almost too much, and I'm sure she can feel the way my heart is pounding. For the first time since that summer, I allow myself to wonder if she's right.

The guilt doesn't vanish, but her words change something inside me—allowing the faintest whisper of hope to shine through. I told Iris she deserves more than she gives herself credit for, but maybe she's not the only one. Maybe it's time to stop punishing myself.

And if I'm going to try to build something new, I want to do it with her, even though it scares the hell out of me.

The thought of building anything new terrifies me—not just with Iris, but in general. I've spent so long defining myself by what I've lost, by the rubble of my past mistakes. The idea of clearing that wreckage away and starting fresh feels like a betrayal of everything that's happened, everything I've done. It's easier to exist in the ruins than to risk constructing something that could collapse all over again.

But staying in this holding pattern isn't living—it's just surviving. And somehow, despite all my defenses, Iris has made me wonder if I'm ready to try something more than just getting through each day. If I'm ready to hope again, to plan again, to believe that I might deserve more than this purgatory I've built for myself. I might just be ready for more.

"What are you doing tomorrow?" I ask as I press my forehead to hers like it's just the two of us in the world right now.

She laughs softly. "Uh, working? Being the mayor and campaigning to continue being the mayor."

I pull back and grin down at her. "Even the mayor deserves to play hooky every once in a while."

She looks affronted. "I've never played hooky from anything. Not a day in my life."

"Let tomorrow be another first." I kiss the edge of her full mouth. "One day, Iris. No schedules, no responsibilities—just you, me, and the mountains. It'll be fun." And possibly the promise of something more.

Her laugh is soft and feels like a victory. "A half-day," she concedes. "You can pick me up at noon. But if the town falls apart, it's on you." It feels like she's handing me the key to a door we've both been afraid to open.

"I don't want secrets between us," I say, even as a flicker of guilt sparks across my skin. Spencer Charles isn't a negative, but it's still a lie and I need to tell her.

She jerks back at the same time there's a knock at the door.

"Is everything okay?" Char asks as she peeks her head in.

"Yep," Iris says brightly and spins on her heel like she hasn't spent the past five minutes peering into my deepest soul. "We're ready for our solo."

Maybe she was reacting to the knock, or perhaps she heard the click of Char's heels, but something tells me she pulled away for a different reason. There's no time to question her as we head back into the studio with everyone's eyes on us.

We take our places, and when her hand settles into mine, I can tell she's as happy to be in my arms as I am to have her there. I guide us into the first steps, forcing myself to put aside the sliver of doubt that there's more to her tears than she's letting on.

As the last notes of the song fade, I hold her gaze for a moment, our connection buzzing in my chest.

"Very good," Char says as the rest of the class applauds.

Iris steps back and gives the instructor a thumbs up. "We're getting better." Her voice is light, and she avoids my eyes. "And we owe it all to you."

"You okay?" I ask as we line up for the next number.

Her smile is so thin I can practically see through it. "Fine. All good."

When Char finally claps to signal the end of class, Iris pulls away like the floor's on fire. "I'll see you tomorrow," she says, already heading for the door. Her voice is strained, and she doesn't wait for a reply.

I glance at the clock, considering whether to follow her or let it go. Pushing doesn't work with my gorgeous, prickly girl, and I'll have all afternoon with her tomorrow to coax out whatever she's hiding. And hopefully find the courage to tell her about my secret.

I'm going to get it right this time—the dancing, my future with the foundation. And, most importantly, Iris.

29

JAKE

I say goodbye to Grandpa and the rest of the group, grab my jacket, and follow her out into the bright October afternoon. The sun is warm on my back as I walk the two blocks to the diner where I'm meeting Daniel Pearson for lunch.

He's waiting at a table near the front and waves enthusiastically as I approach. I think about Iris's comment and the ramifications of me basing the foundation in Austin if and when I take over.

"I'm glad you asked to meet," the program officer says as I slide into the chair across from him. "I love working for your grandpa, but I have a gut feeling you're going to be good for the future."

I smile as the waitress approaches and places a menu in front of me, even as doubt slices across my gut. What would Daniel think if he knew my plan to relocate the headquarters to Austin? What would my grandfather say?

A cold shiver runs through me at the thought. The foundation has been rooted in this community for decades—his life's work and legacy. The rational part of me knows this is the right business decision, but I can't help wondering if Grandpa will see it as a betrayal of everything he's built.

The waitress taps her menu pad and grins. "We've got a real

treat for you today. There's a guest chef in the kitchen—kind of an on-the-job interview—which means a couple of amazing specials."

"I'm all about amazing," I tell her with a grin.

She winks. "I just bet you are, sugar. First up, we've got a meatloaf patty melt on toasted rye with caramelized onions and a tangy tomato aioli." She taps the menu pad again. "It's like fancy mayo. And if breakfast for lunch is more your style, we have homemade waffles with crispy chicken strips and a drizzle of hot honey."

"They both sound delicious. Which is your favorite?"

"The meatloaf. You don't want to miss it."

"Then I'll take that," I tell her, "along with an iced tea— unsweet."

"Same for me," Daniel says as he hands the waitress his menu.

"Coming right up," she promises.

Daniel holds up a hand, palm facing me, and I realize he's looking for a high five. "Already we're on the same page," he says as I give him one.

My stomach lurches, and I remind myself change is inevitable. "How long have you been with the foundation?"

"Almost my entire career," he answers with a sheepish smile. "I got my undergrad and master's in nonprofit administration from UNM, so I worked in Albuquerque during the school year. But every summer, I came back and interned with your grandfather. When he offered me a full-time position after graduation, it was a no-brainer."

"And no interest in trying something different?" I ask after the waitress delivers our drinks. "I understand the constraints of working for a family foundation. If you were with a community agency or a trust that operated with a bigger fund, you'd have more impact, more power."

He glances down at the table. Is the man blushing?

"Having power isn't my main motivator."

"What is your main motivator?"

He thinks about it before answering. "My three sisters and I were raised by a single mom who relied on scholarships and community-funded activities. We didn't have much, but she made sure we didn't feel the lack, and your family helped with that. The foundation impacted my life, and now I'm dedicated to offering similar opportunities to people who wouldn't otherwise have them."

It's a good answer. One I admire. "Would you consider moving away from Skylark?"

He frowns. "I can't imagine not living here. It's my home."

"But you don't have a family of your own," I point out.

"Not yet, but I'd like to someday." He clears his throat. "How was your date with Jodi? The two of you seemed to be having a good time at the rodeo."

"Yeah, but we won't be going out again."

"Why not?" He sounds legitimately baffled. "She's perfect."

"We just didn't have a connection."

"But she's perfect," he insists.

"Why haven't you asked her out?"

His head snaps back like the question is painful to consider. "Jodi and I are friends," he says, his voice a little too casual. "I'm not going to take a chance on ruining that."

"If you don't take a chance, you'll never know if it could be something more."

"Friendship is enough."

"Not always."

The waitress brings our food, and there's a pause in the conversation as we both dig in. Our server was right—this sandwich is the best thing I've tasted in a long time. The bread is toasted perfectly, thin slices of grilled meatloaf covered with Swiss cheese are balanced by the tangy sauce. I don't know where that guest chef came from, but they'd be fools not to hire him for real.

"I think you have a shot with her," I confide as I dunk a crispy fry in the ramekin of dipping sauce the waitress explained is a fancy mix of ranch dressing, ketchup, and the chef's secret spices. "Sometimes love isn't loud—it's about being steady, showing up, and trying again." That's what I'd like to believe with Iris, anyway.

Daniel pushes his plate forward an inch like he's suddenly lost his appetite. "Be real, Jake. I'm a geek through and through, and I realized it long before the first day of second grade when Logan Martin announced it to the class." He taps a finger on the corner of his thick glasses—the kind that would make Clark Kent proud. "I'm okay with who I am, but I've seen the type of guys Jodi dates. Most of them look like you. Like they flip cars or bench press horses for fun."

"Bench pressing a horse wouldn't be fun," I assure him with a laugh. "Don't sell yourself short just because some asshole called you a stupid name or tried to make you believe something about yourself that doesn't have to be true."

He blinks and glances toward nearby tables. Yep, people are staring after my overzealous reaction to his geek comment. It's a name I was never called, but I've heard and believed plenty of others, all to my detriment.

"Okay." He nods again. "You're persuasive, Jake. And passionate. The foundation would be lucky to have you at its helm. I hope your grandfather and the board see that."

"They're already lucky to have you," I counter. "Jodi would be, too. You're a hell of a catch, man."

He laughs self-consciously. "No one has ever called me a catch."

"Get used to it." I grab the check the waitress left on the table when she delivered the food. "For the record, I don't do hype talks if they aren't warranted."

"Thank you." He stands and shakes my hand. "For the record, I wouldn't back you as your grandpa's successor if I didn't think you could do the job."

"That means a lot." I hold his eyes for a minute, then he nods and heads for the door. He walks out of the diner, his shoulders a bit straighter than when he came in, while I pay at the cash register.

A tingling along my neck makes me glance over my shoulder, and I see a familiar face walking down the back hallway that leads to the alley behind the building.

"I should have known you made that sandwich," I say as Nick turns to see who's followed him out into the afternoon sunlight. "It was amazing, by the way."

He takes a long swig from his water bottle. "Getting nothing but raves. Sometimes simple is best."

"There's nothing simple about you returning to Skylark."

"I think the same could be said about you." He lowers himself onto the wrought iron bench that faces toward the alley. There's an ash bin sitting next to it for the restaurant employees who take their smoke breaks out here.

I gesture toward the can. "Do you smoke?"

"Of all the vices I've had, which you know better than most have been numerous, nicotine has never been one of them."

I acknowledge his answer with a nod, then ask, "Why are you in the diner's kitchen today?"

"The head cook's looking to retire, and I'm pretty sure I nailed my interview to replace him."

"You're staying in Skylark?"

"Do you have a problem with that?"

I raise one brow. "I've said it before—only if you're going to cause trouble for Iris."

He shades his eyes as he glances up at me. "And I don't care what bullshit line either of you gives me about dance partners, you're together, which means she's going to get hurt. It's why I asked you to stay away from the start."

My temper flares. "What makes you think I owe you that?"

"I don't know." He shrugs. "Friendship? Loyalty?"

"Loyalty like the way I let her believe for years that night was my fault?"

"Our mother perpetuated that lie."

"You could have corrected that. Told her the truth."

"The truth is she's way too good for either of us."

"One hundred percent." I take a seat next to him. "But I promise she's in control of what's happening between us. If it makes you feel any better, I'm probably the one who's going to end up a big, sad, brokenhearted pile of dookie at the end of it."

He eyes me carefully. "Then why start?"

"She might be too good for me, but I won't be the one to tell her. So, are you really thinking of settling down in Skylark?"

"It's a small town," he answers, "but there's a lot of space here. It's the kind of space that helps keep my head clear, so I'm going to give it my best shot. What about you?"

"Like I told Iris, once my grandfather decides about the foundation's future, I'll be heading back to Texas either way."

"What about my sister?"

I manage a laugh. "She's bound to realize I can't make her happy the way she deserves to be." I rub a hand over the back of my neck, already hating how the thought of leaving makes me feel. "I'm not going to stick around to watch her find the guy who does." The truth of that feels like a knife against my throat.

"Well, if you do stick..." He knocks his fist against the brick wall of the building behind us. "You'll know where to come for Skylark's best sandwich."

I stand up and shake his hand. "I like seeing you like this, Nick."

"Me too," he says. "Remember, man, sticking might be hard, but leaving isn't any easier in the long run. Iris doesn't need you to be perfect. But she does need you to show up."

I head to my car while he returns to the restaurant, wondering if Nick Dixon actually has it figured out. I tried running—from mistakes and guilt and every person I let down. But maybe running is really just a different way of staying stuck.

30

IRIS

"Nick, don't you dare," I shout as the doorbell rings promptly at noon, but it's too late. My brother easily blocks me as I try to muscle my way past him.

"Hello, young swain," he says with a fake-courtly bow after opening the door. Then, even though I'm standing inches away from him, he turns and hollers over his shoulder, "Iris, you have a gentleman caller. He brought flowers. Aren't you allergic to flowers?"

"I am not allergic." He steps to the side when I give him a giant shove, but not because of the force of my push. Nick wouldn't move if he didn't want to. My brother's even more stubborn than he is strong.

Jake looks effortlessly rugged in a soft flannel shirt, sleeves rolled up to his elbows to reveal his muscular forearms. His jeans are well-worn and fit just right, with a sturdy pair of hiking boots completing the look. The shadow of stubble on his jaw is a little more pronounced than usual, and my face warms, imagining how that scruff would feel across my bare skin. But it's his teasing grin that makes my heart stutter.

"New butler?"

"I'm about to fire him."

"You're not allergic, right?" he asks as I take the flowers. They're a mix of warm fall colors tied together with a simple burlap ribbon.

"Only to my annoying AF brother."

Nick leans over my shoulder. "Her *older* brother who could kick your ass with one hand tied behind his back."

"He's not going to kick your ass." Jake doesn't look the least bit worried. "You aren't going to kick his ass," I tell Nick, elbowing him in the ribs.

"Oof. Not unless he gives me a reason to."

"I don't plan on it," Jake says.

Something about his tone makes a shiver of awareness—or maybe it's longing—trail down my spine.

Embarrassed by my reaction, I glance down at the flower arrangement. "Oh, these are from Meadow Blooms." I place a finger on the tag hanging from the ribbon. "That's my friend Molly's flower farm. That makes them even more special. Thank you."

"You're welcome," he answers, his voice low.

Nick pretends to cough behind me, and I clearly hear him choke out the words, "Suck up."

I turn and shove the bouquet—with more force than necessary —into my brother's chest. "Be a peach and put these in water for me."

"If I was a fruit, I'd be a blueberry," Nick answers. "You're the peach, Iris." He points the flowers toward Jake. "You're an ugli fruit."

"I know you are, but what am I?" Jake counters without missing a beat.

I groan and step onto the porch before their game of insults can gain steam. "I won't be late," I tell my brother. "No need to—"

"I'll wait up," he interrupts, then heads toward the kitchen with the flowers.

"Sorry about that," I say as I shut the door. "I don't know what his problem is."

"He's being protective." Jake places his hand on the small of my back. I should be used to the touch—we do it enough during dancing—but goosebumps erupt along my skin. "You've taken care of him for way too many years. It's about time he returned the favor."

"Do I need to be protected from you?"

He pauses as he opens the passenger side door of the truck. "I hope not." He runs a hand through his hair. "I think the opposite might be true."

"No." I lean around the edge of the door and kiss his cheek. "We're in this together, Jake, for as long as it lasts."

His hazel eyes darken with something that looks like disappointment, and I glance away. We both need the reminder that there's an end date on whatever this is between us.

I like rules and limitations because they make life easier to navigate and keep me safe. But my heart isn't on board with that plan. Instead, it's defying every boundary I set, and I can't seem to —don't want to—stop it.

"Did you just kiss me in public where anyone could have seen it?" Jake asks as he turns the key in the ignition.

"I don't want to sneak around or hide any part of my life." I force my hands to loosen when Jake places his on top of my balled-up fists. He can't understand what those words mean to me, and I don't know how to tell him.

"I don't want to hide either, Iris." The words are right, but I don't understand the tension in his body. Maybe he's just reacting to my anxiety. I draw in a deep breath as the truck rumbles down the street.

Resting my head against the back of the seat, I gaze out the window, willing myself to relax. It's a perfect October afternoon, the sky impossibly blue and the aspen leaves shimmering like gold coins in the sunlight.

"Where are we headed?" I ask as he turns down a gravel road just before we get to the edge of his grandfather's property. "There's nothing out this way."

"I've got everything you need, sweetheart."

He says the undeniably cheesy line with so much conviction that I burst into giggles. His affronted growl makes me laugh even harder. He reaches out with one hand and playfully smacks my jeans-clad thigh.

"Woman, you are terrible for my ego."

"Your ego's doing just fine." I link our fingers, and his smile softens as he glances down at our joined hands.

It's not the first time we've held hands, but it might be the first time I've initiated the contact. It means something to me, letting someone in when I've spent so long keeping everyone out.

Jake tightens his hand around mine without saying a word, like he realizes the weight of the small gesture.

"Been to Echoveil Lake?" he asks.

I shake my head. "I didn't think anyone went up there."

"No one has since Grandpa closed the summer camp. It's been pretty much deserted. Maybe a few hikers snap pics of it. Anyway, I thought we could have a picnic and take out one of the boats." He says the words casually, but his voice is tight.

"Are you sure?"

"It was my grandpa's suggestion, actually, and it's a good one. I haven't been up here since Mikey and I visited as kids."

He moves to pull his hand away, but I hold on as he continues, "I also haven't been on a boat since the night he died. Shit. Today is supposed to be fun, not a trip down traumatic memory lane."

"This month has taught me something important about fun," I say softly.

He keeps his eyes on the road "What's that?"

"Fun is less about *what* you're doing and more about *who* you're with—the camaraderie and spirit of being with a person or people you..." I hesitate. I refuse to use the word love, not

216

with things so tenuous between us. "With people you care about."

He glances over like he knows the omission of that one word is purposeful.

"I could probably have fun with you in a hardware store," I tell him.

"We'll see about that," he says. "You have a loose step on your front porch."

I laugh. "That thing has been there forever. It's a game I play to hop over it, especially when I'm carrying loads of groceries."

"We're going to fix that step." He taps his fingers on the steering wheel. "And it's going to be fun."

"I'll take your word for it. Although it might be fun to implement a naked honey-do list rule," I say.

He shudders. "Hell, no. Naked and tools are not a fun combination."

The road conditions worsen as the truck climbs higher along the winding mountain road. There are potholes the size of the Oklahoma panhandle littering the dirt track, and we come across a few fallen branches. Twice we have to stop and clear limbs out of our way. But at last, the lake comes into view, and my breath catches in my throat.

"This is amazing."

The water ripples in the sunlight, cradled on the opposite shore by rugged peaks that burn with the gold of shimmering aspen groves. The scent of pine fills the crisp air, and I can see where the camp structures must have been. Now there's just wild grass and trees all around us.

"Mike and I used to love it here," he says and pulls to a stop near the edge of the gravel drive. "We'd dive off the end of the dock and race each other to the other side."

"Why hasn't your grandfather done anything with it?"

"Mike's accident hit him hard." He looks over at me. "Grandpa was the one who introduced us to midnight boating expeditions. We'd take headlamps and paddle out under the full moon's light with the sound of the dark forest all around us. It was exciting and dangerous, but my brother and I were dumb enough to think we could recreate that on our own."

He gets out of the car, and I follow him toward the path that curves up a nearby hillside. The air is cooler up here and I pull my fleece jacket tighter. "Are you okay?"

He pauses, frowning as he studies the lake. "The night Mike died was totally different than boating with Grandpa. We should have known a storm was coming. You could smell rain in the air, and the clouds were so thick the water was pitch black even though it was a full moon. We'd been drinking, of course, and then the rain started, making visibility almost nonexistent."

"Jake, you don't have to tell me this," I say, stepping closer.

He shakes his head. "I want, or maybe I need, to say it out loud. No one in my family talks about him, or that night."

My heart twists at the vulnerability in his voice. I brush my hand against his arm, wanting to give him whatever space he needs, but also letting him know I'm here.

"We'd been arguing. He was enrolled in Harvard for fall semester, even though he'd been accepted at Stanford, his dream school. But my dad wanted his firstborn to be a Harvard man."

"That's a lot of pressure," I murmur.

He barks out a harsh laugh. "Yeah, well, Mikey also had no desire to major in finance like my dad expected. He pretended like he was resigned to the future, but he was so angry and unhappy."

"It's hard to see someone you love struggling like that."

"I wouldn't let up, pressuring him to do what he wanted to do, be the person he wanted to be." He drags in a ragged breath. "He jumped in the water to get away from me."

His words hit me like I'm the one taking the plunge into that icy darkness. "Oh, Jake."

"We weren't far off shore, and he was plenty capable of swimming that distance. At first I was pissed because it meant I'd be steering the boat back on my own in the darkness. Then the rain picked up, and the lightning and thunder started. I knew something was wrong. I called for him and shined the flashlight all over the water's surface, but it was impossible to see anything. I had to trust that he'd make it back."

"Only he didn't."

"I didn't realize we'd floated into a shallow area." His voice is low and a little rough. "He hit his head on a rock. They said he died instantly."

"There was no way you could have known," I tell him, wrapping my arms around him and pressing myself against his side.

"I know," he whispers and turns to face me.

I glance up, but the shadows that have haunted his eyes since that summer aren't there.

"I finally get that it wasn't my fault. It wasn't my dad's fault, either, even though I wasted a lot of time blaming him. What happened to Mike was an accident—a tragedy. But I'll do more to honor his memory by letting go of my guilt and anger than I have by holding onto them like a lifeline. You showed me that, Iris."

He places a kiss on the top of my head, then takes my hand as we continue up the path. "You've dealt with a lot of shit, but you keep moving forward and trying to do better. Maybe I've taught you a few things about fun, but you've taught me about the value of having peace in my life."

"Peace and fun. I like that combination."

"I want to show you a different kind of fun. Something I used to love that I don't want to be off-limits anymore."

"Are you sure?"

"Yeah, I'm sure. I can't imagine anything I want more except..." He stops and kisses me again. "Ever done it in the woods?" he asks against my mouth.

"Uh, no way, no how," I tell him.

He chuckles and his hands move underneath the hem of the

sweatshirt I'm wearing under my jacket. "We might have to change that."

I push at his chest. "One, bears. Two, sap. Three, bears."

"I'm going to enjoy changing your mind. You'll see how much fun we can have," he tells me. "No sap necessary."

"Are you leading me up this path to some deserted caretaker's cabin to have your wicked way with me? This isn't a historical romance, Byrne."

He cocks his head. "I don't know what that means, but if it involves you wearing a fancy dress with a low neckline, and I get to untie the laces in the back, I'm all for it."

"You'd make a good Lord of the Manor." I laugh. "But I thought your grandfather tore everything down."

Jake nods. "He demoed the main cabin and smaller structures but left the equipment shed standing. Said even though the accident happened thousands of miles away, the water reminded him of Mike. I planned to rent something from the co-op in town for this outing, but he told me the boat we used to take out is still here."

He pulls a set of keys from his jeans pocket and approaches the door of the structure, its wooden planks weathered from years of exposure to the high-altitude elements. "He couldn't bear to get rid of it. Said the memories were good, even if it was too much for any of us to revisit the past."

"He's okay with us taking it out today?"

The smile Jake flashes looks more like a grimace. "I have a feeling he thinks my coming up to the lake is an example of my commitment to starting over in Skylark."

Those words put a damper on my good mood. "Even if you don't live here full time, you'll come back for visits and for foundation meetings. That will mean something to him."

But will it be enough for the two of us?

"Have you ever caught a fish?"

"If by catch, you mean order sushi, then the answer is yes."

"Come on."

He unlocks the door. The shed's interior is dim and musty, and I see the boat propped against one wall and covered with a canvas tarp.

"I think you call this a dinghy," I tell him when he pulls off the fabric.

"It's a skiff," he clarifies.

"Is it seaworthy?" I knock on the edge of the fiberglass boat. It's small but sturdy, paint faded to a dull silver from years of use.

"I wouldn't take it out on the open ocean, but it's perfect for Echoveil Lake."

"I wonder if I get extra points in the book club for doing more than what was initially expected for my bucket list item."

"A gold star for being an overachiever?"

"A *fun* achiever."

"I've got a reward in mind," he says, a devilish glint in his eye.

"So after the Lord of the Manor stuff, we're going to move right into teacher-student role play? Got it."

He indicates that I should take the narrower end of the boat, and we lift it and pull it out into the daylight.

"Yeah, but I'm more a hot-for-teacher kind of guy, so we might have to play that a different way."

"Oh, naughty schoolboy kink. Is that your thing?"

"You're my thing," he clarifies.

Once we get the boat outside into the fresh air, we flip it onto the ground, and Jake returns to the shed for the paddles. It's not heavy, and we have no trouble carrying it down to the bank. He grabs two rods, a tackle box, and a small cooler from the truck's bed.

"What else do you have in there?" I ask, standing up on tiptoe like I'm trying to peer over the side. "A small puppy?"

"No puppies. But I have a couple of really nice blankets that will solve your sap problem."

"What about bear spray?"

He rolls his eyes. "Sweetheart, I'm going to have you screaming so loud, animals three states away will be frightened."

I open my mouth for a snappy comeback, but all of my brain cells have stopped working, traveled south, and are currently doing their own version of a salsa as visions of Jake's mouth and tongue on my body, not to mention him pumping inside me, fill my mind.

"You know it's true," he says, and walks over to plant a deep kiss on my mouth. "And if you don't shut down that dreamy look in your eyes, we're not even going to make it out onto the lake."

Part of me thinks that wouldn't be the worst thing in the world. I know he's not exaggerating his ability to make me scream, but going out on the water means something more. And the fact that he's bringing me along means I've done it. I've gotten past some of his defenses. I'm not sure when that started being a goal, but it sure feels like a big one to accomplish.

"We'll manage the sap later," I tell him, and he laughs again.

My mom had it all wrong. Fun doesn't have to mean breaking the rules or flaunting convention or creating chaos. Fun can also be found in the quieter, more meaningful moments. And there's no one I'd rather spend them with than Jake.

31

IRIS

JAKE ARRANGES THE RODS, tackle box, and cooler in the boat bobbing next to the weather dock. I climb in, gulping when it rocks from side to side.

"It'll be fine once our weight is evenly distributed," he reassures me.

Then he grabs the fiberglass edge and holds it steady, panic flashing in his gray-green eyes. "Iris, you can swim, right?"

"If you mean keep my head above water while I doggy paddle like my life depends on it, then yes, I'm a capable swimmer."

He smiles but studies me more closely. "Not that you'll need it, but do you want me to run back up to the equipment shed and find an old life jacket for you?"

"A life jacket that's been used as a cozy home for a family of mice for the past decade? Hard pass." I give him what I hope looks like a confident grin. "If I need rescuing, I trust you've got me." It's not just a joke. I need to believe someone's got me, for once.

"I've got you," he agrees, emotion darkening his gaze. He lowers himself into the boat and leans across the bench seat in the middle to kiss me.

We wobble, I shriek, and Jake laughs, breaking a bit of the tension pulsing between us.

He pushes off, and soon the sound of the oars dipping into the water echoes in the quiet. The bright sun and the gentle swish of the paddles slicing through the surface are almost hypnotic, and my nerves ease.

When we're in the center of the lake, Jake casts the fishing rod and then hands it to me. "Just hold it steady and wait for the magic to happen."

"I'm not sure I have the magic." I grip the rod tightly, and he leans forward to guide my hands with his.

"You're doing great."

Much to my amazement, I feel a tug a moment later. "I've got one."

"Time to start reeling," he says with a laugh at the look of horror I can't hide. *I've got one.* "Nice and slow."

When the fish finally breaks the surface, I can't help my squeal of excitement. "He's tiny." I glance at Jake. "How can something that small be so strong?"

"He's a fighter," Jake confirms and helps me pull it into the boat. He easily unhooks the brown trout and holds it out to me. "Not bad for your first time, Dixon. Want to do the honors of putting him back?"

He lifts a brow as if he expects me to be squeamish about touching the scaly fish. To be fair, I am, but I'm also caught up in the thrill of it. I take the squirming fish from his hands and try not to grimace. "Have a good life, buddy," I tell the wiggly creature, then set it in the water. The fish stays frozen on the surface for a few seconds before disappearing from view.

"I caught a fish," I murmur. Not something I would have placed on my fun list if you'd asked me two weeks—or even two minutes—ago. And maybe something else I didn't know I was searching for.

Jake casts again, then holds out the rod. "Are you ready for more?"

My smile feels like it's lighting up my whole body. "You bet."

We stay out there for hours as Jake regales me with stories of the adventures he and his brother used to have. I share some of my own childhood tales, most of which have a vaguely heartbreaking undertone since most of my memories involve times when our mother left Nick and me alone, and we kept each other entertained. Jake seems to find the humor in them, helping me realize that while our upbringings were different, they were also similar in a lot of ways. We both had parents who arguably had their own interests front of mind when it came to raising children.

As an adult, I'd like to give my mother the benefit of the doubt that she tried her best. I'd say the same for Jake's mom, whom he speaks of with quiet affection, and who seemed so used to living in the shadow of her domineering husband, she couldn't break out of it even for the sake of her two sons.

With Jake's help, I catch and release four more fish. "Let's face it," I say as he rows the boat toward shore, "I'm a natural fisher whisperer."

"You came to slay." Jake seems perfectly content not to have cast a single line for himself, but to find joy in my joy. I could watch that all day.

It dawns on me that the best part of the afternoon was not catching the fish, although I did love feeling that first tug on the line. The real beauty of it is sharing my happiness with Jake and feeling his in return. I'm not trying to impress him, and he doesn't have to show off. Neither of us have to prove anything or make up for past mistakes.

I want more of this feeling—with him and because of him. And let's be honest. I've never been one to truly go for my dreams, or even believe I deserve them to come true. I've been so busy trying not to be my mother, I lost sight of—or maybe I never really thought about—who I was becoming in the process. And whether or not I liked that person. For the first time in forever, I'm not afraid of wanting.

He rows the boat to shore, then helps me out with a steady hand and a gentle kiss.

I know with certainty that I like who I am with Jake. Not the serious, practical version of me who is always in lock-step with my schedule. Or the frightened girl who held onto control with a death grip.

As we unload the gear, my cheeks almost hurt from smiling so much. I watch Jake drag the boat onto the sandy shore but don't follow him toward the truck.

"You know what would make this day even better?" I ask as I toe off my sneakers.

He glances over his shoulder with a teasing grin. "I have a few ideas. Dixon, what are you doing?"

I give him an exaggerated wink as I undo the zipper of my jeans and ease them and my panties over my hips. "Let's go for a swim."

He throws his head back and laughs. "It's October, woman. Ever heard of shrinkage?"

I continue my awkward strip tease. Although the sun is just starting to dip below the nearby peaks, the air is still warm enough that I can't blame my trembling fingers on that. It's nerves.

I don't do flirting. Or seduction. There are too many past recollections of how sensuality—and even sexuality—is tied up with emotional pain and manipulation.

But everything feels different with Jake. I'm different.

He hasn't joined me in undressing, but my confidence is bolstered by the way his eyes linger, his nostrils flaring with every inch of skin I reveal.

"Seriously going to kill me," he mutters and takes a half step forward before shaking his head. "There's a hot spring not many people know about tucked between this property and my grandpa's ranch. Let's drive over there."

"Maybe it's time you embrace a little spontaneous fun, Jake." I step closer to the edge of the water. "Because I'm here for all of it, even the polar plunge kind."

"Do I need to explain to you how snow runoff works?"

"Stop being so serious," I say as I whip off my sweatshirt.

He growls in response, low and dangerous like he's seconds away from devouring me. "I guarantee hypothermia is serious."

The breeze ruffles my hair and—yikes—not having the sunlight makes a difference in the temps. Goosebumps erupt along my skin, but I'm not stopping. I am fully invested in my unintentional fun.

"Just a few minutes won't kill us." I crook my finger as I back up along the sandy shore.

When gravel pokes into the bottom of my feet, I try not to wince, realizing I should have thought this out a little better. *I can do hard things.*

Jake is slowly moving forward, and I point a finger in his direction. "Take off your clothes," I command. My voice booms out, echoing across the still water.

He smirks. "Now she's getting bossy."

I reach around, unclasp my bra, and then throw it in his direction.

"Fucking hell," he whispers.

"If you like what you see, come and get it," I shout before turning to rush into the lake, only to shriek and freeze mid-step. Freeze being the operative word.

Because, yeah, I've never dipped a toe in a Colorado lake, never mind swam in one.

I figured it would be like the water in Minnesota and warm up enough to make it tolerable over the summer and into early autumn. It gets way colder in and around Minneapolis than it does in Colorado over winter.

But glacier-fed lakes in the mountains are a whole different ball game. Right. I get it now.

I hear the low rumble of Jake's laugh directly behind me, and before I can fully turn, he's lifted me into his arms, holding me close against his chest as he strides toward his truck.

"Well, I don't know how you're feeling, but that was a shit-ton of fun from where I was standing."

"You're mean," I whisper, but I'm laughing along with him as I shiver closer. "Why didn't you warn me?"

He chuckles again. "Obstinate woman," he mutters. "You told me you trusted me to save you, so think of me as your foolish fun cavalry."

He opens the truck's passenger side with one hand, deposits me gently on the cloth seat, then leans across my body to turn the key in the ignition.

He adjusts the temperature dial all the way to hot before brushing a strand of hair from my face. "Chill out here for a minute—or warm up."

"I need my clothes," I say.

"The hell you do," he answers, then captures my mouth in a long, tangled kiss that leaves me breathless. Then he's gone.

I scooch further into the truck cab, close the door, and wrap my arms tight around myself, feeling embarrassed and exposed. So much for spontaneous fun.

Jake appears only a minute later, and I gesture to his empty hands. "Where are my clothes?"

"I told you. You don't need them." He reaches to the back of his neck and pulls his T-shirt off by the collar. "I'll be your personal space heater. It's all part of the cavalry service." He takes a step closer. "Lean over and turn off the truck, sweetheart."

I do what he says, and when he opens the door and holds out his arms, I launch myself into them.

"And I don't think you need to worry about bears. That scream you let out when your feet hit the water scared them all away."

I sniff. "That was a sexy shriek."

"It sounded like a cat with its tail stuck in a door. Trust me, I know what you sound like when you're sexy screaming, and I'm ready to hear it again."

"I'm cold," I protest, even though the heat from his body is quickly warming me. Both because he's holding me tight against him, and because he's holding me tight against him.

"Not for long," he says conversationally as he walks toward a cluster of trees, but I know the hitch in his breath isn't from carrying me.

He places me on my feet on the blanket he's spread over a clearing of flat earth. "I got rid of the sticks and stray pine cones just for you."

Given my earlier bravado about skinny dipping, I feel oddly self-conscious standing naked in the forest, watching Jake kick off his unlaced hikers.

He takes a condom wrapper out of his back pocket and then, with what feels like practiced efficiency, shoves down his pants and boxers, his cock jutting out like it's reaching for me. My mouth goes dry.

"I don't know…" I begin, but he wraps an arm around my waist and pulls me forward.

"I do." His big palms cup my ass, and all my doubts disappear. "I can't wait, Iris." He holds my gaze and then whispers, "Please let me have you here."

He reaches a hand between us, and the tip of one finger slides across my center. "You're already wet."

A sound somewhere between a laugh and a groan escapes my lips. "Should I apologize?"

"Fuck no. I love it."

He lowers both of us to the blanket and indicates he wants me on my knees, then positions himself so I'm straddling his face. It's too much—too intimate—but when he licks me long and slow, a vague protest dies on my lips.

I don't want him to stop, and he seems to have no intention of it. He kisses and sucks, then gently bites the inside of my thigh. If not for his hands cradling my breasts, I'd fall forward from the pleasure spearing through me.

He thrusts his tongue deep, and I cry out then sink lower on him. He groans his approval, the sound vibrating along my too-sensitive flesh. His fingers squeeze my nipples as he finds a rhythm with his mouth that has heat and need pulsing along my spine. He's in control, but I'm the one to surrender—and I've never felt safer.

I'm not sure how he knows exactly how to touch and taste me to send me hurtling toward the edge of control, but I have enough experience to be grateful for his expertise and enthusiasm.

The cool air of the waning afternoon slices across my breasts when he releases them. He uses his thumbs to spread me wider and lightly sucks my clit. Without warning, the orgasm rips through me like a tidal wave, and I can't help myself—I'm grinding against his face like I have no inhibitions. Like he's here to please me. And the power of it makes me gasp for air.

When my body finally stills, Jake kisses my now hollowed-out center before releasing me to slide down his body.

"You're so damn beautiful," he whispers.

"You're so damn talented with your tongue," I counter because there's something in his voice that has my heart hitching even as it returns to a normal pace.

With shaky hands, I reach for the condom and roll it over his length.

"You need a minute, sweetheart?" he asks, placing those warm, calloused hands on either side of my hips.

"Need you," I say and lower myself onto him.

He arches upward with a groan, and my nipples harden again. His thick cock is as deep as I can take, and we begin to move, Jake rocking into me as the tension starts to build inside me again, this time coming from someplace deeper.

That first release is still echoing inside me, but I let out a groan as his thrusts become erratic.

"Can't make it last," he tells me with a hoarse laugh. "God, what you do to me, Dixon."

I press my hands on his muscled chest and circle my hips, rubbing my clit against him as he sits up to wrap his arms around me. His teeth graze my shoulder, and I'm gone again, pitching over a cliff without any thought of the landing below me.

Jake follows seconds later, groaning against the base of my throat and then trailing kisses along my skin, his embrace still tight like he'll never let me go.

And even though I know it makes me the biggest fool on the planet, that's what I want. To be his for always. That dream no longer feels reckless. It feels like coming home.

32

JAKE

How am I going to walk away from this woman? It's the only question reverberating through my mind as Iris collapses on top of me. Every instinct in me screams that I can't, but I ignore all of them.

I'd love to fool myself into believing we can make it work with my pitiful offer of a long-distance arrangement, but she deserves more. Look at how she's put herself out there at every turn—not only for the sake of fun, but because she's brave.

And I'm a goddamn coward.

Because even if I wanted to stay, it wouldn't be enough. It's never going to work when I haven't even shared the biggest part of me.

My ego would like to believe the biggest part of me is currently deep inside her, but every fiber of my being is screaming at me to acknowledge the career I've kept a secret for so long. My writing is important. It defines me as more than the slacker so many people believe me to be—a role that's been easy for me to play. Easy with everyone but her.

"Hey, where'd you go?" She cups my face with her hands and kisses my forehead.

"Pretty sure I died and went to heaven." I move my hands up and down along her naked back as a shiver runs through her. "But we need to get you dressed and fed."

She climbs off of me, and my body screams in protest as I let her go.

This isn't the end, I remind myself. Not yet. And maybe it won't have to end at all. I just wish I knew how to avoid that fate when the path forward feels too damn complicated.

I wrap the blanket around her, pull on my boxers and jeans, slip into my shoes, and carry her back to the truck.

I sit her on the seat again, and she waits while I gather her clothes. She doesn't say anything as she dresses, but watches me with a pensive gaze.

"How do you feel about charcuterie?" I ask, as if feeding her is my most pressing concern at the moment.

"I feel good about meat and cheese." She offers an almost shy smile. "I feel good about everything right now."

If the sex doesn't kill me, her sweetness will. I press a long kiss to her mouth. "Me too, Dixon."

The blanket now spread over the tailgate, we settle in as the last rays of sunlight spread golden across the lake. Iris tucks her legs under her, her cheeks still a little pink, brown eyes soft like melted chocolate. I want to believe I gave her that rosy glow. We're mostly quiet as we eat the simple setup I packed-—slices of salami and smoked cheddar, plus crackers and a cluster of grapes.

"You did good, Byrne." A smile tugs at the corner of Iris's mouth as she reaches for another slice of cheese.

To my surprise, I feel my face heat at the simple compliment. "Nothing fancy."

"But perfect," she whispers.

"Yeah," I agree. The air buzzes with all the things neither of us are willing to say. Not yet. And maybe they aren't necessary. I want to believe we both know what this afternoon meant.

Her gaze drifts to the dusky sky, which is slowly fading to a palette of soft pinks and purples. I'm content to watch her, a lock of soft hair trailing over her cheek, her long lashes fluttering against her creamy skin. My chest expands and contracts simultaneously, fitting for how Iris has turned my life—or at least my heart— inside out.

No matter what happens next, the memory of this afternoon is going to be one of my happy places for a long time.

We finish our picnic, and although I'd like to stay longer, I can tell by the way she's started to shiver every few minutes that she needs to warm up for real. I want to whisk her away to an actual mountain escape with hot water, thick towels, and thousand-thread count sheets and keep her there for weeks until I get my fill of her—if that's even possible. Instead, I blast the heat on the way home, and she relaxes against the seat back next to me. Lock the world out and live in her warmth.

It's not late, but as soon as I pull up to the curb, a shadow passes in front of the window at the front of her house.

"He wasn't joking about waiting for you," I say, reaching over to take her hand. I can't seem to get enough of touching her.

"You could come in?" she suggests softly. "Stay the night."

The invitation is so damn tempting, but I shake my head. "Highly doubt your brother would approve."

Her lips press together. "Nick is a guest in my home. If I want to invite another guest over, it's none of his business."

"As much as I hate to admit it, he's got a good reason for not trusting me. Yet." I kiss her mouth and smooth the hair away from her face. "I'll take a rain check."

The truth is, I'm at a loss to describe how such an ordinary afternoon can feel like it changed me in some profound way.

"Today was fun," she says.

Although it doesn't come anywhere close to describing it, I nod.

"I'll see you at class."

Since Fun Fest is less than a week away, Charlotte has stepped up the frequency of rehearsals, at least for her two stars. And I'm not going to complain about more chances to spend time with Iris. "Have a good night."

She places a hand on the door but looks back at me with a teasing grin. "To be honest, I have another date planned for later this evening."

I raise a brow. "Stepping out on me already?"

She grins. "My book club meets next week. Things have been so busy, I haven't had a chance to finish the latest Ellie Spaulding mystery."

A vague sense of panic settles at the base of my spine even as her smile widens.

"I'm going to spend my evening in a hot bubble bath with Spencer Charles."

My breath catches in my throat and I try to hide my shock.

"Jake, it's a joke." She reaches out and places her hand over mine. "Who knows—maybe Spencer Charles is the pen name for some sweet old grandma."

I force a smile and squeeze her fingers. "I never thought I'd be jealous of a book, but here we are. Just remember, it isn't going to make you scream in pleasure."

"You have a special skill set," she assures me, but just as I start to relax, she adds, "But so does Spencer Charles." Each word I've ever written under that name suddenly feels like a confession.

She laughs again and heads for her front door while I'm left to drive home, my thoughts whirling. The Ellie Spaulding series is already popular, and the spotlight will be even brighter once the first season of the series that's filming in Vancouver makes its debut.

As much as I love her, Ellie Spaulding needs to go.

I climb the steps to the apartment above the barn two at a time and burst through the door, divine inspiration blasting me with adrenaline. It's an idea for the tenth installment of the series, the final book, after which I can leave behind my secret persona and just be me.

It wasn't the plan, and there's no doubt I'll miss this part of my identity. Even on the most challenging days, when the words won't come, and the plot feels like pea soup in my brain, I love writing. I love the process and the satisfaction of finishing a first draft. I love it as much as Ellie loves solving the case.

If I'm going to say goodbye to her, it will be in grand fashion—the case of her life.

I grab my pad of paper and start scribbling an outline. The plot points flood my brain. The villain takes shape, the red herrings and clues I'll drop. I work until three in the morning, then climb into bed, exhausted.

When I open my eyes again, it's to find light streaming in the bedroom window. I pick up my phone from the nightstand. How have I slept until ten? I was supposed to have breakfast with my grandpa an hour ago to review and give input on the foundation's grant cycle for the next twelve months.

I have three missed calls and twice as many texts from him, along with one from Iris, wishing me a happy morning and good luck at the meeting. I don't even remember telling her about it, but the fact that she remembered means the world to me.

Except I can't think about that because I haven't overslept like this in years. I hate that it will only confirm my reputation for irresponsibility, which is ridiculous. I've never missed a deadline, and my writing is a joy to edit—at least according to my editor—because of my thorough research and attention to detail.

One missed meeting, and I feel like a kid again. The screw-up everyone in my family believes me to be.

I scramble out of bed and tap my grandfather's number, but a phone rings nearby.

"What the hell," I mutter as I stumble into the main living area.

Grandpa sits at the table, bathed in morning sunlight and

surrounded by my notes plus the eight Ellie Spaulding mysteries published since the start of the series.

I open my mouth to apologize for missing the meeting, but trail off after, "I'm sorry," because there's so much more that needs to be said. And I don't know where to start.

"You want to start at the beginning and explain this to me?" he asks, like he's reading my mind.

33

JAKE

"No one was supposed to see those notes."

His thick brows draw together. "I got worried when you didn't answer your phone or my texts. The truck is here, so my rational mind knew nothing bad happened up at the lake."

His gaze shifts as he massages a hand over his wrinkled forehead. "Then I wondered if something bad did happen because...well, that's where my mind went."

"I'm sorry," I repeat, and he waves off the words.

"I let myself in and saw that you were sleeping. But when I turned around to walk out, I saw..."

He gestures to the papers spread across the table. "What the hell, Jake? Are you Spencer Charles? Mike's middle and Grandma's maiden name put together."

The decade-long secret feels like it's choking me as emotion clogs my throat, but I nod. "It seemed a fitting way to honor them both."

Gilbert Byrne smacks a heavy hand on the table. "Don't you think a better way to honor your family is to put your own goddamn name on the cover?"

His anger surprises me, and I raise a hand to my chest as if I've been dealt a physical blow.

"It isn't that simple. Or at least it wasn't when I started. Now it feels even more complicated." I incline my head. "You're a fan?"

He snorts out a laugh and runs a finger along the pile of books. "Son, half the world is a fan of Ellie Spaulding. Spencer Charles is up there with the greats. Patters—."

I raise a hand to stop him. "I don't need to have my name up there. I want the books to speak for themselves."

"But you *wrote* the books." He glances down at my chicken-scratch notes, then back to me. "Every word, right? No team of ghostwriters helping?"

His doubt stings but doesn't surprise me. "All me." I rub a hand over my jaw, then move toward the kitchen. "I've imagined this conversation a hundred times in my head, but not like this. I'm going to need caffeine and some food to give it the attention it deserves."

"You always were a crabby ass first thing in the morning." His smile is sentimental. "Your brother woke up like he was the second coming of sunshine. You, not so much."

"Let's face it," I answer as I pour coffee grounds into a filter, "Mikey was better in every way."

"That's not true." He stands and opens the fridge then looks me up and down, carton of eggs in hand. "Shower and get dressed while I make breakfast. After you eat and down the caffeine, you can explain to me why my grandson is one of the most popular authors in publishing and no one knows it."

"You know why," I mutter, but head for the bathroom after hitting brew on the coffee maker.

I want to call Iris for moral support, but she can't help me because I haven't told her the truth either.

I think about what I want to say to my grandfather as the hot water streams over me. After toweling off, I throw on jeans and a Longhorns sweatshirt. As promised, a steaming cup of coffee and a perfectly cooked fried egg sandwich with cheese is waiting when I return to the kitchen.

Grandpa sits across from me, his rough hands wrapped around a ceramic mug as I dig into the sandwich.

"Perfect," I tell him after eating half of it in two large bites.

He smiles. "One of my few culinary skills."

"Me, too," I tell him. "Have you heard Iris's brother is back in town?"

Other than a slight tightening of his fingers on the mug, he doesn't visibly react. But when he lifts it to his lips for a long sip, those fingers aren't quite steady.

"How's Nick doing these days?"

"He got a job at The Pinecone Grill as the new chef."

Grandpa makes a noncommittal sound. "I didn't know he'd gone to culinary school."

"Don't think he did, but the guy's got mad sandwich skills, and he's going to put them to good use."

"Wonder if he'll last."

"He's not the asshole kid he was when we were teenagers," I feel compelled to point out.

"Neither are you," he reminds me.

"I was never an asshole. My forte was in the skilled underachiever arena."

He reaches out and taps on the stack of books. "Hardly. You've been lying to me—to everyone."

"It wasn't exactly lying."

He lets out a disbelieving snort. "You let me think you were bouncing from one thing to the next, living off the family trust. All this time..."

I place the last bite of the sandwich back on the plate and try to ignore the guilt curling in my gut. Taking another fortifying swig of coffee, I pick up the first book in the series, *Absolute Darkness*. "The title was Mikey's. It was *his* dream. How can I take credit when it should have been him?"

Confusion dulls the anger in my grandfather's eyes. "I don't understand. You wrote these books with your brother before—"

"No. We didn't write anything down. But we made up stories to entertain each other. Mom would go on one of her girls' trips or wellness retreats." I use air quotes around those last two words, and his mouth tightens. We both know several of those wellness retreats were in a mental health facility. "Dad liked to entertain while she was gone."

"Women," Grandpa's whisper is harsh.

"So many women." I take a deep breath as memories assail me from all sides. "So many parties. They got loud and rowdy. Mike and I would climb into the attic, where we couldn't hear them." My gaze shifts to the book. "And there was—"

"Absolute darkness," Grandpa finishes.

I offer him a small smile. "We spent hours making up stories. Ellie Spaulding was originally Elliot Spaulding," I tell him. "I changed our protagonist to a woman when I started book one."

He shakes his head. "You had all of these books outlined by the time of your brother's accident?"

"No, but the initial idea was his. I'd imagine the plot twists because I had a flair for the dramatic. The plan for a book series was Mike's. He didn't want to go to Harvard or major in finance. He wanted to be an author—a storyteller. He wanted to write stories that mattered."

Grandpa's eyes fix on me, but I can't tell if he's mad, disappointed or both. "You've done that, for both of you."

I think about Mike crouched down in the darkness, spinning story ideas like they were the safety net that would keep us from falling into the endless pit of our parents' dysfunction. And now that I've started my confession, the words come flooding out of me.

"I started writing to feel closer to him. I never expected it to turn into...this." I glance at the stack of books.

"But why keep it a secret?"

"Do you know the first thing authors get asked in an interview? *Where did you get your start? What's your inspiration?*" I shrug, my throat tight. "What am I supposed to say? I stole the idea from my dead brother? It should have been him."

Grandpa picks up a book with each hand like I haven't seen them before. "These are your words, Jake, your work. Even if you and Michael came up with the idea together, you've written eight books. It's your voice on every page."

"Nine," I correct. "The next installment is due to my editor in a couple of days, and last night I came up with the idea for number ten. It will be the final Ellie Spaulding book—the last book Spencer Charles will ever publish."

"Why?" he demands. "You're talented, Jake. You—"

"I'm sick of hiding," I whisper, my voice hoarse with emotion I can't seem to contain.

"Then tell people. Does Iris know?"

"Of course not." I sigh and run a hand through my still-damp hair. "Ironically, she's a fan. Her book club is reading my latest release this month. Her friend Sloane keeps reaching out to my agent—Spencer's agent—trying to convince him to make an appearance at their meeting."

"You need to tell her."

"It will be a non-issue after the final book releases. I'm not going to be a writer anymore."

"I don't think that's how being a writer works." He places his coffee mug on the table. "And damn skippy, your brother would be the first one to say how proud he is of you."

"You don't understand," I tell him, my voice quivering with the emotion I can't seem to tamp down.

"I understand enough to know that walking away from something you love leaves scars." He shakes his head. "You have enough of those already."

"So what now?" I demand as panic tightens my stomach. "Are

you going to reveal my big secret? Put Dad in charge of the foundation to try and convince me not to give it up?"

"If you truly believe I'd do either of those things..." He pushes back from the table and stands. "You haven't been paying attention. I'm not going to make your decisions for you. Be a man and make them yourself. I did hope that by now besting your father isn't the only reason you're here. The foundation is part of my legacy," he says quietly. "But you're the most important part."

His words hit me square in the gut. "I'm here to honor your legacy. What the foundation does matters to people. To me." I get up and wrap my arms around his thin shoulders.

We've spent a lot of time together this past month, but I can count on one hand the number of times I've given him a hug. I need to do it more. I should take every opportunity to let this man who means the world to me know that I love him.

"Tell Iris, Jake. I know you love her, but keeping a secret, even one that feels innocent, isn't the way to show her."

I pull back. "Iris and I are just friends." The denial sounds ridiculous even to my own ears, but I plod ahead like the fool I am. "I care about her, but I don't do love."

Except I do, and it terrifies me.

"Then you aren't the man I believe you to be," he says softly. That parting shot lands like a sledgehammer against my chest, and I stare numbly at his back as he walks away.

"You forgot your books," I call after him when he's at the door.

He turns around, a smile lifting one corner of his mouth. "Bring them back signed by the author. They're first editions, you know. I've been a fan of yours from the beginning."

The proof that someone believed in me before I ever did means more than I can say.

34

IRIS

There's a knock at the door to my office, and I look up from the computer to see Gloria studying me like she's been there for a while.

"Do you have a minute?"

"Yes, of course," I say and gesture her forward. Jodi is at her weekly nail appointment, so it's just me in the office. "I need to head out in a minute to pick up my yard signs from the printer. I know I'm a little behind, but I'm getting things going this week." I offer what I hope is a confident smile. "Between the signs and a bigger slate of community events, not to mention the excitement around Fun Fest, I think I can win this election. Do you want to walk to the printer with me?"

She shakes her head and closes the door. "We need to talk in private."

"Oh." I rack my brain, trying to figure out what would make her look so serious. "Are you endorsing Joey?" I ask with a nervous laugh.

"It's not me," she says as she sits across from me.

My heart drops to my toes. The question was a joke, or so I thought.

But Gloria continues, "I got a call from the national committee chair this morning. Governor Wilhelm's plans for the next primary are ramping up." Her voice is professional but carries an edge of something I don't recognize—pity, maybe? "There are concerns about you becoming... About your continued presence on the political scene."

Shame and regret come rushing back, the need to curl in on myself overwhelming. But I square my shoulders and meet Gloria's steady gaze.

I force myself to process her message. "Skylark, Colorado, is hardly a national stage, and no one outside of his immediate circle knows about us. They told me to leave Minnesota and lay low for a while. I've done that."

"You're the mayor," she reminds me. "It's a public role."

"I was appointed."

She inclines her head as if conceding that minor detail. "Six months ago, but now you're gearing up for a campaign. You also asked for my support with a career path that will take you to D.C. if things work out."

The truth slams into me like a wave. "They didn't mean lay low for a while." My voice is flat. "This will follow me forever."

Gloria's jaw tightens. "You know how the game works. History is never forgotten. It's not personal."

"It feels pretty damn personal." I raise a hand to my throat because it's hard to breathe as my whole body struggles under the weight of her message. "If I'd known he was married—"

Gloria slaps a hand on the desk. "You *knew*."

"Separated," I say weakly. "I thought they were legally separated."

"He lied and misled you, and now you're paying the price for believing him. It might be time for a fresh start. I reached out to a friend who runs a think tank in Seattle—"

I choke out a laugh. "I've never even been to Seattle."

She doesn't flinch even though I practically spit out the

words. "It's green and lovely—the mountains are different than Colorado but just as beautiful. Winters can get a little rough, but get yourself one of those SAD lights and you'll be good to go."

"What if I don't want to *go*? I've done everything right. Skylark is thriving, and people like me now." My voice cracks, and I draw in a breath. "I'm the *fun* mayor."

She shakes her head. "Fun doesn't win races."

Ironic considering I thought being an uptight stick-in-the-mud was my problem. "Are you trying to kick me out of the race *and* the town?"

"I'm trying to give you options," Gloria says. "I like you, Iris. I admire your dedication and resilience. You have a lot to offer a community, but it's not going to be in politics."

"I can work in another capacity and—"

"What's changed, Iris?" Gloria leans back, hands folded in her lap. "Because a few weeks ago, you made it clear that Skylark was just a stepping stone to something bigger. Is staying in town really what you want?"

Of course it is, I want to tell her. But with everything on the line, I can't shake the doubt creeping in.

At the start of my campaign for fun—Sloane's bucket list challenge—I was no more ready to commit to this town for the long run than I'm ready to put my heart on the line for a chance at a future with Jake. Is he part of my future or just another reminder of who I've always been? I know that if I want to be treated differently, I have to *be* different. A new version of myself. I just don't know who she is quite yet.

"I don't know," I admit, my voice trembling. "I don't know what I want. But I appreciate hearing this from you."

"It's not fair, Iris." She shakes her head. "You had to live down your mom's reputation. Now you're paying a hefty price for the mistake with Robert Wilhelm, while the cheater gets off easy. It's not fair," she repeats.

"It's not," I agree. "But he has to live with himself—and his wife."

"Although I'm not a fan of revenge," she says evenly, "I wouldn't blame you if you wanted it."

"Did the party ask you to gauge whether or not I'm going to come out of the woodwork down the road to try to ruin him?"

She sighs. "Maybe, but this is me telling you as a friend that you need to do what's best for you."

"Hurting Robert won't help me."

"Then figure out what you want. Not what the committee, Governor Wilhelm, or even this town expects from you." She leans across the desk and pats my hand. "Decide for yourself, Iris."

She's right. It's past time for me to decide. Yes, I've made mistakes, but I'm no longer hiding.

"I'll see you later at class," she says as she stands.

"Sure, see you later."

After she leaves, I turn and stare out the window at the view of the town square I've come to love, waiting for the tears to come. Ever since I popped my crying cherry, I get emotional at everything. But my eyes remain stubbornly dry.

Maybe that's a good sign. I'm returning to being numb—my method of choice to keep the world at bay. My mother's chaos taught me early that feelings are just weapons waiting to be used against me. Emotional distance helped me stay in control even when I was barely holding on.

But I'm damn sick of this white-knuckled grasp. I'm sick of everything at this point.

I scribble a note to Jodi explaining I'm sick and need to take the rest of the day off. The nice thing about old-school communication is I don't have to worry about her text reply or follow-up questions.

I pick up my order from the sign shop, forcing a genuine smile when the owner tells me he appreciates my commitment to small business. "You've got my vote," the man says, holding up his palm for a high five. I give it to him, then place the signs in the back of my car, knowing they'll never see the light of day.

Once home, I quickly change into sweatpants and a sweatshirt. If my brother weren't staying with me, I'd take my bra off too, but out of respect for him, I leave it on.

Keeping up the "I'm sick" ruse, I text Char and Jake that I won't be able to make the class this afternoon. Jake immediately responds that he can bring chicken soup or whatever I need, and as tempting as it is—because I need a hug—I decline.

Instead, I curl up on the sofa to finish the final chapters of *Absolute Determination*, wishing I had half the guts of Ellie Spaulding. She wouldn't let anyone push her around or run her out of the life she wanted. Maybe it would be easier if I truly knew I wanted the dreams I'm chasing—an election, a career in politics.

All I know is that this place feels like home. Jake feels like home. And I desperately want a home.

Nick walks through the front door two hours later. One look at me on the couch and he shakes his head. "Jake came into the cafe this afternoon and told me you're sick. He said I need to check your vitals and then get back to him."

"How's this for a vital?" I ask as I flip him the bird.

"Right." He gives me a thumbs up. "I'll let him know you're good to go. Do you need me to open a bottle of wine?"

I place the book on the coffee table. "Nick, I cleared out every ounce of alcohol in my house the morning after you got here."

He nods. "I noticed that and appreciate it, but I figured you kept a secret stash. Most people do."

"Secrets have gotten me nowhere, so no stash." I straighten a little bit. "But I have a carton of vanilla ice cream, frozen strawberries, and a great blender."

"Milkshakes coming up."

"I'll text Jake and let him know I'm doing okay."

"The guy's seriously whipped."

The smile I offer him wobbles at the corners. "What can I tell you? I'm irresistible."

"Runs in the family." He disappears toward the kitchen, and I pick up my phone, which is set to Do Not Disturb.

> Me: Thanks for having Nick check on me. I'm fine. Just a bad headache.

> Jake: Want me to come over and massage your temples?

> Me: Appreciate the offer, but I'm going to bed early.

> Jake: Want company?

> Me: Not tonight, but thank you for—

I don't know how to finish that sentence. *Caring about me* sounds stupid. *Your concern* is too formal.

What I'd like to say is *Thank you for making me feel loved*, but talk about how to lose a guy in one text.

> Me: For everything.

He responds with a kissy face emoji, and I smile. Jake is a big fan of emojis, which would probably surprise most people who know him. It surprises me every time one pings on my screen.

"What's going on?" Nick demands as he hands me a frothy milkshake.

I close my eyes to savor the creamy perfection. "This tastes like heaven and nirvana had a food baby. How do you do it?"

"It's three ingredients," he says with a chuckle. "Not exactly complicated."

"That's my point. Three ingredients. When I make a

milkshake, it tastes good. This one is an ideal summer night at the local drive-in movie or county fair. It's happiness in a glass."

Nick shakes his head but I can tell my effusive praise makes him happy. "I do add a few tears of the unicorn I have chained in your basement to everything."

"You wouldn't even have to chain the unicorn," I tell him. "Any creature would happily do your bidding just to be part of this moment."

"You give me too much credit, Iris."

"That's funny, because I sort of thought I wasn't giving you enough."

He pats my leg. "Come on, Sis, tell big brother your troubles."

"I can't. You'll hate me. Or think I'm an awful person."

"You're joking, right?"

He slurps his own milkshake, then turns to face me fully on the couch. "Iris, you gave up your dream house savings account to pay my debt one last time. If that's not rock bottom, I don't know what is. If you think there's anything that will make me turn on you, you are sadly mistaken."

I stare at the melting ice cream in my glass, my voice barely above a whisper. "I had an affair with a married man."

Nick continues to polish off the milkshake, vacuuming the bottom of the glass with the straw to get every last bit of goodness.

"Are you going to finish that?" he asks, reaching for mine.

"Yes," I tell him, pulling it away. "Are *you* going to react to what I just told you? I'm just like Mom."

He barks out a laugh. "That's a stretch."

"Nick, he was *married*."

"I heard you. Is that why you dated him?"

"Of course not."

"Then you aren't like Mom. She craved the drama and chaos her actions caused as much as the romance it resulted in. You aren't the same. And I'm guessing there's more to the story than you're telling me."

"It doesn't matter. I'm not going to make excuses for my behavior. I hurt innocent people."

"I'm guessing you were also hurt."

"*I* don't matter."

"You're wrong. You *do* matter. You matter to me. To your friends. You matter to the people of this community, where you've somehow made a home despite the destruction left in mine and Mom's wake."

He reaches out and taps a finger on the top of my head. "Use that big brain of yours. Do you think I would have gotten the job at the diner if it weren't for you?"

"I didn't pull any strings."

"You don't have to pull strings. People here like you. They respect you."

"They wouldn't if they knew what I'd done. I'm not going to take a chance on anyone finding out. I'm dropping out of the mayor's race and taking a job in Seattle."

I take another sip and wait for the cold concoction to help with my overheated cheeks.

"You're joking."

"No."

"Iris, I almost killed innocent people by being stupid and reckless, and I'm back here. Facing my past. Are you going to let one mistake steal your life?"

"It's not only about me."

"Maybe it should be."

"If I don't do this, innocent people could suffer."

"The man's wife and kids?"

"Yes," I whisper. "I don't want to go into details because if it ever comes to light, I don't want you to have to lie."

"Iris, I'll lie for you. I'll kick ass for you. Let me help."

"Not with this. You have to trust me."

"Okay, you drop out of the race. So what? You don't have to leave Skylark. You love this town. But...hell, I'm not even sure you want to be elected."

"What's that supposed to mean?"

"You want to do good. You want to help families—kids who need it like we did. But the handshaking and community cheerleading? It's not exactly your wheelhouse."

"I'm *fun*," I insist, wrinkling my nose. "I've rehabbed my image. Ask anyone."

"I'm not debating your fun factor. Half the reason I came here is because you're my favorite person in the whole damn world. You don't need to prove anything to anyone. You're great just the way you are."

"I'm a porcupine," I tell him.

He rolls his eyes. "To me, it's more feral cat energy. People love asshole cats. Remember the cat with resting bitch face? That asshole pussy made tons of money."

I laugh at his crass joke. "I'm not Grumpy Cat, Nick."

"You're my grumpy sister, and I love you. If leaving Skylark is what you want, fine. I'll support you. But if you think you can be happy in this town, I want that for you too."

"Okay."

"Okay, what?" he counters.

"Thanks for your support."

"Admit you love it here."

"I love it here," I mutter.

"You want to stay."

"Maybe." I don't know what I want yet, but I'm damn sure going to figure it out. Maybe staying in Skylark really could be an option?

"I'm the best brother you could ever imagine."

I smile and hand him the last of my milkshake. "The very best. Your animal is a capybara."

"The giant rodents from South America?" He tilts his head, a slight smile curving his lips. "I can accept that. Now, do you want to talk about the fact that you're in love with Jake Byrne?"

"Ye—" I punch him in the arm even as my heart lurches. "You aren't getting me to admit that."

"You don't need to. For once, the emotions are written all over your face."

"It doesn't matter." Between the mess I've made with Jake and the election fiasco, my situation here feels hopeless, but is it? Is anything truly hopeless if I have hope? I consider the possibilities —following Jake when he inevitably leaves, or begging him to stay. Neither feels right, but the thought of letting him walk away feels even worse.

"Stop saying that."

"Can we stop talking altogether and watch some mindless TV?" I ask weakly. I need to stop thinking for a while. My brain and heart are too mixed up to figure out how my life unraveled so quickly and what I can do to fix it.

He flips through the channels, finally landing on *The Office*.

"You and Jake are like Pam and Jim."

I snort. "Not in any way."

"I totally see it." He gives me a sideways glance. "The slow burn and banter."

"You're stupid," I mutter, settling deeper into the couch.

Nick nudges me with his elbow. "All that undeniable chemistry."

I snort like he's an idiot, but hope blooms deep in my soul. I'd like to believe I might get a Pam and Jim-worthy happily-ever-after. And just maybe—once the dust settles—I can have it with Jake.

35

IRIS

I SLINK into the office around noon the following day, assuming I'll find it empty since Jodi is a regular at a lunch-hour Pilates class at the local studio. Only, I hear voices when I walk into the reception area. And they're coming from my office.

Daniel Pearson jumps about ten feet when I open the door, the bag of chips he tossed in the air raining potato snowflakes all over the carpet in front of my desk.

"I thought you were sick," Jodi says from where she sits in my chair.

There's no apology from her, no scrambling to vacate the seat behind my desk... which nearly makes me laugh. I stand in the doorway like I'm the one who doesn't belong. And in a lot of ways, that's true.

"I thought you did Pilates on Tuesdays."

She tips up her chin in acknowledgment. "Daniel brought lunch. We're discussing the foundation's involvement in the initiative."

"In my office with the door closed?"

"There's a class of loud third graders touring town hall for a field trip."

"Huh. I didn't see any kids when I walked in."

I can't help but wonder what's going on between the two of them. Whatever it is, I'm happy for Jodi if she's happy.

"I should go," Daniel says as he bends down to scoop the fallen chips.

"You don't need to go," Jodi and I say in unison.

I draw in a deep breath. "I'm glad you're both here. I have something I need to tell you."

I incline my head toward Jodi. "Mostly you, but it's probably good that someone from the foundation hears this as well since they sponsor so many community events."

Daniel frowns. "Shouldn't Jake be part of the conversation?"

"Jake doesn't work for the foundation yet." That's not why I haven't told him my news, but Daniel doesn't argue.

"Did you pick up your signs?" Jodi asks. "I haven't seen any yet."

"I'm not putting them out." I walk forward, my hands balled into tight fists at my sides. "Daniel, don't worry about the chips. I'll vacuum later."

"I can vacuum," he offers, glancing at Jodi with a shy smile.

"Have a seat," I tell him.

Jodi places her half-eaten sandwich in a paper wrapper on the corner of my desk.

"Sorry for using your office," she says. How funny she's apologizing now when she's taken far bolder liberties over the past six months.

"You're welcome in here anytime. I'm sure your cousin will feel the same when he takes over."

"No negative thinking." Jodie shakes her head. "You have a good chance of—"

I hold up a hand. "I'm dropping out of the race."

She and Daniel both gape at me before blurting out, "Why?" in identical tones of confusion.

"Personal reasons. The bottom line is that as much as I enjoy making a difference in the mayor's office, politics isn't my true calling. I like *initiatives*." I smile at Daniel. "I love working with the foundation. But the other parts of the job—pancake breakfasts and the public persona of the glad-handing small-town mayor—they aren't for me."

"But you're making it work." Jodi sits back in her chair—*my* chair. "Your whole make-the-mayor-fun operation is working."

"And I've had way more fun than I expected." I shrug, thinking about my brother's words and all the cute porcupine images I have on my phone thanks to Jake. "I'm glad I learned to loosen up a bit, but I don't want the pressure to prove I've changed. I don't want to change any more than I already have. If I continue in politics, I'd have to become someone fundamentally different. I like me, even if I am an acquired taste."

Jodi doesn't look convinced. "Are you sure? You have a decent chance of winning."

"I appreciate all the support you gave me," I tell her, "but I'm sure."

I turn to Daniel. "The initiatives we've started—the parks improvements, small business grants, the youth programs—are too important to let fall apart because I'm not in office. I want to make sure they continue, whether I'm mayor or not."

His expression shifts from surprise to something more thoughtful. "Most people would walk away and let the next guy deal with it."

"This town means too much to me," I say firmly. "The people here mean too much. Even if I'm not mayor, I still want to help."

He smiles and adjusts his glasses. "You've done a lot of good here, Iris. I hope you know that."

"So what's next?" Jodi asks.

"Gloria has a friend who runs a think tank in Seattle. She's offered to put in a good word for me."

"You're leaving Skylark? But you have plans for your initiatives. You can't manage them from Seattle."

"I have friends—and now family—here, so I'll be back to visit."

"What about Jake?" Daniel asks. "Will you be back to visit him? Because I'm almost certain he'll be named the next president of the Byrne Family Foundation."

"Jake won't be—" I stop myself.

"Jake won't be what?" Jodi asks me, then turns to Daniel. "If he's running the foundation, he's going to be here, right?"

"I assume so." He pauses, then says, "There's a satellite office in Austin, but his grandpa has always been committed to keeping the foundation headquartered in Colorado."

"What about when Gilbert isn't running it anymore? Is there anything that would force Jake to keep it here?" Jodi asks, concern lacing her tone.

"Jake's going to do what's best for everyone," I say brightly, regretting what I almost let slip. That isn't my secret to share, and I have no right to reveal it.

Sloane chooses that moment to burst through the door, skidding to a stop and taking in the scene in front of her. Jodi is sitting in my chair with her lunch on my desk while I stand in front of her like I've been called to the principal's office, and Daniel, who's back on his knees, is scooping chip dust into his hand.

"I have a lot of questions," she says slowly, "but right now, I need to talk to Iris in private."

She raises a hand to adjust the knit cap covering her bald head, blinking rapidly like whatever she has to say is serious.

"Of course," Jodi says as she pops out of the chair.

"Right," Daniel agrees as he shoves his hand into the front pocket of his beige slacks to deposit the crumbled chips.

I study Sloane, trying to gauge her emotions. She doesn't seem upset, but it must be serious if she's barging into my office and demanding to talk to me in private. Has something happened with her treatments? Or maybe she's received a new cancer update?

"You're sure this is what you want?" Jodi asks me as she comes around the desk. "Because I truly believe you can be—"

"We'll talk later," I interrupt, flicking my eyes to Sloane. I don't want to bother her with my piddly problems if she's facing some new hurdle on her health journey.

I reach out and place a hand on Daniel's arm as he starts to move past me. "You're good for this town, too, Daniel."

"I appreciate that, Iris. You have the right kind of vision." He nods and then follows Jodi out of the office.

Once the door clicks shut behind them, Sloane grabs my arms and squeezes tight. "That was weird, right? Like I said, I have questions. But first, I have news."

"Is everything okay?" I squeeze her hand in return.

"Not even a little." Her eyes flash with obvious excitement. "My news is amazing, mind-blowing, and you can't tell a soul."

My grin is genuine. "I'm up for having my mind blown."

"Spencer Charles is coming to book club tonight."

My mouth drops open. "Shut the front door."

"Oh, girl. I'm opening the door of *my* bookstore to *your* favorite author. His agent called today, and she sounded as surprised as I feel. He's in Colorado and willing to attend. No pictures, no social media, and nobody outside of the book club can know." She whisper-shouts, "But he's coming. Spencer Charles is *coming*, Iris."

"How did you manage it?"

She shrugs. "I might have used the cancer angle, but only because I love you."

"You manipulated a best-selling author to come to book club? For me?" Cue the tears.

"We've been friends forever, and you've never once asked me for one thing, Iris. Not even a bite of my food, and I'm clearly the superior menu orderer. This month has been a lot, and even though going to a dance class or singing karaoke at a dive bar seems easy—easier than, let's say, finding the courage to punch a V-card with an NFL god—"

"Turned out okay for Sadie in the end," I assure her.

"Exactly. It's going to turn out okay for you, too. Tonight's book club is going to be the best because you're going to meet one of your heroes."

I let out a tiny squeal and then hug her as the reality of it sinks in. "I love this for me." The weight of my life feels not so weighty at the moment.

"I love it for you too," she says, hugging me back. "But you can't tell anyone, not even Jake."

"Are you sure?" I don't want another secret from Jake. "I know he's read a few of the Ellie Spaulding books. Maybe he could—"

"No, it's just us. If I'm being completely honest, I have a vision of your eyes locking with Spence's across the room and watching the sparks fly."

"Oh, he's Spence now?"

"I feel like he's going to be Spence by the end of the night, for sure. What if he falls instantly in love with you?"

"Yeah, right. We both know I'm not the type anyone falls instantly in love with. Even if he did—" I sigh, sinking more deeply into the hug.

"You're in love with Jake Byrne," she murmurs.

"I didn't mean for it to happen." My voice is muffled by her jacket but she hears me all the same.

"Any chance you can un-fall?"

"I have a feeling I'm going to have to." I pull back, hoping a deep breath will help me find some inner strength, but I seem to be fresh out. "It's going to take a while."

"We'll get you through this, lady. And Spence might be the perfect rebounder. Based on his bestseller status, he's got to be loaded. He can whisk you away to the remote mountain cabin where he writes all of his books and—"

"Hold up." I grip her shoulders, willing her to take this—my heart on the line—seriously. "I'm super excited to meet him, but when I say I'm going to have to get over Jake, aren't you supposed to assure me things could work out?"

"Things could work out," she repeats.

"You don't believe it." I wish I could say I'm surprised, but...

"I don't know that Jake Byrne knows how to do a relationship, and you're not exactly an expert, so the two of you together, well—"

"You don't even know if Spencer Charles is hot. He could be ninety years old with a stoop and a cane."

"He writes like he's hot," she says. "Plus, there's the whole mystery writer mystique...I'm pretty sure he's hot. Or maybe disfigured, like the Beast."

"Except *Beauty and the Beast* isn't my vibe," I tell her. "You're the one with the library of books, skipping and singing through the town."

She rolls her eyes. "I've got exactly zero interest in romance, unlike some people I know."

She cups my face in her small hands. "Whether or not it works out with Spencie, you *aren't* going to have your heart broken by Jake Byrne."

My heart feels like a lead weight in my chest, but I wiggle my hips and manage a grin. "Jake Byrne who? I'm meeting Spencer Charles tonight. This is one of my dreams come true, even if he is a wrinkled old man."

"I'm all about dreams." My friend sounds delighted with herself, which she should.

"Thank you for making it happen. Talk about the cherry on my fun sundae. Whoever goes next in the bucket list challenge is going to have some pretty big shoes to fill."

Sloane grins. "You went all out. I'm proud of you, Iris." Her eyes gleam as she studies me more closely. "Am I going to make you cry?"

I laugh and press a finger to the corner of my eye. "Is that your goal?"

"No sad tears, but I like you in your feelings."

"I have a lot of them these days," I admit.

I should tell Sloane about my plans and the potential of moving to Seattle, but I don't want this moment and tonight to be overshadowed by anything. Something else I've learned about true fun during my foray into it? Fun is easier when you stay in the moment instead of worrying about the past or the future. It's not an easy task, but I'm getting better at it every day.

I walk Sloane out, then turn to Jodi, who's staring at me from her desk. I can't decide whether it's judgment or empathy in her gaze.

"So...lunch with Daniel? That seemed cozy."

She sniffs and pretends to examine her nails. "I see you trying to change the subject, but it was a business lunch." She points to the brown paper bag on the corner of her desk. "He brought a sandwich for you as well."

"I thought the two of you went on a date the other night?"

"Yeah, and it was amazing. But he didn't kiss me at the end of it."

"Maybe he was being a gentleman?"

"Maybe he realized he can do better."

"I highly doubt that."

"We'll see," she says with a flick of her wrist. Although she sounds casual, there's something more in her eyes. But I'm in no position to judge somebody's fears or insecurities when I'm full-up dealing with my own.

"Stop trying to distract me," she says with a soft laugh. "Are you really going to pull out of the race?"

I nod. "It's the right thing to do."

Her eyes narrow. "For whom?"

"Me, I hope." I can't tell her what's prompting this decision, but appreciate that she doesn't probe for more, even though I can tell she wants to.

"I'll miss you, Iris." She shrugs. "I've gotten used to your porcupine energy."

"I'll miss you keeping me on my toes," I answer with a smile. "Will you text me your cousin's contact information? I want to talk to him before I make an official announcement."

"Of course."

"I'm sure this will make everyone in your family happy. Will you be okay working with your cousin?"

She makes a face. "I'll be turning in my resignation when Joey takes office."

"Seriously?" I'm shocked. "Why?"

"Me working in the mayor's office is what my family wants—what my mom expects. Maybe it's part of our family's legacy. But it's not my dream."

"What *is* your dream?" I ask, genuinely curious.

"I'm going to go to aesthetician school," she answers, her voice an unexpected mix of nerves and excitement. "I've been thinking about it for years, and it's time."

"Good for you," I murmur, a little bit dazed at this conversation. "Will your family support you?"

She laughs, but there's an edge to it. "My mom won't be thrilled, but I'm done letting other people decide what my life should look like."

Her words reverberate through my chest, a warmth spreading outward until it pulses through my body like electricity. Me too, I add silently, not wanting to take anything from Jodi's moment.

She doesn't need my approval, but I'm proud of her—and a little jealous if I'm being honest. "Good for you."

"You can do it, too," she assures me. "Make whatever you want happen. You just need to figure out what it is."

I'm not sure I deserve her confidence, but I grab hold of it like a lifeline. My heart beats faster—not in panic, but with yearning. And a flare of hope. If Jodi can fight for her dreams, maybe I can too.

36

JAKE

THE BOOKSTORE APPEARS dark as I approach, but the door is unlocked, and I hear voices from the back of the store.

What the hell am I thinking? This is a terrible, horrible, no good, very bad idea. Maybe it's not too late for me to change my mind. I tuck my computer bag more tightly under one arm, then startle as Sloane appears around one of the tall bookshelves.

"Oh, hi, Jake," she says, looking confused about why I'm standing inside her store. "Iris is booked for tonight." She holds up her hands, indicating the surrounding shelves. "Get it, she's booked."

"I'm not exactly here for—"

"We're having a book club meeting." She's studying me intently now, like I'm slow on the uptake.

I've never been one for cardigan sweaters with leather patches on the elbows or whatever other stereotype of a mystery writer they might have. I should have brought the thick-framed glasses I wear when I'm writing to protect my eyes from the computer light. I could have done the reverse Clark Kent thing and made myself look like an author. I only brought my laptop in case I need to convince these women I'm Spencer Charles.

"Is it him?" Molly asks as she joins Sloane, holding a small plastic cup of red wine. "Oh, hey, Jake."

At some point in almost every story I write, the characters go off script, the narrative taking on a mind of its own, with unexpected plot twists or a snippet of backstory I didn't see coming. If I were writing this particular scene, this would be the moment I lose control of the story.

The rest of the group joins Sloane and Molly, each of them staring at me like I don't belong, including Iris.

"Evening, ladies."

Iris offers a soft smile. "Hey, you. Sorry I haven't been around much."

"I'm—"

"We're in the middle of something. This is not the time for googly eyes between the two of you." Sloane steps in front of her. "Jake, you're killing the vibe."

She glances at her watch. "We've got a special guest coming, and he—or she—is about to—"

"Spencer Charles is the guest," I blurt.

Sloane looks over her shoulder at Iris. "You weren't supposed to tell anyone."

"I didn't."

"Which one of you blabbed?" Sloane demands, and it's like watching a kitten being fierce and commanding.

"My agent told me and..."

My voice cuts out as six pairs of eyes stare at me again. So many years of keeping this secret. As much as I'm ready to claim my alter ego, I'm surprised at how difficult it is to say the words aloud.

I clear my throat. "I'm here for the meeting. I'm Spencer Charles. Or, he's me." I shrug. "My pen name."

There's a beat of weighted silence before Avah barks out a laugh. "Impossible. You're a charming slacker with an enviable trust fund, but you're not a chart-topping author."

"No mincing words," I say with an answering chuckle,

although the judgment—while not surprising—stings. "I don't need to live off my trust fund because I do fine writing the Ellie Spaulding mysteries."

I pull a copy of the latest release out of the computer bag. "You spoke to my agent, KJ Preston," I tell Sloane, but I'm hoping Iris will meet my gaze. No such luck as she keeps her eyes averted. "She confirmed my appearance tonight."

"Anyone can find out an agent's name," Molly answers.

"Why would Jake go to the trouble to lie?" Sadie asks, and I appreciate the measure of confidence, even a small one.

After another few seconds of silence, the room erupts.

"No way!"

"This is wild!"

"You're Spencer Charles?!"

Amid the chaos, I look at Iris again. Her eyes are locked on the book, her face pale, her jaw tight. Not exactly the reaction I hoped for.

"Why now?" Sloane asks, and I notice she shifts to block Iris more fully from my line of sight. Like she needs to be protected from me. Which is ironic considering a big part of the reason I'm finally coming forward is because I want her to know the truth.

I want her to know I'm more than my former reputation. I have goals and ambition and a *life*. A good one, even if it is lonely. I want the excitement she has when she talks about the Ellie Spaulding books directed at me, not just my author persona. More than anything, I need her to understand how much the past month has meant to me. That she's a big part of why I'm doing this.

"I'm tired of hiding," I say. "I want people to know." By people, I think they all understand I mean one person in particular. A person who is still not looking at me.

"Do you have proof?" Avah demands. "Because I'm a little gobsmacked, to be honest. And what's stopping you from taking credit for another person's work? How would we even verify it?"

Molly nods. "I just finished watching season three of *Bridgerton*, and this exact thing happened. Cressida—"

"Let him answer the question," Iris interrupts. Her voice is quiet—almost a whisper—but the murmuring and outright questioning stops.

"I have proof." I pat my bag. "I've written all the books on my laptop, along with notes, outlines, and pages of character profiles. They're all date-stamped. I'm not sure I can rattle off the more obscure details about some of the older books the way my super fans do. My publisher has really good continuity editors, though. They keep a series bible."

I give a crooked smile, trying to tamp down the discomfort prickling under my skin. Iris continues to study a place directly over my left shoulder, as if she can't bear to make eye contact with me.

"Okay then." Sloane grabs Iris's hand. "Welcome to our book club meeting, Spencer Charles." There's nothing welcoming in her blue eyes. "Do you want us to call you Spencer?"

I shake my head. "No need."

"We've got drinks and snacks plus a list of questions about the book and your writing process."

"Can I have a minute with Jake?" Iris asks, her tone eerily quiet. I'm not a fan of her reaction to this news. Dread settles like a layer of hot ash over my gut. I didn't expect her to start gushing over me, but...well, I wouldn't have said no to a little gushing.

Sloane looks like she has no intention of leaving Iris alone with me. Maybe she's more ferocious than a kitten after all.

Sadie steps forward and places a hand on the bookstore owner's arm. "We can give you guys all the time you need. Talk about a plot twist. The rest of us will be in the back...um... processing."

She waves a hand in my direction. "You're a very talented writer, Jake. Congratulations on your success."

"Who else knows?" Iris asks when we're alone, although it

doesn't feel like we're alone. The books lining the shelves seem to be leaning in, listening and waiting to hear my answer as much as Iris is.

"My agent, obviously," I say. "The senior editor at my publisher, but no one else."

"Who *here* knows?" she asks through gritted teeth.

"You and my grandfather, but he found out on his own. You're the first person I've told, Iris." I move closer, but she takes a step away. "You're the first person I've *wanted* to tell."

I need her to understand what this means to me—for us and our future. I *will* her to understand why I'm revealing this now.

"But you didn't tell *me*," she points out. "You told my book club. You were looking at Sloane when you did your big reveal."

"She was standing in front of you." I run a hand through my hair. "What does it matter anyway? I did this for *you*. You were the one who wanted Spencer Charles—me—to come to your book club." I lift up my hands. "Here I am. This is me."

"Sure it is." She laughs, but there's an edge to it. "Have you been laughing at me for the past month? All those times I encouraged you to believe you're better than other people's doubts." She holds out her hands. "You must have thought I was clueless giving advice to someone who didn't need it."

"No. Your confidence meant the world to—"

"You *knew* you were better than the doubters. You dominate the freaking New York Times bestseller list like it's your job." She laughs again. The sound is too wild for my taste. "It *is* your job. You don't need me or my support."

"I do, Iris." How can I make her understand? "You helped me believe I was worthy of claiming this."

"Worthy? You wrote the books, Jake. You're not just worthy. You're exceptionally talented." She takes another step away, and I want to growl in frustration. "You're not who I thought you were."

Alarm bells go off in my head. There's an unspoken

conversation happening between her sentences, but as good as I am with words, damn if I can figure out what it is.

Then my mind turns to a possible reason she's acting like this, and anger spikes through me without warning. "Do you have a problem with the fact that I'm not actually a slacker?"

"What's that supposed to mean?" She looks genuinely confused. "I never believed you were a slacker."

"Come on. Everybody believed it. I encouraged the reputation. And we both know extending a hand so far down from your pinnacle of perfection is easy. Maybe it's harder to accept that I'm not the loser everybody wants me to be." The idea of this slips out before I can stop it, and I hate myself for thinking it. For believing it.

"Nobody wants you to be a loser, and certainly not me." Her mouth presses into a thin line. "I can't understand why you didn't trust me."

"It isn't you, it's everyone..." I draw in a deep breath. "Mostly it's me. I never believed I deserved this success. My brother was supposed to be the writer."

"He'd be so proud of you," she says softly. "I'm proud of you."

I move again, and so does she. "Then why do you keep backing away from me?" I demand. "This isn't how the night is supposed to go."

She shakes her head like she can't understand it either.

"It's not you," she says. "It's me." Although I told her the same thing minutes before, I don't like the way those words land. Her eyes are guarded, like this has changed something between us, and not for the better.

"Any chance we could start the meeting?" Sloane asks as she peeks around the bookshelf, her gaze trained on Iris.

"Be right there." I hold up a hand but don't move. "Why do I feel like this thing that I want to be good for both of us is anything but?"

Iris shakes her head. "Like you said, it doesn't matter at the moment. Everyone's so excited about meeting Spencer Charles. Let's not bring down the mood."

"Fuck the mood."

She makes a face. "We should join the group. I loved *Absolute Determination*, by the way. Might be my favorite of the series. I don't want what's between us to ruin this night for my friends. The show must go on and all that."

I close my eyes and bite back a sigh. What a fool I was to think this would be easy. I've just complicated everything. Ruined my chances for a future with Iris by revealing my secret. "I'm sorry I didn't tell you before now—that I didn't tell you first."

I know Iris to her core. How did I think she'd appreciate being blindsided by hearing my big reveal along with everyone else? Maybe I was being a wimp and hoping she'd go along with the moment and not ask the hard questions—why now, why after all this time? Questions I wish I could answer.

"It's fine."

It's clearly not fine, but I follow her to the back of the bookstore, a tight knot settling in my chest. I have to make this right. I just wish I knew how.

Iris's friends are not thrilled that she's upset, and I can tell they blame me. Hell, I blame me, so at least we have that in common.

Sadie, who seems to take on the role of peacemaker, begins asking questions, and I'm shocked at how good it feels to talk about my writing. To take credit for my hard work while still giving, recognizing Mike for the times we spent weaving what would become the first Ellie Spaulding mystery.

The women don't seem shocked or disappointed that my late brother was involved. Sloane voices the idea that I'm honoring Michael's memory through my words. My grandpa said the same thing, but somehow, tonight, it hits home. I have the choice to believe I didn't steal his dream.

And although my parents always made it clear that it should

have been me who died that night in the water, that's not how accidents work.

It's a tragedy that my brother is gone, but his life wasn't more valuable than mine. All life is precious. I hope my parents—my father—will be proud when I tell them about my career. I'm not so enlightened now that I don't still crave that. But even if they can't appreciate it, I hope they'll understand that part of my motivation is to feel close to the brother I still miss every day. If not, it's their loss.

The questions fly fast once the discussion gets going. I should feel elated, but I keep glancing at Iris. She's quiet, her usual spark dimmed. Every now and then, I catch her friends sneaking her concerned looks. When the meeting ends, they all wrap her in hugs.

"I'll walk you out," I offer as she puts on her jacket.

She nods but doesn't speak.

Outside, the cold October air bites at my skin. I shove my hands in my pockets. "Iris, I...can I call you later?" I ask, suddenly uncertain of the answer.

Her smile is hollow. "Tomorrow. We should wait and talk tomorrow."

"We have our final class and dress rehearsal tomorrow," I remind her. "Tonight doesn't change that. We're partners, right?" I can't stop sounding like a sniveling fool begging her not to walk away.

"I'll be at the dance studio."

"Iris, I—"

She stops me with a small shake of her head. "I need some time, Jake. That's all."

Her words hit me like a gut punch. I watch her walk away, and all I can think is that the secret I thought would make it all better, might have ruined the one thing that matters most.

37

JAKE

I DRIVE HOME with the windows cracked, willing the crisp night air to clear my head. My grandfather's house is dark when I pull down the long driveway, which is disappointing because I'd love to share this night with someone.

I want to share it with Iris, but I'm giving her the space she asked for. Despite the sense of emptiness inside me, exhaustion takes over when I close my eyes, and sleep comes easy.

The next morning, I head to the main house before eight. Grandpa and I have a meeting with the foundation's senior staff, one I'm not as prepared for as I should be. I've spent the bulk of my time the past couple of days enmeshed in the world of my new story, determined to give Ellie Spaulding the farewell she deserves.

When I walk in, he's at the kitchen counter, bent over his daily crossword puzzle.

"Are you ready to head out?" I ask.

"Grab a cup of coffee and have a seat." He keeps his gaze lowered.

"Should I take it to go so we can talk in the car? I don't want to be late for—"

"We aren't going to be late," he says, his voice clipped.

A quick glance at my watch says otherwise, but I won't argue.

I add a splash of creamer to the dark brew, then sit down next to him at the island, his thick fingers tapping on the granite countertop.

"Are you planning to move the foundation's headquarters to Austin?"

I blink, caught off guard. "Where did you hear that?"

"Is it true?"

"I've been considering it." I place my mug on the counter with a decisive clink. "Nothing's finalized yet."

"You bet your ass it isn't."

I rub a hand across my jaw and force myself not to look away from his sharp gaze. "It's not a big deal, Grandpa. It won't change—"

His face darkens. "It would change everything. You want to uproot the foundation I spent a good portion of my life building in this community. How is that not a *big deal*?"

"There will still be a presence here," I answer. "We'll keep a satellite office to manage the local grants, but Austin is a bigger stage to expand our reach. Help more people. Isn't that what you want?"

"The Texas office was never meant to be the headquarters, and I don't give a rat's ass about a bigger stage. This foundation means something to this town, Jake."

"Nothing needs to change—for a while."

"For a while," he repeats. "Jake, this is my life's work, my tribute to your grandmother and what this community meant to her. Moving it sends a message, and not a good one."

"We need to grow if it's going to keep making an impact."

"You sound like your father." Disappointment and challenge clash in his eyes. "That's not a compliment."

His words feel like a slap in the face. "Fine. We'll keep it based here. Like I said, nothing is finalized. Why is this such a big deal, and how do you even know?" No one knows I'm not planning to stay except... "Did Iris say something to you?"

He inclines his head. "She raised her concerns to Daniel. Jake, you can't run away when things get real. If that's all this town means to you—"

I should respond to his run-away remark, but one word fills my head. "Concerns?"

Did Iris purposely throw me under the bus? I wonder if this has something to do with last night. It was clear she felt betrayed by the fact that I hadn't told her first about my writing, and while I'd understand, it's hard for me to believe she'd channel that into this kind of retribution.

He lets out a slow breath. "You have a good career, son. One that means something to you and a lot of fans around the world. Maybe you should focus on—"

"I want this, Grandpa. It's why I'm here."

"Yet you're willing to leave at the drop of a hat."

"You don't get it." I feel like a kid caught with my hand in the cookie jar. "Austin isn't about me. It's a better location. The connections and infrastructure—"

"Running back to Austin isn't going to fix your life, Jake. You need to stop running and figure it out for yourself."

I can't answer because his words slice across my chest, stealing my breath.

"So what next?" I manage after a few seconds.

He shakes his head. "I've said it before, you're my greatest legacy. But the foundation belongs here, Jake. If you can't see that...see what you're throwing away by leaving, then maybe you should."

He leans back, his expression softening. "I canceled the meeting this morning. Take the time you need, Jake. But if you decide to stay, you need to be prepared to stay for real."

I flinch at the finality in his tone. "Thanks for the advice."

He doesn't respond, just goes back to his crossword.

I stalk back toward the apartment, then switch direction and climb in the truck, needing to get away.

Part of me thinks it would be easier to leave. Go back to Austin and not worry about messy emotions or complicated relationships or letting anyone down.

Would Iris care if I left? Or would it be more proof that I was never worth trusting in the first place? My chest aches as the truck speeds down the two-lane highway. Maybe she's better off without me. Maybe they all are.

38

IRIS

I'm unsure what to expect when I walk into the dance studio for our final rehearsal before the showcase. My mind and heart are still reeling from Jake's revelation.

Sloane came over after she closed up the bookstore, absolutely sure Jake wanted to reveal his identity as the author of the Ellie Spaulding books in large part because he didn't like deceiving me. But I'm still having trouble letting go of the fact that he did. Plus, the accusations he leveled at me—that I believe he isn't anything more than his long-ago reputation—sting.

I don't think it's true. I don't want it to be true. Was I patronizing him with my support?

It feels like all those times with my mother, when I believed she wanted something more than the affairs she engaged in over and over. I always believed she was changing—she'd be different, and our lives would be different. And my heart was crushed again and again when she'd make one choice after another that hurt Nick and me. Or destroyed my chances at keeping the friends I'd created in some new town. Or the future that I wanted.

I can't help but think that if Jake truly cared about me, he would have told me before the rest of my book club found out. Would have trusted me with his most guarded and treasured secret.

I was always the last to know Mom's secrets, and I vowed not to be so naively trusting as an adult.

But look at where that got me. I'm losing my job because of an affair, which is jeopardizing the chance to make Skylark my home.

So maybe this is about me and my penchant for self-sabotage. I'm so afraid of being hurt by someone that it's easier to mess things up on my own.

Gloria gives me a questioning look as I walk in, and I offer a smile, hoping she won't see beyond it. I still haven't publicly announced my decision to withdraw from the mayor's race, but I haven't changed my mind about dropping out. Joey and I are scheduled to meet before the start of Fun Fest. It's one thing to strive for happiness—it's another to try to force it.

I can't help the way my heart skips a beat as I see Jake follow Char out of her small office. I wish I didn't have this kind of reaction to him. It would be easier if I hadn't fallen in love with this infuriating contradiction of a man, but I did. I'm also genuinely proud of what he's accomplished as Spencer Charles. He deserves the fame and accolades, and I hope he lets himself enjoy them now that his secret is out.

Char claps her hands as she always does to begin class, but gives me a funny look as a way of greeting that makes something uncomfortable twist in my stomach.

"Before we begin, I have an announcement to make," she says, and we all draw closer. "Unfortunately, one of our students is not going to be able to attend the Fun Fest showcase this weekend."

I glance around. Is it Tom? Did something happen to Janie?

"Jake has to go back to Texas for an emergency."

My eyes lock on him, but he's looking anywhere but at me.

"Can it wait?" Gloria asks, disbelief and disappointment warring in her voice. "We're two days from the event."

"I'm afraid it can't," Jake says, a muscle ticking in his jaw.

Everyone looks at me, and it's clear by their sympathetic gazes they think I've already heard the news.

"Are you sure about this?" his grandfather asks. By the way Gilbert's jaw is working, he's no happier about it than the rest of us.

"It's for the best," Jake says.

For whom? I want to demand. "I guess I'm out of the performance, too," I say, not sure how I'm supposed to react.

Quite honestly, the showcase is the least of my worries at the moment, but it's safer to focus on that rather than the fact that my heart feels like it's splitting in two.

"I was just on the phone with a friend of mine in Denver," Char says with a tight smile. "He's a dance instructor in the city, one of the best I know. He's going to drive up for the showcase. We won't let our mayor sit on the sidelines."

A smattering of applause echoes through the room, and I feel my cheeks heat.

"He'll be here early Saturday, so you two have time to meet and do a short rehearsal before our curtain call."

A short rehearsal? It took me weeks to get comfortable enough with Jake not to look like I was stumbling all over the dance floor.

But mostly, we started looking like we belong together because I started to feel like we belong together. I have a hard time believing that will work with a new partner.

"Jake's going to run through this last rehearsal," Char tells the group in general, but I feel her eyes searching mine.

"Great," I say with a tight smile.

Jake's shoulders are stiff, his expression unreadable as he approaches me.

"Are you okay?" He finally looks at me, the regret in his eyes making my chest ache.

"Fine," I lie, not fooling either of us.

The music starts, and we fall into step. It should be awful

dancing with him right now, being so close that the warmth of his body heats my icy skin. It's anything but. His hand on the small of my back is firm but gentle, guiding me across the studio. Even though he's leaving me—like everyone leaves—my heart races with each spin. I want to soak up every touch. Fall into the way our bodies fit like they were made for each other.

I can feel the tension in his body, as if he expects me to stomp on his foot or offer some big argument about his choice.

I don't. I won't.

I've fallen in love with him, but I have no claim to his heart. He doesn't owe me his loyalty. He's done everything I asked and then some.

Each dance is bittersweet and the hour passes far too quickly. Near the end of class, Char turns on the music for our solo dance. If Jake notices my trembling hand as we begin, he doesn't say anything. What we're doing here feels like more than a simple dance.

It feels like a question, an apology, and goodbye all rolled into one.

How can it end like this? Maybe that's my luck. Maybe it's just me.

Our performance is perfect. And it breaks my heart.

The other members of the class break into applause when we finish.

"Your guy better be very special," Tom tells Char, "because these two would light that showcase on fire."

"You'll do great without me," Jake says quietly.

The word on the tip of my tongue—stay—fades. Sloane told me I should ask for what I want, but I'm not going to get it. Asking will just make the rejection sting worse.

"I have all the faith in the world in your friend," I say to Char as I take a step away from Jake. I wanted to put my faith in him. I placed my heart in his hands, that's for sure, and it's come back to bite me in the ass.

I gather my stuff and walk out the front door. I don't stop when he calls my name because I'm unsure how long I can hold back the tears pricking my eyes. Life was so much simpler when I wasn't a crier.

The cool air feels refreshing against my flushed skin, and sunlight slices through the golden leaves of the cottonwood trees lining the sidewalk. Today, the beauty of the season feels like an insult—the world doesn't care that my heart is breaking apart.

I'm at the corner when a firm hand closes around my wrist.

"You can't have more surprises in store for me," I say, half-joking, as I pull my arm away. "We don't have an audience."

His jaw is tight, and his eyes search my face. "You told my grandfather I'm not staying in Skylark." It's less of an accusation than a statement of fact.

Except...

"I didn't tell your grandfather anything."

He waves away my denial. "You told Daniel. A secret for a secret."

I think back to my last conversation with Daniel and Jodi and shake my head. "It wasn't like that. I didn't—"

"I get it. I should have told you about Spencer Charles."

"Is that why you're leaving? Because your grandfather found out your plan for the foundation because of me?"

"I shouldn't have kept it a secret. I've kept too many secrets from people I..." He pauses, and it feels like my heart stops right along with him. "From people I care about. I don't want things to be awkward for you."

A broken heart isn't awkward at all.

"I know you love this town. Me being here complicates things, so..."

"I'm not running for mayor," I blurt. "I'm not...I might not even stay in Skylark."

"Why?" His thick brows draw together. "I don't understand."

"You're not the only one with secrets."

He laughs softly and reaches out to touch one finger to my cheek. I swallow hard but don't pull away. "Secrets are easier to deal with," he whispers, "if you tell someone."

"I had an affair with a married man." My voice cracks, and I hate him seeing me like this, but I continue, spilling everything into the space between us. "I thought they were separated. It was stupid, but I was desperate for someone to love. He made me feel like I mattered...until I found out I didn't." The irony isn't lost on me and I straighten my shoulders. "I don't want it to be made public."

Jake stares at me like I'm a puzzle he can't solve. "You think it will if you become mayor?"

I shrug. "Maybe it will now. Maybe later. But it's made me... the possibility has made me understand I don't want a career in the limelight. I want to help people, to do good work. To make sure kids like my brother and I have places to go where they feel safe and a community to support them. I can do those things behind the scenes."

"What are the consequences for the jackass who cheated?" Jake demands, his words heavy and charged like the first crack of thunder in a rainstorm.

"He's not my concern anymore."

"It's not fair, Iris. I don't know if you're aware of it or not, but you have so much to give. I know how much you want to make a difference. You are—"

"Thank you for that," I say, cutting him off. "You helped me see that it's okay to be who I am." I reach up and cup his cheek. "It's okay to be who you are, too—both the writer and the grandson."

"You don't need to leave, Iris. This is your home."

"Maybe having roots doesn't suit me." How do I explain that it doesn't suit me if I can't have a home with him?

"Go home to Austin, Jake. I hope you find the life you're looking for. You deserve happiness. Whether you're there or here, I hope your grandfather puts you in charge of the foundation. I know you'll honor his legacy."

Before he can say anything more, I turn and stride away. We've made so many mistakes with each other, but a part of me knows giving up on him—on us—might be the one I regret the most.

39

JAKE

STANDING at the edge of the summer camp's lake, I hear the car pull up the long drive. Gravel crunches under slow-moving tires, a sharp contrast to the hush of the surrounding pines. I don't turn around. There's only one person in the world who could have found me here.

My grandfather insisted we share locations when I first returned to Skylark, as if I was a teenager who needed monitoring.

To be honest, I didn't mind. After so many years on my own in the mostly solitary life of a writer, there were moments—particularly during grueling deadlines—when I wondered if anyone would notice if I disappeared completely.

Isn't that what I've done in a lot of ways? Disappeared into the books? Into the role of Spencer Charles, reclusive author. Only crawling out from my self-imposed exile when absolutely necessary. Sure, I've started doing more with the foundation in Austin recently, but that had more to do with appeasing my long-term guilt over losing Mike and appropriating the career that should have been his than some philanthropic fire burning inside me.

But it's not really his. This life is mine. My unwillingness to claim it might have cost me not only the career I love, but also the woman I love—a woman I don't think I'll ever stop loving. As stupid as I was at seventeen, falling for Iris remains one of my smartest moves.

I pick up another smooth stone, test the weight in my hand, and run my thumb over the flat top. The surface is warm from the day's sun, but the air around me has cooled as dusk approaches. With a flick of my wrist, I send the stone skipping across the water. One, two, three hops before it sinks below the surface.

"I taught you well," Grandpa says in his gravelly voice as he comes to stand next to me. "But you're releasing too soon."

I hand him the rock I'm holding in my other hand. "Show me how it's done, Obi-Wan."

He chuckles but takes the stone. I watch his fist curl around it, testing the weight the way he taught Mikey and me to do when we were kids. He shifts his feet on the uneven shoreline, then, with more grace than I'd expect, he pulls back his arm, and in one fluid motion sends the stone flying. Five skips across the water, nearly making it to the lake's center, before it sinks.

"The old man still has it," I say with a slow clap.

"The dancing has limbered me up. It's good for the old joints —lubricates them."

I huff out a devilish laugh. "You know, the find my phone app goes both ways," I tell him, wiggling my brows. "I've noticed your location at Gloria Johnson's house several times in the past few weeks. Looks like your joints aren't the only thing being lubricated."

My grandfather shakes his head. "You need to mind your own business and show more respect to your elders."

"All respect," I clarify. "Glad those dance lessons paid off."

He scowls, but a smile plays at the corner of his mouth.

"Gilbert Byrne still has the rizz." I'm enjoying myself now. "The old man has moves."

"Enough." He holds up a hand. "Do you want to hear my go-to move?"

"Absolutely not," I answer.

"Listen anyway." He puffs up his chest. "My best move is getting out of my own way. I don't let the past predict my future."

I pick up another rock and hurl it toward the water, not surprised when it lands with a plop instead of skimming the surface. "I'll take your word that it works."

"I didn't come up here to skip stones, Jakey. We need to talk." He draws in a deep breath and turns to survey the property that has been in our family for years. "This is the first time I've come up here since that summer you were here."

The wind picks up slightly, rustling through the tall grass further up the shoreline. A hawk swoops overhead but doesn't dive toward the water.

"Why haven't you sold the camp? I'm sure there are people who'd want to make something of it."

He shakes his head. "I couldn't force myself to come up here or let it go. This place reminds me of your brother. Of the two of you and happier times. I didn't mean to stay away. In my mind, I told myself I was going to tear down the old structures and build something new. Maybe a retreat center, or…"

He bends down, picks up a rock, and holds it out to me. "Someplace where kids who need help could go and actually get it. Not like that hellhole your father owned in North Carolina."

I take the rock from him, amazed that it's the perfect size and shape for skipping. The sun has slipped behind the distant peaks, but the stone is warm in my palm, still holding onto the afternoon light.

"When we give the past too much power, it becomes bigger than we can handle," Grandpa says, running a hand through his white hair. "It overtakes not only the future but the present, too. Everything."

"I get it, Grandpa. If you don't learn from those lessons, you're bound to repeat them."

"But if you stay stuck without learning, you'll stay stuck."

"You should embroider that on a pillow."

"You should stop hiding behind the kid you used to be."

"Is this your not-so-subtle way of telling me you're putting Dad in charge of the foundation? Because I can't be trusted?"

"Who said anything about you not being able to be trusted? No. You're so deep in your head, pretending it's my voice or your father's voice or your brother's voice talking all this shit—" He jabs me in the bicep with one gnarled finger. "It's you. You're the one telling yourself you can't do this."

"Or I'm repeating what I've heard my whole damn life."

"Then change the channel if you don't like what's playing. You're not a T-Rex with tiny little arms."

I laugh at that comparison. "Scientists now think the T-Rex had a bigger brain than they used to believe."

"Then you have that in common," Grandpa says, smirking. "For the record, a brain works better if you use it."

"Duly noted. Back to the foundation's future..."

"Jake, you are Spencer Charles. Or he's you. You have a natural, God-given talent. Do you really want to give up being a writer in order to run the foundation?"

"I want to do right by Mikey's memory."

"Stop. Do you know how pissed your brother would be to know you were using him and his memory as an excuse to play small? You and Mike came up with those first stories together—but you are the writer. Everything else aside, do you love writing books?"

I swallow when emotions try to clog my throat. "Fuck yeah," I whisper.

"Finally some truth. Do you want to keep doing it?"

"I don't want Dad to get his hands on the foundation, Grandpa. Not just because of my shitty relationship with him. I might have only been involved from the periphery, but I know what you do is important. The values, our family's name, your legacy...it means something to me."

Grandpa swipes a hand across his cheek. "You mean the world to me."

He watches the water for a long time before speaking. "I'm naming Daniel Pearson Executive Director of the foundation," he says. "He's got the experience to run the whole thing day to day. But I want you to take on a piece of it—your own program area. Something that reflects your values. Maybe you bring this camp back to life, turn it into a retreat center, a space for healing."

I stare at him, wondering if he's serious. "You want me to run part of the foundation? And keep writing?"

He nods, grinning. "That's the idea. You've got a good head and a bigger heart than you let on. Use both. Build something that lasts, Jake. Not just for yourself."

My breath whooshes out of my lungs as I think about what I want to make last in my life. Who I want to build it with. "I don't know if I'm the right guy for—"

"You are," he says, like it's already been decided. "You're the right guy for Iris, too. I see the way you look at her. Don't let fear rule the day. Be a man who's willing to fight, Jake."

I stare out at the lake stretching wide in front of us and feel a spark catching fire inside me. Like I finally know what's worth fighting for—my future, this place, and Iris.

40

IRIS

My first thought when I wake up Saturday morning to the sound of muffled voices is that I'm being burgled. Nick had an early shift at the diner, so I should be alone in the house.

But just as my pulse starts pounding in my ear, Sloane's distinctive cackle rings out, followed by Molly shushing her like only a mother can.

Relief and confusion flood my veins as I stumble from the bed, the hardwood cool against my bare feet. As I round the corner, laughter greets me, my book club friends buzzing around my kitchen like human honeybees. My gaze is drawn to the shiny balloons tied to the backs of the dining chairs. They spell out the message *you're a star*.

"What is all this?" I slowly move forward, still a bit dazed and definitely confused.

Sloane turns from the stove, spatula in hand. "Surprise! We're here to hype you up for your dancing debut."

"Lucky for you," Avah adds, looking me up and down, "Sadie stopped by The Roasted Sky and had Sally make a double-shot latte. You look like shit."

Molly elbows our blunt friend. "She means you look like you didn't get a good night's sleep."

"I'm sure I look like shit," I agree, running a hand through my tangled hair. "I feel like shit."

I take the coffee Avah hands me along with a tight hug. "Helium and caffeine hyping works," I tell her, blinking back tears.

"We've got you." Taylor joins the hug.

I let out a watery laugh. "I don't think porcupines cry."

"You aren't really a porcupine." Sloane plants a soft kiss on my cheek. "And you can handle Fun Fest."

"We'll make damn sure of it," Avah promises.

"What would I do without you all?"

"If you stay in Skylark," Taylor says gently, "you won't need to find out."

"We're not convinced Seattle's right for you." Avah wrinkles her nose. "I don't think hair like yours does well in humidity."

Sloane slides two perfectly fried eggs onto a plate and places it on the table. "More importantly, we want you to stay."

Sadie wraps an arm around my shoulder. "I might have mentioned your potential plan to Sally. She wanted me to tell you that you've got a job at The Roasted Sky whenever you want it."

"From mayor to barista?"

Sloane pushes me into a chair in front of the eggs and hands me a fork. "You could do worse. They have a killer tip jar."

I glance up at her. "I'll think about it."

"Think hard. Seattle is too far away." Her voice softens. "You belong with the people who love you."

"That's us," Taylor adds.

I press a hand to my chest. It feels like my heart is splintering again, but for a totally different reason. "You guys are the best."

"And we're better together." Avah flips a lock of chestnut hair over her shoulder. "Now eat your eggs, and then I'm going to do your hair and makeup."

Molly claps her hands together like an excited kid. "Yeah, we're going to get some sexy pictures of you and Char's instructor friend and make Jake Byrne rue the day he walked away from you."

"*Rue* it," Sloane confirms with a smirk.

I smile, but my throat feels tight. "Not necessary," I say. "But I'll take the hair and makeup anyway."

As much as I appreciate having these women in my corner, I miss Jake. He's been gone less than twenty-four hours, but I miss him every minute. His absence feels like losing something precious, and I don't know how to make the ache in my heart go away.

After my Fun Fest makeover, complete with kohl-rimmed eyes and hair that would do a Vegas showgirl proud, I head to the dance studio, the weight of the day starting to press down on me again.

The dress Char helped me order for the performance hits just below my knees, with a flared skirt that swirls with every spin. The sequins on the sleeves are a little flashy for me, but I appreciate the built-in bodysuit that keeps everything in place. My new partner is just as talented as Char claimed, with a laid-back smile that puts me at ease despite my nerves and toe-trodding. Fortunately, I'm not quite as bad as I was when Jake and I first started.

Apparently, falling for my partner made me a better dancer. A better person.

Even though I'm nervous, sad, and unsure of the future, spinning around the dance floor is still fun. My mind keeps wandering to Jake—the way he steadied me and made my heart skip a beat when he spun me. The way we just clicked.

"You've got this in the bag," Derek tells me with a high five after we run through our solo routine a second time. He's being kind, but I'm okay with that.

Imperfection is okay, even when it's me who's not as good as I want to be. I'm more willing to accept my missteps and stumbles because at least I'm trying. There's something freeing in the realization that I don't have to be the flawless version of myself I've been chasing all these years. Maybe the person I actually am deserves some long-overdue grace.

Once Char is convinced I'm not going to embarrass her or ruin her reputation, she releases me, and I head toward the fairgrounds. I find Joey helping a group of volunteers set up chairs in front of the festival stage.

His eyes narrow as I approach.

"Good morning, Madam Mayor." He crosses his arms over his chest, his hair newly clipped and his wide jaw clean-shaven. In his crisp white Oxford shirt with one button open at the collar and the sleeves rolled up to his elbows, he looks the part. And while that isn't everything, he's going to do okay for the town. I have to believe that.

"Are you here to scare me off?" he asks slowly. "I know your popularity is on the rise—at least my cousin tells me I don't stand a chance against you. The crew over at Tony's report you can belt out Journey with the best of them."

"Don't stop believing, Joey," I answer with a smile. "I've learned a lot about the community during my time in the mayor's office."

"I get it. You've got the on-the-job experience that I don't, but my name carries weight. And Cy—"

"I know you have plenty of money to dump into this campaign," I interrupt. "Your signs are everywhere."

"Did yours get lost?"

I shake my head. "After the showcase, I'm going to announce that I'm withdrawing my candidacy."

He runs a hand through his thinning brown hair, his expression skeptical. "You don't think you can beat me?"

"I think I'd have a hell of a chance to win. I'm a good mayor, and I love this town with my whole heart." I point to the marquee sign for the weekend's festivities. "I'm also fun. Remember to be fun, but more importantly, have fun. Do the dunk tanks. Let people smash a pie in your face. Take care of the community, but have fun while you're doing it. It took me a minute to understand that both of those things are important, and why."

"So why quit?"

"I'm not quitting." My voice is steady, and so is my heart. "I'm choosing something different. I don't want to keep trying to live up to expectations I didn't set for myself."

He looks away. "No one in my family believes I can succeed as mayor. They think I'm too dumb because I started working at the auto shop right out of high school." His gaze shifts back to me. "I could have gone to college, but I like cars."

"There's nothing wrong with that."

"That's not what my aunt says, or what my father thought."

"Only allowing ourselves to become what our parents wanted would be a pretty sad state of affairs for most of us."

He laughs softly. "Amen to that."

"One other thing this town—this office—has taught me is fear might be along for the ride, but I can't let it drive my life. It might not be the path your family wanted, but it's yours. You own a successful business in Skylark, which gives you a unique perspective. You're honest and hardworking. You can figure out the rest. Most of life is figuring it out as we go along. There's nothing wrong with not having all the answers."

He rubs a hand along the back of his neck. "After a speech like that, I'd vote for you."

"Not gonna happen, but I appreciate your confidence."

"Best of luck to you, Iris."

"You too, Joey."

We shake hands, and I walk away feeling lighter, a weight lifted from my shoulders.

By the time I take my place with the rest of the class, Fun Fest is in full swing. And it looks like the entire Skylark population has turned up. The crowd buzzes with energy and the smell of popcorn and funnel cakes is thick in the air. There are craft booths and face painting and a small petting zoo on the far end of the midway. It's everything fun and perfect, and I should feel great in this moment. I want to feel happy. I'm just not sure how with the way my heart feels like it might never recover.

But the show must go on, and Derek takes my hand as we line up for the first routine. No matter what happens next, I'm a part of this community in a meaningful way—something I didn't even realize I wanted at the start of my bucket list journey.

This class taught me so much. Not just about dancing, but also how to live life to the fullest. I just wish Jake were here to share it with me. I want to experience this moment—and all the moments going forward—with him. To share the good and the bad, the fun and the challenges.

But the emptiness without him feels like it could swallow me whole if I let it.

I take a deep breath and rein in my emotions. I'm done blaming myself for either of our mistakes and missteps. Like me, Jake has to figure out what he wants from life, and I hope his path makes him happy in the long run.

Do I secretly hope he realizes he can't live without me? Um, *hell yes*.

Do I believe that's going to happen? *No.* Which is another reason why the job in Seattle might be the right next step for me.

Even if Jake returns to Austin permanently, he'll come back here to visit his grandfather. I'm not sure I can take the chance of running into him—not quite as literally as our encounter a month earlier—and have my heart break all over again.

The music starts, the speakers crackling, and nerves threaten before muscle memory takes over. The crowd claps and cheers, and the music vibrating under my feet carries me through the first two routines.

While the other students take their positions for the third number, Derek and I exit the stage. We'll go on for our solo next, and my nerves return in full force.

I'm covered in sweat, my breathing ragged, but Char grins and hugs me tight. "You were perfect."

There's only one thing that could make this moment perfect, but I return her hug and force a smile.

As we wait in the wings, ready to make our entrance after the applause dies down from the group dance, Derek flashes a confident smile. "Don't worry, Iris. I've got you."

"Actually, I've got her for this one," a familiar voice interrupts.

My heart stutters, and awareness tingles along my skin. Before I can fully register what's happening, Jake's warm hand presses against the small of my back, making my knees go weak. I can't imagine his touch ever doing anything else.

"What are you doing here?" My voice shakes as I stare at the man responsible for the thousand butterflies that have taken flight across my middle.

He looks handsome and a little tousled, like he ran the whole way back from Austin.

He offers a crooked smile. "I think it's called pulling my head out of my ass." His gray-green eyes soften as he studies me. "Turns out, I was right where I belong all along."

I'm saved from answering—not that I'm in any shape to put together a coherent response to that—because Char is introducing us. She must have known about the switch as she doesn't seem surprised to see Jake leading me out onto the stage.

The crowd goes wild.

"Byrne, baby, Byrne!" Sloane's voice rings out over the applause and cheering.

So many questions tumble through my mind, but the music starts.

"Dance with me," he whispers, then spins me, my dress twirling out, and suddenly there's no audience. There's no confusion or missteps. There's only this moment with the man I love and the dance that brought us together in the first place.

We fall into step like we never missed a beat. He draws me close as the music fades, but instead of the bow we're supposed to take as the audience roars, Jake cups my cheeks and kisses me.

It's like every dream I didn't know I had is coming true at once.

But there's no time to process what Jake's return, our kiss, and the fact that he can't seem to take his eyes off me mean for my galloping heart and our future. As the audience continues to cheer, the rest of the class joins us on stage. The Fun Fest crowd gives us a standing ovation, and Sadie's friend Sally, the event's emcee, talks up the dance studio before the next act, a local magician, takes the stage.

We shuffle off, and there are more hugs and congratulations as family and friends join us backstage, separating Jake from my side before I'm ready to let him go. Again.

"I'm sorry I missed the solo," Derek says as he lifts me into a celebratory hug, "but you two clearly belong together."

His words puncture the bubble of happiness enveloping me, but I smile and accept his praise.

"Iris."

I turn to face Jake, who's made his way through the crowd to stand in front of me.

"Well done, Byrne." Avah pats his shoulder.

He nods, but his eyes remain fixed on mine. "Iris, I—"

"Let's not do this here," I tell him, not wanting to prolong the agony if that's what's coming. Given how we left things, how can I think it will be anything else? I know now he's too decent to just disappear—Jake would want to explain it away to make sure I understand it's not my fault, even though we both know it is. "It can wait for—"

He takes my hand in his and links our fingers. "I don't want to wait another minute to tell you that I love you, Iris." His eyes swirl with emotions—hope, joy, and uncertainty. "I want to be with you. Give me a second chance. I'm not saying I deserve one. I've been a fool and a coward and an idiot."

"A pigheaded idiot," Gilbert clarifies as he joins the group of people surrounding us.

Jake grins sheepishly. "All those things and much more. Well said, Gramps."

Murmurs of agreement come from my book club friends.

"No one needs to offer more," I call out, raising my free hand. Jake also captures that one, lifting it to his mouth to brush a soft kiss across my knuckles.

"You love me?" Something fragile flutters in my chest, a glimmer of hope I'm almost afraid to nurture. That simple question feels too big for this moment and yet not enough.

"Probably since we were seventeen, but I was definitely too much of a fool to do anything about it then. You taught me to be brave and embrace every part of my life. But none of it matters without you, Iris."

A champagne fountain of emotions erupts inside my heart. I'm fizzy and light, as if I could float away in the crisp autumn air. He fills every hollow place I thought would stay empty. This is what I want, who I want, but—

"You're going back to Austin."

"Not if you say yes." He shakes his head. "Skylark is my home. *You* are my home. I never knew my place could be a person—until you."

I blink. "I have an interview next week in Seattle."

"You have a job offer right here," Sally shouts from the back of the crowd.

"More than one," Jake's grandpa says as he steps forward. "We have an open position at the foundation for a program manager to work in Skylark and the surrounding communities. You'd be perfect for that role, Iris."

I feel my mouth drop open, and I'm not sure how to react.

"Will you give us a chance?" Jake asks. "I know it might not be easy, but I don't want easy, Dixon. I want you and me. The messy, beautiful, imperfect everything. All of it as long as we're together. Every version of life I can imagine is better when I'm with you."

"Yes," I whisper as my heart fills. It might not be easy, and I might not have all the answers, but I know I want to figure them out with Jake.

This is my future, and I'm not going to let it go. Not this time.

I don't realize I'm crying until he brushes a thumb across my cheek. "You mean that?"

"Yes," I repeat. "I'll give you—us—all the chances we need."

I wrap my arms tight around his shoulders and kiss him.

"Then you're stuck with me, Dixon. Forever." For the first time, forever doesn't feel scary. Because I know I'm exactly where I'm supposed to be.

"Forever," I whisper with a soft laugh. My heart is overflowing with happiness knowing Jake and I will figure out how to make our future everything we want it to be. Not because it will always be easy, but because it will always be us.

Every step forward with him–dancing or otherwise–is the home I want. A home where I can be fully seen and completely myself, a love that shows up in every moment, and the promise that we'll always choose each other.

FOR AN EXCLUSIVE BONUS EPILOGUE, join Michelle's newsletter via her website or at the address below. Happy reading!
https://dl.bookfunnel.com/8ge5jrhcjh

AND TURN the page to get a sneak peek at SOMEONE TO HAVE, coming to a bookshelf near you July 24th, 2025!

SOMEONE TO HAVE
SNEAK PEEK

Taylor

I STAND on the sidewalk in front of Tony's, the most popular local bar in my hometown and wonder—not for the first time—what am I doing here?

Not in an existential crisis sort of way. There's no debating the meaning of life or my purpose on the planet. This is more a question of *why haven't I left Skylark, Colorado?*

Wouldn't I be happier someplace where I could create who I want to be from scratch instead of staying stuck as the me everyone thinks they know?

My teeth chatter as the January wind whips along the street—the buildings of Main Street encased in winter frost. All except for the one I'm staring at. It's half past eight on the first Sunday of the new year, and the old Victorian structure, with its chipped gray paint and faded white shutters, is lit up with colored twinkle lights flashing like a beacon in the darkness.

A wreath hangs on the door, adorned with *empty* shot bottles

—don't want to tempt the local teens. The words painted on the front window wish everyone a Merry Beer-mas.

This is stupid, and it's only going to get worse inside. I should be at home, polishing off the last of the stale holiday cookies I baked with my nieces and watching something on BBC America. A British accent makes everything better.

As I'm about to scurry away, Molly McAllister and Avah Harris pull up in Avah's BMW. She parallel-parks the compact SUV like it's her job. It's kind of annoying that Avah does everything well. Heck, she could make scooping cat litter look cool —not that she's a cat lady. That's my area of expertise.

"Come on, Barbie, let's go party," she calls as her head appears above the top of the vehicle. How does she keep her car so white when round-the-clock plowing after a recent storm has left a border of dingy snowbanks on either side of the street?

I lift a mittened hand to acknowledge the greeting, even though no one is going to confuse me with Barbie. Avah's the one who looks like a brunette version of the anatomically impossible doll with her shiny hair, perky boobs, and tiny waist.

"Are you freezing out here?" Molly places her gloved hands on my cold cheeks. "Why didn't you let us pick you up?"

"I'm only a couple blocks away. It's easier to walk. Besides, whoever moved into the apartment across the hall from me is playing their music way too loud. There's only so much old-school metal I can take in one evening."

Avah joins us on the sidewalk, shimmying her hips. "Maybe your new neighbor isn't a card-carrying member of AARP like the rest of your building."

"My neighbors are nice and quiet. We look out for each other." Both statements are factual but also a weak argument.

"Your hallway smells like Bengay and cough drops."

"Muscles get tight when it's cold. It's a Colorado thing."

"It's an octogenarian thing." Avah shivers against the cold air. "Seriously, why didn't you go in? You look like a human popsicle."

I know what cold does to my face—my nose gets red like Rudolph, and my eyes start to water. It's not pretty.

"I might take a rain check." I glance toward the bar. "I can see my brother and his friends through the window. I don't know why Toby is out when I'm sure he's still nursing a hangover from New Year's Eve."

"Relatable." Avah links her arm with mine. "Jon and I went to some fancy corporate party at the Four Seasons in Denver. We stayed the night, and since neither of us was driving home and the champagne was complimentary...midnight is a bit of a blur."

I snort, thinking about the takeout and Netflix binge I indulged in two nights ago to ring in the new year. "Are you trying to make me jealous? Because it's working, and I want to punch you in the face."

"I don't condone physical violence," Molly says with a laugh, a strand of red hair blowing into her face thanks to another wind gust. "But I support you getting your drink on tonight."

"And you don't want to punch me in the face," Avah says, trying to tug me forward. "You're too sweet for that, Taylor."

My booted feet remain planted on the sidewalk. At five-eleven, I've got six inches and probably forty pounds on Avah. My dad used to say I'm a "solid piece of work", until my mom told him it hurt my feelings, which baffled him since he meant it as a compliment. But still...the upside of solid is that no one is dragging me anywhere I don't want to go. "Can we try somewhere else? My stupid brother's going to make a big deal about seeing me out at a bar."

"It's not an exclusive club and he's not the boss of you," Avah reminds me. "Tony's is for everyone."

"But *why* exactly am I here?" I ask as I allow her to lead me forward.

"Because you go back to work tomorrow. This is your last hurrah." Molly tries to sound enthusiastic, but her voice is pinched.

"A *hurrah*. Since when do I need a hurrah?"

Avah opens the giant wood door. The typical bar noise and the scent of stale beer and roasted peanuts spills out. At least it's warm inside. "Let's discuss it over a drink."

I don't like the sound of that, but I'm not one for standing my ground despite being physically capable. I'm more the type to step in quicksand and be swallowed up by the whims and wishes of the people around me. I used to make a New Year's goal to get a backbone, but it was always such a giant failure that I don't bother anymore. This year my goal is to read more. Easy-peasy.

"Can we at least go to the back so my brother doesn't see us?" I do my best to shrink down behind Avah's svelte form.

Toby's voice booms from across the bar. "Tink, over here!"

"Can we talk about why your brother calls you Tink?" Avah asks with an eye roll.

"Not even a little," I answer.

"We'll get a table while you say hi." Molly gives me a thumbs up. There's something weird happening with my friends, and I wish I knew what it was.

I'm also wishing—or at least hoping—that the visit with Toby, who is six years my senior, will be short and sweet.

"What are you doing in a *bar*, Taylor Marie?" he asks as I approach, hands on hips and scowling in a convincing imitation of our father.

"I know you know I'm twenty-six, Toby. Plenty legal. And you've seen me in Tony's before tonight."

He makes a show of looking past my shoulder. Toby is six-three, while our older sister, Elise, is six foot even, making me the smallest of my siblings. That's not saying much. "I haven't seen you with Avah Harris. She's hotter now than she was back in high school."

"She's also got a serious boyfriend. They're practically engaged, so don't make an ass of yourself and embarrass both of us."

"Practically," he repeats with a wink. "That's not fully engaged and nowhere near married." He slaps the back of the man standing next to him. "Am I right?"

I *practically* swallow my tongue as the man, who has at least an inch on my brother, turns and a pair of all-too-familiar dark chocolate eyes stare down at me.

"Anderson, this is my sister, Tink."

"Taylor," I correct automatically, surprised I can form those two simple syllables or even remember my name with the object of most of my school girl fantasies standing directly in front of me. There was Eric Anderson and Mr. Darcy. The Colin Firth version, of course. Classics are classics for a reason.

"You probably don't remember her," my brother continues like the big oaf he is, and I run a finger across my bottom lip to confirm I'm not drooling. "She was a pipsqueak when she used to come to our college games."

Eric lifts the hand holding a beer bottle and points in my direction. "You sat in the stands reading a book." It sounds like an accusation.

I feel a little flattered that this tall, dark-haired god of a man remembers twelve-year-old me.

Eric was my brother's roommate and captain of the Colorado College hockey team for two of the four years my brother played there. He's a couple of years older than Toby and left school early to turn pro in some European league.

As all-encompassing as my girlish crush felt, I didn't keep track of him after he left, but I know he doesn't live in Skylark. He must be passing through, which explains Toby's night out—showing off for his buddy.

A couple of the other firefighters in Toby's crew greet me, and I'm grateful for a break from the intensity of Eric's gaze.

"I wasn't into hockey," I say when I finally return my attention to him.

"Sounds sacrilegious coming from Marty Maxwell's daughter."

My dad is a legend in the hockey world, right up there with Wayne Gretzky and Mario Lemieux. He retired the year I was born, which might explain my lack of interest in the holy grail of sports. Toby used to tell people I got dropped on my head as a kid.

"The sports gene kind of skipped me."

"Tink was adopted—left on our front porch by a band of roving book nerds."

Another one of my brother's his favorite explanations. I flip him the bird.

Eric rubs a hand against the back of his neck like he's not sure how to respond. "You were adopted by a wonderful family." The dark blue sweater he's wearing makes his skin look golden, like he spent Christmas in the south of France. For all I know, he was on a yacht with his supermodel girlfriend and the son of some Russian oligarch. Okay, maybe I've been hitting the dark romance section of the library too hard lately.

"I wasn't adopted," I mutter.

"Dude, I'm messing with you." Toby smacks Eric on the shoulder. My brother is touchy-feely in the most annoying ways. "Tink looks exactly like our mom. She's just weird."

"Yeah, I get that," Eric answers casually.

He casually thinks I'm weird. Lovely. There goes my childhood crush, crashing and burning in a fiery death. Thank god I still have Mr. Darcy.

The irritation must be written on my face, not that I'm trying to hide it, because Eric visibly cringes.

"I didn't mean you're weird. I remember your parents coming to games. You look like your mother."

It's the nicest compliment a person can give me, and I guess it's true. I have the same dark hair, pale skin, and clear blue eyes as my mom. I look like her, but the resemblance stops at the surface.

My mom had this way of making people feel like they

mattered. Where she was fearless, I hesitate. She filled a room with laughter, while I shrink into corners, awkward and unsure. Although she died four years ago in a car accident, the mention of her still causes a tight ball of emotion to clog my throat. Tears prick the backs of my eyes, and I know Eric notices because he looks like he wants to bolt.

Why can't men handle a crying woman? They're emotions, not the clap.

My brother orders another round, then turns to me again. "Seriously, you think I've got any chance with Avah?"

"About as much as a snowball in hell, and leave my friends alone."

"How are you and Avah Harris friends?" he demands but hands me a beer when the bartender places a bucket of them on the scarred wood bar. "She was the ultimate cool chick in high school."

"Are you being more of a dick than usual on purpose or am I just lucky tonight?" I assume my brother knows it's a rhetorical question.

To my horror, he answers anyway. "Don't get your granny panties in a twist."

I can't believe he just told Eric Anderson, who's now looking less like he wants to escape and more like he's trying to bite back a smile, that I wear granny panties.

"They're hipsters, Toby. If you'd fix your washing machine, you wouldn't need to bring your laundry to my place."

"I'm not complaining, Tay-tay. First, you buy those beads that make me smell like spring. Second, I don't like to think of my little sister getting any, and I know for sure you're not while wearing those things."

He holds out his hands, indicating to Eric the giant girth of my underpants. I'd be much obliged if the ground could swallow me up whole at that moment.

"For the record, I'm going to tell Avah you still suck your thumb," I fire back.

Toby lifts his hand to give me a high-five that I don't return. "Maybe she'll ask me to call her Mommy."

This time, Eric doesn't hold back. He laughs heartily, tipping up his head to reveal the strong column of his throat. If I were another type of woman—or not standing in front of my brother and a guy too hot to give me the time of day—I might lean in and drag my mouth across it. Press my lips to his Adam's apple and—

"Tink, stop," Toby commands. "Gross."

I blink and touch a finger to the side of my mouth. Still no drool. "How is standing here listening to you be a sexist pig gross?"

"You're staring at Anderson like you want to take a bite out of him. Trust me, I've seen that same look on dozens of faces back in college—and even tonight. Pretty sure Malone has dibs."

Megan Malone is a firefighter on my brother's crew. She has dark eyes, naturally wavy hair and curves for days. She's also funny, sweet, and a total badass. Megan and Eric Anderson would make beautiful babies together, that's for sure.

"I'm not looking at him like anything," I say.

"He's a man-whore, Tay," Toby announces. "A man-whore with a heart but not anywhere close to right for you."

"Thanks for the vote of confidence, man." Eric seems to take the insult in stride although his smirk goes a little tight around the edges.

"Dude, you can't help it—it's pheromones."

Toby jabs a finger in my direction. "You *can* help it. Be gone with you and your granny panties."

"I hate you," I tell him, then switch my gaze to Eric Anderson, who's still smirking with a tiny bit of glower added into the mix. While the combo is sexy as hell, it's also just as annoying. "I hate you by association."

I offer my middle finger once again. "I'm giving this

conversation zero stars. Would not recommend. Have a lovely night, gentlemen."

Both of them salute as I turn away and weave through the crowd of firefighters, greeting several of them, until I reach Avah and Molly at the table in the back.

"Who's your brother's friend?" Avah asks. "Talk about easy on the eyes."

"He's a conceited hockey jerk, and you've got a boyfriend." I take a long swig from my bottle of beer.

"I was looking for Molly. It's time she got back out there."

Molly chokes out a laugh. "I'm a single mom of twins who lives with my late husband's mother." She ticks off items on her fingers like she's reciting a grocery list. "I haven't shaved my legs since Thanksgiving, and I'm pretty sure my bra is a holdover from when I was still nursing my kids."

"Girl, that's sad." Avah shakes her head. "Even for you."

"Why am I the sacrificial set-up lamb?" Molly asks. "Taylor is more single than me."

"No need to make it a competition," I protest. My siblings and dad like to make everything a competition. Since I never have a chance of winning, I don't bother to try—in most areas of my life, if I'm being honest.

"Tall, dark, and could-be-a-Hemsworth-brother isn't Taylor's type," Avah says. "She likes guys with small hands."

"Bryan doesn't have small hands." I roll my eyes. None of my friends understand the crush I have on Bryan Connor, one of my co-workers at the high school. But they're wrong about him *and* how perfect he is for me. Nothing like Eric "Hemsworth-look-alike" Anderson. "Just because he isn't some 'roided-up hockey meatstick that bags every puck bunny who steps in his path doesn't mean he isn't attractive. Call me crazy, but I'm not looking to add an STD to my New Year's bingo card."

"She didn't mean that how it sounded." Avah stares at a spot past my shoulder as Molly cringes.

"I had blood work done last month," a deep voice says from behind my chair. "Got the all-clear. Those puck bunnies better be on their A-game."

I shift in my chair and find myself once again staring into Eric Anderson's dark eyes. He's definitely not smiling now.

ABOUT THE AUTHOR

USA Today and Top 5 Amazon Bestselling author Michelle Major writes swoon-worthy stories full of heart, heat, and guaranteed happily-ever-afters. When she's not dreaming up romance, you'll find her hiking the trails (or avoiding housework) in her home state of Colorado.

Connect with Michelle
website: michellemajor.com
Instagram: @michellemajorauthor
Facebook: michellemajorbooks